"I see the way you've been looking at Katie-Lynn."

"What way's that?"

"Like you've still got feelings for her."

"Dead wrong." Cole raised his bottle for a drink to shield his expression. Travis was as sharp-eyed as a hawk, reading people and situations in an instant. A good trait for a sheriff. Not so good in a brother when you were hiding something...

"I hope so," Travis said. "Just remember what happened after she left you."

"Nothing happened."

"Except you disappearing for three months."

"I was driving cattle."

"Sleeping out on the range, never coming home..."

Cole drained the last of his dark malt and handed it to a passing waitress. "Are we done here, Sheriff?"

Travis pinned him with a steady, hard look before nodding. "You're free to go...with a warning."

"Which is?"

"Don't repeat a mistake you already learned from. Anyone messes up once. Doing it twice is just plain stupid."

Dear Reader,

Have you ever wished you were part of a fictional family? Growing up, my sisters and I would call, "Good night, Jim Bob. Night, Mary Ellen," like the Waltons, and we'd braid each other's hair like the Ingalls sisters. The Cades and the Lovelands in my Rocky Mountain Cowboys series embody what I love most about family: love, togetherness and support...a shoulder to cry on, a forever friend, the person who always has your back, who knows you better than anyone else and loves you no matter what.

In this fourth book, these feuding families are about to be united on the eve of their parents' wedding. Their temporary truce, however, is threatened when TV show host Katlynn Brennon returns to her hometown and enlists the aid of her ex, Cole Loveland, to solve the scandalous mystery surrounding the kidnapping, murder and priceless jewel theft that began the feud over a hundred years ago. She needs to face her difficult past to score high ratings to save her show. Cole needs to keep the woman who once broke his heart from destroying his father's happiness. If they dig deep enough, they might just resolve their own history along the way...

I hope this story captivates you and keeps you turning pages. Stay tuned for Jewel Cade and Heath Loveland's love story, coming soon in 2019!

Until then, with love and thanks,

Karen Rock

HEARTWARMING

A Cowboy's Pride

———

Karen Rock

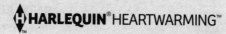

Recycling programs
for this product may
not exist in your area.

ISBN-13: 978-1-335-63380-4

A Cowboy's Pride

Copyright © 2018 by Karen Rock

This edition published by arrangement with Harlequin Books S.A.

For questions and comments about the quality of this book, please contact us at CustomerService@Harlequin.com.

Printed in U.S.A.

Award-winning author **Karen Rock** is both sweet and spicy—at least when it comes to her writing! The author of both YA and adult contemporary books writes sexy suspense novels and small-town romances for Harlequin and Kensington Publishing. A strong believer in Happily-Ever-After, Karen loves creating unforgettable stories that leave her readers with a smile. When she's not writing, Karen is an avid reader who also loves cooking her grandmother's Italian recipes, baking and having the Adirondack Park wilderness as her backyard, where she lives with her husband, daughter, dog and cat, who keep her life interesting and complete. Learn more about her at karenrock.com or follow her on Twitter, @karenrock5.

Books by Karen Rock

Harlequin Heartwarming

Visit the Author Profile page at Harlequin.com for more titles.

To "Beanie"—the best French braider, foreign-film discoverer, homeopathic health experimenter and big sister I could have ever wished for. You're the yellow heart to my pink.

CHAPTER ONE

"ACTION!"

At her director's prompting, Katlynn Brennon aimed her sincerest smile into the television camera, stuck out her forehead and tipped down her chin for her best angle. Her weary eyes chased the racing teleprompter all while striving to ignore her "slimming" undergarment's malicious dig.

What number was this take?

Infinity?

"Babe Paley, the socialite wife of CBS founder, William S. Paley, once said, 'A woman can never be too rich or too thin,'" Katlynn intoned, voice steady despite the boom mic's close dip to her head. "However, many of her fellow glamour queens might have added that riches don't guarantee contentment. Heiresses may even share a unique kind of adversity."

Beneath blaring lights, Katlynn willed back the damp forming on her forehead.

Glow not glisten.

Glow.

"On tonight's episode of *Scandalous History*, we'll dig into the secret lives of seven 'golden girls' who inherited their share of troubles along with their fortunes."

She paused, maintaining her pose for Editing, who appreciated extra room on the ends of takes. Dozens of eyes peered at her from the shadows.

Nope. This wasn't awkward at all...

Perfectly natural to grin at nothing like a loony statue...

"Cut!" bellowed her director, Gabe French, and she blew out a breath. A gray-haired, slouchy man, Gabe's heavy-lidded eyes and rumpled clothes belied his legendary perfectionism. "Great job, Katlynn. Just amazing. Now, can we do another take with you repeating the intro salaciously?"

Mary, the studio's overzealous hair and makeup person, rushed Katlynn with a fistful of spritzes, brushes and powder. De-frizzing spray blasted in a coconut-scented cloud.

"Salaciously?" Katlynn choked out as Mary smoothed down microscopic hair wisps only an expert stylist or a circling hawk could spot.

"Like you've got a tasty, juicy bit of gossip to tell." Gabe's eyes gleamed. "Give me a knowing smile with your left eyebrow lift."

"How's this?" Katlynn shot him her best Mona

Lisa impersonation while Mary scurried around in a cyclone of powder.

"Perfect!" he crowed before turning to the lighting director. "And can we warm up the lights? Katlynn's skin looks like a corpse."

"Give us a sec," the gaffer grumbled, huddled with his crew.

Katlynn hid her wince, concealing her growing worries about aging in a youth-obsessed industry.

"And Mary, do something about those dark circles under her eyes." The director peered at the camera's monitor.

Mary whispered, "If he calls you a corpse one more time, I'll put *him* in a grave."

"I'm thirty-two," Katlynn reminded Mary as she dotted concealer under Katlynn's eyes. "Ancient by LA standards."

"Pee-shaw," Mary clucked. "You're the most beautiful woman on TV. *People* magazine said so."

"Five years ago," Katlynn reminded her. Yesterday's news. What would happen when she wasn't young enough, pretty enough, to headline a show? Would she disappear, fall into the same obscurity she'd grown up in? Become no one again?

She shook the crazy thought aside. Six seasons and still going strong, *Scandalous History* was here to stay, her hosting position assured.

So why hadn't the network confirmed next season's renewal?

Mary lint-rolled Katlynn's dress then hustled out of frame when the key grip lifted three fingers for the countdown. He curled down one finger, two, then pointed the third. The director yelled, "Action!"

Katlynn leaned forward, lifted her left eyebrow and curled her mouth conspiratorially as she delivered the next take "salaciously."

One hour and eight takes later, Katlynn briskly strode from the taping room, every step agony as the heels Wardrobe paired with her tight sheath dress strangled her toes.

"Hi, Ms. Brennon."

"Hey, Bob." She flashed their set designer a broad smile without stopping. The minute she reached her dressing room she'd shut the door, kick off her shoes and wriggle free of the straitjacket masquerading as shapewear.

A couple of interns flattened against the wall when she approached, wide-eyed and silent as she passed.

Katlynn held her head high, soaking in the attention accompanying stardom on a major primetime show. Twelve years ago, she'd been a no one from Nowhere, Colorado. Growing up poor, the youngest of twelve children, she never had much, especially attention from her hardworking parents. She'd struggled to be seen and heard, to feel important, valued.

One time she'd even run away for two days to draw their attention. When she'd returned home, she discovered a humiliating truth. She hadn't even been missed.

"Your new eyelashes arrived, Katlynn," Mary huffed beside Katlynn, striving to match her long-legged stride. "If you have a sec…"

Despite her hurry, Katlynn slowed. "Sure." She shoved down her need for five minutes of blessed quiet and a non-cinched waist. She was a professional, not a prima donna.

"Also, Jennifer would like to squeeze in a fitting," Mary continued, referring to the show's wardrobe supervisor. "You're going to love this dress. It's a sheath, which'll show off your amazing figure. Plus, the rose color will be gorgeous with your blond hair and blue eyes. I've already picked out a custom lip color to match."

"Sounds great," Katlynn enthused, disguising her dismay. Another "body-conscious" dress. She made a mental note to call her trainer about extending her grueling workout sessions. Yay.

"I knew you'd like it!" Mary seized Katlynn's arm and steered her toward Wardrobe.

"Katlynn!" One of the show's producers approached, tie askew and slightly out of breath. "Tom's calling a meeting in five."

Alarm bells shrilled. Tom, their executive producer, usually followed a strict schedule, one that included an afternoon round of golf. What was important enough to make him miss his coveted tee time? News about their show's renewal? Surely, he could have just emailed them, unless...

"Sorry, Mary." Katlynn's heartbeat sped. "Tell Jen I'll stop by after the meeting, okay?"

"Thanks. You're a doll." Mary clomped away in square, comfortable-looking heels.

How long since Katlynn had worn anything practical like those to work? Even when running errands, she dressed up, maintaining the classy "brand" her PR agency insisted on, aware of lurking paparazzi eager for the "Stars, They're Just Like Us" money shot. Since landing in the tabloids when she dated a famous actor for a hot minute, they'd stalked her...a dream for her PR team, and, she'd admit it, a thrill for her. Still, what she'd give to shop in a pair of comfortable jeans and worn cowboy boots like back home.

"Everything okay, Braydon?" she asked as they practically galloped down the corridor.

"What's going on?" asked Ted, one of the show's writers, joining them.

"He didn't say." Braydon stopped abruptly and lowered his voice. "But according to his secretary, Mr. Warner called him an hour ago and they spoke *at length*."

"The new CEO?" Katlynn breathed, her internal alarm bells now shrieking. Recently acquired by another parent company, their network braced for changes, changes she feared included her being replaced. Out with the old; in with the new. "That's…interesting."

Ted crossed himself and mumbled something inaudible.

"I just saw the email about the meeting." Their head writer, Stella, emerged from the writer's room. "Are we canceled?"

"Not officially," Braydon groaned as they resumed their hurried trek to the conference room.

"Stay calm, everyone," Katlynn said through a smile when they reached the glass doors leading to the conference room. She pushed one open and glided in, projecting confidence and star power.

Never let them see you sweat.

"Katlynn, you look beautiful as usual." Tom stood, exchanged two air kisses with her, then drummed his fingertips on the long, mahogany conference table.

Somber-faced staff filed in and slid into their seats. Katlynn's cheeks hurt with the effort to keep her lips stretched upward. Eyes swerved between her and Tom. Someone coughed. Someone else tapped a pencil, a snare-drum sound.

Katlynn slid into her seat once everyone took their places. As the show's star, she was looked to for direction by the staff, and she wouldn't project fear. Beneath the table, though, her fingernails dug into her palms.

"Our acquisition by Ultima will allow us to reach a larger market share and produce a wider range of shows." Tom paused and gulped whatever his LA Lakers' mug contained. By the smell, Katlynn guessed whiskey.

She glimpsed Braydon pantomime slashing his throat and nudged the tip of his dress shoes beneath the table. When he mouthed, "What?" she lifted her eyebrows, a silent, "You know what." Followed by, "Stop." He was scaring the staff, given their wide eyes.

"We're thrilled to be under Ultima's umbrella," Tom continued, looking slightly sick, his skin tinged green. "However—"

"Here we go!" Braydon exclaimed.

Chairs creaked and fabric swished as several staff members fidgeted in their seats. Someone knocked over a coffee cup. Others fiddled with their phones beneath the table, frantically contacting their agents, Katlynn suspected…something she'd need to do, too. Possibly. If the show was getting the ax.

She gulped back the sour taste of fear and lifted her chin, her expression serene.

Fake it till you make it…

"It's not as dire as you think," Tom assured

them, dabbing at his perspiring brow. He shrugged off his jacket and draped it over the back of his leather chair, revealing wet stains beneath his arms.

Katlynn blinked. In all her years working with Tom, she'd never seen him without his suit coat. It was disconcerting, and the simple act felt like it heralded the apocalypse.

Was her dream of living in the spotlight, a person who counted, mattered and was noticed, over?

She'd arrived in LA twelve years ago with a broken heart and a job offer at a local news station. Since then she'd worked tirelessly to climb the ladder, meeting influential people, making the right connections, taking night classes to finish her broadcasting degree, even revamping her appearance and style from country mouse to LA chic. She would not go back, not when she'd come so far, sacrificed so much, including the man she'd once thought she'd love forever.

"What is it, then?" blurted their head writer, Stella. "Are we canceled?"

"No," Tom said, and a collective sigh of relief rose from the table. Katlynn released a long, shaky breath. "However, they're taking a closer look at the viability of some of the current programming, and *Scandalous History* is on the list."

"So, what's our status?" Braydon grabbed a mint from the bowl in the center of the table and struggled to unwrap it with shaking fingers.

"TBD," Tom stated flatly, his lips leached of color.

To be determined—purgatory for a television show—a temporary stop before cancellation.

No.

"We have to wow them, folks, and show an uptick in ratings to avoid the chopping block." Tom dropped his elbows on the table and leaned forward. "Let's brainstorm."

"That's our department." Stella's protest was joined by her nodding writers.

"We're in this together," Tom insisted. "We need a grand slam."

"What about Area 51? The sixties are far enough away to be history," suggested Braydon.

Tom shook his head. "Too sci-fi. We need something that screams Americana. An unsolved mystery maybe. Something to capture the viewers' imaginations and create watercooler buzz."

"I like that!" Stella scribbled on a pad then peered up through the square glasses perched on the tip of her nose.

"How about a missing ship, like the USS Wasp?" suggested their gaffer. "It headed to Bermuda after the War of 1812 then disappeared."

"Lots of great shots in the Caribbean," their director, Gabe, mused, his eyes now three-quarters open. "Plus, we'd get to film our gorgeous star on the beach." He squared his hands and framed Katlynn in them across the table. "The wind blowing through her platinum hair…a sarong around her bikini…"

Katlynn made a face at him, mostly embarrassed but also appreciative of the staff's approving glances.

"I'm a serious journalist, people. Put me in a one-piece at least," she joked, earning her a larger laugh than she deserved. Funny how fame amplified life. Everyone and everything was bigger, better, more beautiful. She no longer knew if people laughed at her jokes because they were funny, if others were nice because they liked her, or if they did favors without expecting something in return.

LA was a lonely place, despite all the attention. Still, it beat Carbondale, Colorado. She'd been invisible there except, for a brief time, when her ex-fiancé made her the center of his world. Yet, before their wedding, he'd shoved her needs aside like everyone else and broken her heart.

No.

He'd shattered it.

You could fix broken things, but shattered meant irreparable… Besides a few lackluster dates, she'd avoided romance since, determined to never open herself up to hurt again.

"USS Wasp…" Tom rubbed his chin, considering, then shook his head. "Sounds too military. We need something juicy and personal. Murder. Revenge. Stuff like that…"

Mystery. Scandal. Americana, murder and revenge. Katlynn's body froze as an idea detonated into her mind, nuclear-blast bright and just as devastating.

When a choking sound escaped her, staffers jumped to offer bottles of sparkling water.

"Are you okay?" Braydon thumped her back and appeared ready to perform the Heimlich.

She held up her hand as she swallowed a long, cold gulp of water. "F-fine."

Only she wasn't okay, not when she knew the perfect idea to save the show was one that might destroy her in the process.

"Anyone else?" Tom demanded.

"We could return to New Orleans," Stella suggested. "Dig up more on the Ax Man serial killer."

Tom's eyebrows crashed together. "No. We need something new. Something people sitting at home can relate to. A scandalous story about a family, maybe. Star-crossed lovers. Betrayal. Anything?"

Silence descended, and Katlynn's throat swelled,

the answer to the show's dilemma on the tip of her tongue.

"We're sunk," moaned one of the writers.

"Better call your agents, folks," Stella joked, not sounding amused.

Katlynn's heart squeezed when their sound tech, seven months pregnant with her first child, swiped away tears. She had to share an idea, which might save not only her career, but also those of this amazing group, who worked hard to make her shine.

At her throat-clearing, everyone quieted.

"Katlynn?" Tom asked, using the gentle voice he reserved for her. "Did you have a suggestion?"

She nodded, temporarily mute at the idea of returning home and seeing Cole Loveland. She'd fled Carbondale to save herself. Now she needed to return to it to do the same.

Oh, the irony.

"The Cade-Loveland feud," she said once she trusted her voice.

Stella stopped writing and glanced up. "I've heard of that…"

"A juicy scandal all right," Braydon added. "The longest-running family feud in America. Wasn't the rumor that the feud started when the poor, younger son of one family kidnapped the other family's heiress daughter and killed her?"

"That's one version. Some believe there was

a secret affair," added Katlynn, recalling more details. Just last month, when her mother finally returned Katlynn's call, she'd declared herself knocked over by a feather. Incredibly, the heads of the Cade and Loveland clans were engaged, and everyone in Carbondale speculated that a Titanic of a wedding disaster loomed.

Stella rubbed her hands together. "Ohhhhh, this is going to be juicy."

"It has it all." Tom nodded slowly. "Mystery, murder, betrayal, love and a jewel theft. Didn't a famous fifty-carat sapphire belonging to one of the families disappear at the time? What was it called? Carolyn's Tear?"

"Cora's Tear," Katlynn corrected, knowing the legend of the priceless stone having grown up in Carbondale, not to mention being engaged to the oldest son in the Loveland clan.

"That's your hometown, right?" Braydon asked.

Katlynn nodded, masking her dread. After leaving twelve years ago, she hadn't looked back. She never wanted to remember the nobody she'd been, the love she'd lost. Could she face her difficult past?

To save her show...yes. She'd have to see Cole to cover the story about his family. Only this time he'd realize he'd been wrong to ask her to give up her dreams, her ambitions. She'd learned to shine on her own so she'd never be diminished again.

"Do you have a connection with the families? An in?" Tom demanded, his voice rising. Excited murmurs circled the table.

Katlynn cleared her clogged throat with a cough. "I'm acquainted with them, yes."

Tom's broad smile revealed capped teeth in a flash of white. "Then it's settled. Katlynn, you've saved the day."

She lingered as the group filed out.

If she solved such a sensational historical mystery, it'd secure *Scandalous History*'s spot in next season's lineup, put them on the map and might even win her an Emmy. Could she handle returning home where her family, and the man she'd once loved, had made her feel inconsequential to do it?

"SHE'S DROPPED HER CALF," Cole Loveland informed his approaching father, pointing to the bellowing gray Brahman lying on the frosted ground. He'd herded the "heavy" into the small field adjacent to the calving shed last night when he'd noticed the beginning signs of labor. Since then, Cole had checked on the heifer every hour, concerned for the first-time mother.

"Doesn't appear interested in her calf." Boyd reined his brown quarter horse to a stop, and they watched the wet newborn shiver in the freezing dawn.

If the mother didn't lick it dry soon, it'd die of hypothermia. Cole's brown and white paint horse, Cash, sidestepped and nickered, sensing Cole's unease.

"She's new to it." Cole steadied his stallion while keeping his eyes on the imperiled calf.

"Might have to pen the two and see if we can't force them to bond." Boyd huddled in his saddle. His fleece-lined work jacket was zipped against the arctic temperature.

Spring officially began a couple weeks ago, but frigid air still gripped their Rocky Mountain ranch. Lingering snow capped nearby Mount Sopris, and the rising sun reflected on the white peak, coloring it rose gold against the lavender sky.

"Let's give her a minute. See if we can avoid stressing them." Cole watched, narrow-eyed, as the exhausted heifer snorted then sank her head to the ground. Meanwhile, the newborn struggled to rise, its sodden limbs heavy and uncoordinated. It bawled, a child's universal appeal to its mother for help. The Brahman continued to stare listlessly forward, though, as if she hadn't heard a thing.

"Can't afford to lose any more calves." Boyd reached into his saddlebag and passed over an insulated coffee thermos.

Cole's fingers, numb despite his gloves, fumbled to open the tab. He lifted it to his nose and breathed in the fortifying, pungent brew. Scalding black liquid burned his tongue as he swigged it back. Instantly, energy zapped his fatigued body, worn through after twenty-four hours of ranch work, anxious vigilance and no sleep. "Saw we got a letter from the bank yesterday."

"Yep," his father answered, noncommittal.

Cole slid a sideways glance at his pa's weathered face, his expression inscrutable beneath the wide brim of his rancher's hat. Tough old cowboy. He never gave a thing away.

"What's it say?" Cole asked as the calf hoisted itself on its front legs before it slipped and fell again. Its mother glanced back and pushed to her knees. A sign they were beginning to bond?

"Final notice."

His father shared the devastating news as if relaying the weather. "Cold out today," Cole imagined him saying. "Mind the ice. And our one-hundred-and-thirty-year-old family ranch is about to be foreclosed on."

Cole swore under his breath. The Lovelands had battled to remain solvent for generations, despite their lack of access to the Crystal River. Property lines ceding water rights to their feuding neighbors, the Cades, required longer, danger-riddled cattle drives to distant water sources, depleting Loveland herds. A recent three-year drought pushed them nearly to the point of no return.

He had to find a way to save the ranch.

And it wouldn't be by benefiting from his father's imminent marriage to Joy Cade, Cade Ranch's widowed matriarch, despite whispered speculation. Lovelands made their own way, provided for their family and didn't take charity.

Besides, Cade Ranch was jointly owned by the Cade siblings, and Joy only owned a small percentage of the property.

"How much time do we have?" As Cole watched, the new mother struggled to her feet and meandered a short distance from her crying calf, attempting to graze. Was she about to abandon it? Cole's anxiety intensified.

"It'll go up for auction within the month."

"Before the wedding." Cole passed the thermos to his father, his dismay compounding. News like this set tongues wagging. It'd further fuel rumors of his father being an opportunist who married for money.

"Yes." The hint of despair in Pa's voice set Cole's teeth on edge. "Unless we accept James Cade's offer."

"No." They'd never allow rivals to buy their land and rent it back to them, no matter how fair the offer. James vowed the deal would be just between them, but Cole's pride wouldn't let him accept.

Being talked about in public got under his skin. The child of an alcoholic parent, he'd grown up in a house full of secrets. When his mother killed herself on his sixteenth birthday, her father, a senator, fed the press fake stories and suggested foul play to pressure law enforcement to open a homicide investigation.

When the press labeled Boyd a murderous opportunist after his wife's inheritance, it'd nearly broken him.

Now, on the eve of a second chance at love, Cole's father might be the subject of malicious, widespread gossip and press again.

No.

He could not let that happen.

The heifer inched farther away, rutting hay scattered over the frozen ground, an eye flicking to her calf now and again. She was curious. If Cole gave them more space, would she take to mothering? Some things couldn't be forced. Even penning them together wasn't a guarantee. His mother had been surrounded by her children and she'd never considered them over her addiction.

His lonely father deserved happiness, a scandal-free wedding and a loving marriage with his former childhood sweetheart. Yet the Cade-Loveland family truce was temporary at best given their

continued water rights and cattle disputes. They'd
be fortunate to get through the wedding peace-
fully without outside pressure riling simmering
tensions.

Tomorrow Cole would ask the loan officers to
postpone the foreclosure until after summer. A
rainy season might turn things around and help
them replenish the herd. Despite the long-shot
odds, he had to try.

He'd devoted his life to Loveland Hills, sacrificed all, including his heart, once. He'd never
leave it voluntarily. Not while he still breathed.
Lovelands stood by each other. His father gave
up his happiness for his kids' sakes. He'd earned
their loyalty, no matter how it'd nearly broken
Cole when he'd had to let go of the one person
who'd meant everything to him.

The calf ominously stopped bawling, and its
movements slowed to mere twitches. An arctic gust billowed Cash's mahogany mane like a
sail. Another five minutes in these conditions and
the newborn would die. Cole's fingers clenched
around the reins.

"Let's bring 'em in." Boyd patted the rope
looped on the side of his saddle. "She's not keen
on being a mother."

Cole watched the now listless calf. His heart
went out to the youngling. A mother should care
for her offspring, dang it.

"Got one last idea." He whistled for their cattle dog, Boomer. The black-and-white border collie sprang from beneath the calving shed's eave, ears up and forward, eyes on his master. Cole ordered Boomer into the field and held his breath.

The clever dog crept across the white ground, body low. The newborn's eyes rolled, whites showing, as it struggled to drag itself away from a perceived threat. The stream of its frantic bleats whipped the heifer's head around. White huffed from her flaring nostrils when she spied Boomer.

"Get him, girl," Cole urged the Brahman beneath his breath, leaning forward in the saddle. Hopefully, his gamble paid off and the "predator" nearing her offspring would arouse her maternal instincts.

"Boomer's got her attention," Boyd observed quietly as they watched the tense standoff.

The collie crept closer, and the heifer stamped her hooves.

Fueled by terror, the calf surged to its feet and trembled in place, its strength expended. Boomer advanced a couple more steps, and the heifer issued a loud warning bellow.

"You gonna call that dog back?" Boyd asked out of the corner of his mouth. "He's likely to get trampled."

"I trust him," Cole replied firmly. As the ranch manager, he trained all their cattle dogs, including Boomer, to herd, load and drive. Despite everything gone wrong in his life—a called-off wedding, failed love life and looming foreclosure, Cole excelled at commanding his working dogs.

Cole watched as Boomer eyed the thousand-pound Brahman, sliding another paw forward, then another, drawing within bite distance of the terrified, braying calf.

Then the mother charged, fueled by maternal fury, surging at Boomer. The cattle dog expertly dodged her deadly hooves and scuttled clear.

Cole held up his hand, halting the collie's retreat. They weren't out of the woods yet. Best keep pressuring.

One eye on Boomer, the heifer sniffed her calf. Her tongue darted out and her rough lick tipped the newborn's head.

"Atta girl," Cole muttered, his chest loosening as he dragged in his first full breath in hours.

"Nicely done, son," Boyd said and the rare praise from his stoic father caught Cole with unexpected warmth. Living life on the edge of personal and financial disaster had a way of threatening a man's pride. He took his victories where he could. They'd saved the calf whose mother now lavished it with a thorough bathing.

Could they save the ranch, too?

"Looks like our work's done." Pa wheeled his

horse around and nudged it into a walk down the rutted lane to their stable.

"I'll keep checking on them." Cole brought Cash up alongside his father's mustang. Boomer kept pace.

Only the twittering of waking birds, and the clip of hooves striking hard ground, broke the silence. Overhead, the iridescent sky glowed. Light now striped the fallow fields awaiting this year's planting, and their shadows rode ahead.

"I'll stop down to First National at nine," Cole said once they'd reached the stable and untacked the horses. The sweet smell of grain rose as he poured cornmeal into Cash's feed bucket, a treat for the exhausted horse.

"No need to waste your time, son." Cool water misted the air as Boyd filled the water troughs. Several horses hung their heads outside their stall doors, nosy about the early activity, nickering to the new arrivals.

"It's not a waste." Cole doled out halved apples to his siblings' mounts. "If I can convince them to hold off a couple months, and we have a good season, we could turn things around."

"I figured out another way without including the bank." Boyd pulled the stable door shut behind them once they finished.

"Good to hear." Cole glanced at his frowning

father from the corner of his eye. Why didn't Pa seem pleased?

"Not sure you'll think so." They ambled closer to the two-story homestead built by their ancestor, Colonel Archibald Loveland, an army veteran. He'd deserted from the Colorado War, married a Cheyenne interpreter and settled here over a hundred and thirty years ago, breathing life into the first of many Loveland scandals.

Must be in their blood.

"Why would I object?" Cole noticed a few green shoots alongside the fieldstone walkway to their front porch. With any luck, they might get three hay crops...

Boyd paused on the porch's stairs. "Was approached by an outfit to do a story about our feud with the Cades. They'll pay enough to cover our mortgage through the season if I give them access to the property."

Cole leaned against the pine banister, absorbing his father's news. Like the rest of the home, it'd been culled from the distant forests and hauled over great distances. Their ranch was a bastion against a landscape of forbidding mountains, its warm hearth and hand-hewn timber beams communicating self-reliance, simplicity and lack of pretentions. His heart swelled at the thought of what his ancestors had wrought.

They'd fight to their last breaths to safeguard

their family's legacy. But a story dredging up old scandals? It'd upset the tenuous peace between them and the Cades and jeopardize his father's wedding. His hard-won happiness.

"What kind of outfit? Something local?" Cole's hands tightened around the banister as he recalled the frenzied media who'd hounded his family after his mother's death.

"Cable show." For some reason, his pa seemed to have trouble meeting Cole's eye.

"National TV?" Cole squinted into the strengthening sunshine and glimpsed an approaching black car bumping down their drive. "We don't want them sniffing around the place, dragging out old skeletons."

"Better than being thrown off our land before the wedding," Pa countered.

Cole shoved his balled hands into his pockets, unable to counter the argument. "They'll drag up stuff about Ma."

The vehicle neared, its engine's smooth purr sounding expensive, foreign. Out-of-towners. Someone lost?

"Got assurances to the contrary." Boyd stepped off the porch and, to Cole's astonishment, waved two hands overhead as if he expected whoever was driving.

"Who's this?" Cole strode to his father's side

and peered at dark-tinted windows as the town car slid to a smooth stop.

"The show's producer and host."

"This is a done deal!" Cole exclaimed. "Why'd you keep it from me? Does anyone else know?"

The door opened and a fetching pair of slim, shapely legs in black heels emerged.

"Nope. You're the first."

A tall blonde ducked gracefully from the car. Something about her struck him as if he knew her, though he wasn't sure with the sun backlighting her, casting her features in shadow.

"I don't understand."

A suited man joined the lady, and they stepped gingerly across the pebbled drive. She held her head high and stared directly at him.

"The show's called *Scandalous History*," Pa said, then hustled to greet his company.

Scandalous History… Now where had Cole heard of it?

Then it hit him, a sucker punch straight to the gut, leaving him off balance.

"Hello, Cole."

His body stiffened at the familiar, silky-smooth voice. A flash of memory—listening to her speak as they'd watched campfires, star-gazed, fly-fished—pulled a lump into his throat. He'd once thought her words sounded like lyrics, her laughter a song. He'd also thought she walked on water until she'd skated right out of his life.

He peered into the beautiful face he'd seen in his dreams, the one he envisioned while riding the range, gorgeous as ever with her perfectly symmetrical features and large blue eyes in a heart-shaped face. Only she looked different somehow. More sophisticated. Elegant. As if someone had slapped a coat of varnish over her natural beauty, making it harder to see who she really was…if he'd ever really known at all.

Old hurt stalked through him, residual anger on its heels. When she'd left, she'd nearly done him in. Was she back to finish the job? Not a chance.

His jaw clamped shut, and he spoke through gritted teeth, minding his manners for Pa's sake until he got rid of her and the threat she posed to him and his family.

"Welcome home, Katie-Lynn."

CHAPTER TWO

KATIE-LYNN.

Besides her family, no one had used her real name since she'd changed it to match her make-over. Katie-Lynn was another person, a ghost from her past.

In LA she was a star.

Remember that girl.

"Katie-Lynn, you're as pretty as ever." Boyd beamed at her as he pulled a can of coffee from a wooden cabinet. He hadn't changed much. Sun streaming through the kitchen's windows glowed on his thick white hair and highlighted unbowed shoulders in a flannel shirt. The extra lines on his craggy face added to his distinguished appearance.

"That's sweet of you. Thanks. And I go by Katlynn, now."

"Help yourself to some fruit if you're hungry," Boyd added. "I could make you some toast if you haven't had breakfast."

"No. This is great." She leaned across the oak table, filched a cherry from a bowl and popped it into her mouth, hyperaware of Cole's eyes trained solely on her. The sensation was unsettling. It reminded her of the buzz of anticipation accompanying a roller coaster's first lurch, one she'd ridden before. This time, however, she knew the drops, twists and corners ahead.

Her limbs stiffened, and her jaw clamped as she fought the crazy urge to squeeze her eyes shut. She practically lived under a microscope in California; why did Cole's scrutiny fluster her?

She squashed the disturbing question—he had no sway over her anymore—and glanced across the table at the inscrutable rancher. Cole Donovan Loveland, the first man she'd ever loved, and the only man who'd ever broken her heart.

His eyes were still that unnerving shade of clear, glacier blue. Clipped black hair showed no signs of gray or thinning. And he was still crazy tall—obviously—people don't shrink in their thirties, least of all a Loveland.

Katlynn's toes tapped the wide-planked floor.

Cole was as mountain-size and rugged as his surroundings, and he still radiated his enigmatic, I'm-the-puzzle-you'll-never-solve vibe. Oh…no. This was not good.

"Katie-Lynn?" Tom's nose scrunched as if he smelled something bad. In his polished Italian loafers and custom suit, her producer appeared out of place in this rustic setting. Hollywood

called him a shark, but in the Rockies, he resembled a beached guppy.

"I didn't have a say in picking my name," she said beneath her breath. "Then."

Cole's narrow-eyed gaze darted between them.

"Don't you think she looks pretty, Cole?" Boyd persisted, dumping ground beans into an old-school coffeemaker.

At Cole's noncommittal grunt, her shoulders squared inside the tasteful black dress she'd carefully selected for today.

For Cole.

To impress him; to show him how far she'd come from the mouse he'd once dismissed. To earn his approval...

Why?

Because you're an idiot.

An empty watering can atop a mat in the center of the table snagged her eye. In a flash, she was seventeen again, picking daisies with Cole to fill it.

"Here's one for your hair." He'd tucked a flower behind her ear. "Though you're the one making *it* look pretty."

And she'd blushed, amazed the popular, athletic boy in high school had even noticed her, let alone made her his girlfriend. She'd felt special. Important.

"How about some coffee?" Boyd's question

pulled her back to the present with a jolt, her stomach tipping side to side.

A roasted-bean aroma erupted from the gurgling coffeemaker. Over Boyd's shoulder, a brick hearth covered most of the back wall. Her mouth twitched as she recalled a disastrous strawberry-rhubarb pie-making attempt with Cole using one of the baking slits. They'd spent hours scrubbing goo off those stones…and had a fun time doing it.

How her tastes had changed.

Refined.

A good time nowadays meant a glass of Dom Perignon, preferably White Gold, while attending a star-studded event to see and be seen.

"None for me." Tom stabbed at his cell phone then circled it overhead, searching for a signal.

Her eyes lingered on the coffeemaker's glass carafe. One pot for everyone. No individual cup allowances for mint chocolate coffee or hazelnut vanilla… Here, coffee was coffee. Period. There was a simplicity about it she found refreshing. Sometimes when you had too many choices, you focused on the little things and lost sight of the big picture. Her eyes flicked to Cole again then scurried off, circling the room, landing anywhere but on the magnetic cowboy.

"Katie—I mean, Katlynn?" Boyd gently prompted, as considerate a host as ever. "Coffee?"

"Sounds great."

"It won't be fancy like Starbucks," Cole drawled, his deep, Johnny Cash baritone as gravelly as she remembered. Her heart added a couple extra beats.

"I'm sure it'll be great," she replied firmly, striving to stay "mindful" and in the present moment as her life coach advised. Deep breath in, anxiety, frustration, despair, out.

Deep breath in, returning attraction and insecurities regarding ex-fiancé, way *out*.

"Are you staying at the Holsford?" Boyd asked, referring to the small town's only hotel.

"They've double-booked my suite."

"You're welcome to share mine." Tom's perfectly shaped eyebrows twitched in the limited way his Botox allowed.

Cole's lips pressed into a flat line.

"Or you could stay here." Boyd cast a quick glance at Cole.

Sunlight glinted off Boyd's silver and turquoise bolo tie, the one he donned for special occasions. How sweet that he'd dressed up. "We've got plenty of room now that Cole's living in one of the cabins and Maverick's out on his PBR tour," Boyd beamed. "Oh—and Daryl got hitched a while back. He and his wife have a cottage not far from here. You're welcome to stay."

From a professional standpoint, staying on

Loveland Hills gave her immediate and frequent access to the investigation as well as her location shoots. From a personal standpoint, it'd mean spending too much time around Cole.

Too dangerous.

"Thanks, but I'll stay at my folks' place." She crossed her fingers on her lap. Hopefully...if her mother would return her calls...

"Where can I get a signal?" Tom scooted his spindle-backed chair from the table and stood.

"Signal?" Boyd stared at him, confused, the line between his brows deepening.

"For his cell phone." Cole jerked his thumb at the door. "Try the porch."

Tom mumbled his thanks as the screen door clicked shut behind him.

"We don't have cell service." Boyd poured coffee into a World's Best Dad mug.

The upward tug of Cole's full lips snared her attention. He looked so handsome sitting across from her, his broad shoulders filling out his thermal shirt, his lightly bristled jaw begging to be touched. He cocked his head and caught her staring. Katlynn dropped her eyes, sure everyone could hear her heart thundering in her chest.

"It got him out of our hair at least." His thick-lashed eyes gleamed at Katlynn when her gaze darted his way again, and he arched a challenging brow.

Was he planning on getting rid of her next?

She lifted her chin. Well, he could try. She wasn't as easy to discard as she used to be.

"Cream? Sugar?" Boyd held up a pitcher of foamy, fresh milk.

"Do you have skim milk? Artificial sweetener?" she asked with a sigh. After failing to zipper Jennifer's rose sheath, Katlynn vowed to lose five pounds on this trip.

"No. But I could run to the store."

"She'll survive without fake sugar," Cole asserted, folding muscular arms even a personal trainer would envy. "And a few extra calories would do her some good."

Was he calling her skinny? She was a size six—practically obese in her industry, hence the necessary evil of slimming undergarments. Speaking of which, she shifted in her seat to alleviate their cruel pinch.

"I'll just have it black." She sucked on another cherry, the action seeming to fascinate an intently staring Cole.

"Cole? Want a cup?"

"I'll fix it." He snagged a cup out of the cupboard and banged it down on the counter. As he added a generous amount of cream, his lips twisted in a sardonic grin aimed her way.

"Hope it's not too plain for you." Boyd handed over the coffee then seated himself beside her.

She sipped her drink, enjoying the rich, unvarnished flavor, so different than her usual nonfat latte with a caramel drizzle. Boyd's concerned face relaxed at her smile and nod.

"Really good, Mr. Loveland. Best cup I've had in years."

"Well, now…" Boyd cleared his throat gruffly, looking embarrassed, then switched topics. "Glad to have you back home. We've missed seeing you around the place. Haven't we, Cole?"

"You're back to film a show about my family?" he asked instead of answering his father.

Her eyes lingered on his body as he leaned against the counter—tall, broad and thick with muscle. Cole was dressed in jeans, a thermal shirt and a down vest, pretty much the same thing he'd always worn, if memory served. And her memory seemed to be disturbingly clear where Cole Loveland was concerned.

She gave herself a little shake followed by a coffee chaser.

Get it together. You're a professional. Not a high school girl crushing on the homecoming king.

Not anymore.

"You've heard of my show, *Scandalous History*…?" How strange to talk to Cole again, to drink coffee and behave civilly, like she'd never been in his arms, kissed those lips, cried those tears.

It takes grace to remain kind in cruel situations...

Cole shrugged, and the simple motion communicated one simple truth. She was as irrelevant to his world as ever. Well. Fine, then, since her world had outgrown his.

"Like I told your father," she said smoothly, drawing on her vocal training to sound strong, assured, impervious, as if breathing the same air as her ex had no residual effect. "We do investigative reports about American history."

"Where's the scandalous part come in?" Cole sauntered back to the table and grabbed his seat.

Her muscles tensed. Boyd rushed to her defense. "No harm in speculating about old news—it doesn't hurt anyone."

"Most of your subjects are dead, correct?"

At her nod, Cole turned to his father. "Our situation's different."

Concern spiked. Was Cole thinking about his mother and the media frenzy? "No one will be harmed because of the show."

"Katlynn's only focusing on the feud." Boyd dropped more sugar into his coffee. His spoon clanked against the mug's sides as he stirred.

"What guarantee do we have?"

She met Cole's direct stare head-on, determined to win him over for her show's sake. "My word."

"You gave me your word once before," he said slowly as though the words were razor blades, slashing his mouth as he released them. They cut her deep, too. "I haven't forgotten how that worked out."

"Neither have I."

Boyd's eyes flicked between them in the tense silence. "That's water under the bridge, kids."

A muscle jumped in Cole's jaw, and she carefully pried her clenched fingers from her mug handle.

Boyd was right. Their broken engagement was yesterday's news. Not worth covering. Or revisiting. No matter how the journalist in her wished to excavate their history for the answer to a basic question:

Why hadn't he loved her enough?

"Katie-Lynn? What are you doing here?" A tall, dark-haired man dressed in a tan sheriff's uniform appeared at the bottom of the stairs leading from the second-floor bedrooms. In three giant strides, Cole's younger brother and Carbondale's local sheriff, Travis, swept her into his arms for a tight hug.

"She goes by Katlynn now," Cole said.

"Your father gave my show permission to shoot some episodes about your feud with the

Cades." She eased away and grinned up at Travis extra wide, since it seemed to get under a fidgeting Cole's skin.

"*Scandalous History*, right?"

At her nod, Travis turned to his father. "Why didn't you say something?"

"Wanted Cole to know first."

Travis's broad smile fell and his chiseled features, slightly more refined than Cole's, sobered. "Right." He shot his brooding older brother a long look before heading to the coffee machine. "What've you learned so far?"

"We're still in preliminary stages, so I don't know much beyond what I grew up hearing. I plan on interviewing family members, consulting with local historians and digging through old town records for land surveys and such."

"Will that clear up our water rights dispute?" Cole asked.

She remembered the restrictions keeping the Lovelands' ranch on the brink of bankruptcy back in high school. "It's something I'm going to investigate."

"I'll see if the sheriff's office has anything." Travis poured himself a cup of coffee and drank it black, his hip propped against the counter.

"That'd be a big help. Thanks." Katlynn settled back in her chair and peered at the three handsome men. Lovelands were legendary for their incredible good looks and their willingness to lend a hand when needed. They were strong, principled men of action few dared to cross. "Would any of you know if correspondence between Maggie Cade and Everett Loveland exists? Letters? A journal Everett might have kept?"

Boyd shook his head slowly. "Not that I know of, but you're welcome to check through the house and property."

"We've also got cabins that once housed ranch hands. Some haven't been occupied in decades." Travis drained his mug and rinsed his cup. "If Maggie and Everett met in private, one of those might have been the spot."

"A lover's nest…" Boyd mused.

Her nose tingled, itching as it always did whenever she caught scent of a lead. "Great. No telling where the clues are, but I'm determined to uncover what happened between those two."

"It's not a mystery," Cole said. "The Cades, hotheaded as always, jumped to conclusions when they discovered Everett by their runaway daughter's lifeless body and their family brooch…"

"Cora's Tear," Travis supplied.

"Right, and the jewel missing." Cole passed a hand over his thick black hair. "Then they strung up Everett, no questions asked, since they decided he must have coerced their innocent daughter to steal the priceless heirloom. They dispensed prairie justice like outlaw vigilantes."

"And the murderers broke out of jail and hid in the mountains, harassing our ranch for years." Travis squinted out the window at nearby Mount Sopris as if wishing he could travel back in time to apprehend them personally.

Hopefully, she'd bring the family closure and justice.

"Are you planning on digging up our property to search for the jewel? It'll disrupt operations during our busy season." Cole leaned forward, elbows bent.

"We might excavate a few areas if we have a strong lead," Katlynn said. "I'll follow the facts where they lead me."

"Spoken like a true investigator." Travis shot her a smile, donned his hat then opened the door. "Y'all have a good day."

"The jewel isn't on this land," Cole insisted.

"Guess we'll see."

"What makes you think Everett took it?" Boyd asked.

"He was the last one seen with Maggie, and the Cades don't have it… If your family took the jewel, it'd explain the bump in business for Loveland Hills after Cora's Tear went missing. Some say your family may have sold it and used the money to expand your operation. In that case, the jewel would be long gone... However, my preliminary research reveals no transactions or sightings of the infamous piece."

"This investigation might stir up trouble between our families again. Discord we don't need."

Her heart squeezed when she spied Cole's concerned expression, his gaze on his father. Boyd had gone through a lot, and Cole was loyal to those he loved.

When push came to shove, he'd picked his family, his ranch, his old life, over a new one with her.

"The truth will set you free," Boyd said. "We need to lift this cloud. It's been hanging over us for too long."

"If *Katie-Lynn* proves Cora's Tear was here, and our ancestors sold it—which I doubt—then we may as well give James Cade our ranch. We couldn't pay back its worth."

Katie-Lynn.

He refused to use her new name, see the person she'd become. Knowing Cole, this would be an ongoing battle of wills. "What's James Cade got to do with it?"

At her question, Cole shot his father a warning look. "Pa..."

"She may as well know all." Boyd's lips drooped in the corners. "We're on the brink of foreclosure. A while back James Cade privately offered to buy the ranch at full market value and rent it back to us. It's a more than fair offer, considering what the bank would get at auction. We've put off giving him our answer, but we received the bank's final notice yesterday. Your show's compensation buys us a few more months. Otherwise we'd be deeding this land to James."

"Keep that between us." Cole's face paled beneath his farmer's tan.

A heaviness filled her at the thought of the proud, hardworking Lovelands losing their land. It'd be devastating, especially for Cole, who'd sacrificed for it. He'd wanted it above all else. Even her. "I promise. It's off the record."

"I trust Katlynn," Boyd vowed. "She was almost family."

Almost. Her eyes stung at his staunch support. She would have loved to be a part of the tight-knit Loveland clan, so unlike her own.

"If the public discovers our financial status, people will think Pa's marrying another rich woman for her money." Cole's fingers drummed on the table.

Tom stomped inside. "Who's marrying for money? Sounds interesting."

"Just debating causes for the feud," Katlynn temporized, and the tip of Cole's boot touched her foot beneath the table. Her eyes flew to his, and she melted a little at the glimmer of warmth in their blue depths.

"Throw in as much scandal as you can, and we've got America hooked."

Cole's eyes narrowed on Tom, shooting sparks.

"We'll only report verifiable facts," she hurried to assure Cole and Boyd.

"And speculate on those we can't," Tom cut in, not helping at all. "And you're right, Katlynn. We are in the middle of nowhere. Can't get a signal."

"Could use the landline."

Boyd pointed to a rotary phone mounted on the wall beside a cuckoo clock as old as the house.

Tom studied it a moment, then gingerly lifted the handset, turning it every which way. "Where are the buttons?"

Cole lifted an eyebrow as the left edge of his lips tipped up in an amused smile, his silent "can you believe this" look.

She flared her nose and scrunched her eyes, her old expression for "Shut it." Then she flattened her lips to keep from smiling back at him.

She was here to work. Not flirt. Especially with an ex capable of shaking her hard-won confidence.

Tires crunched on the rocky drive outside. Tom peered through the window then whirled. "Good. The director's found us. Mr. Loveland, would you show us the lay of the land? We need to scout the property for potential shots."

"You got it." Boyd grabbed his coat and shoved his arms through its sleeves. "It'd be a relief to resolve the feud before the wedding." Boyd settled a wide-brimmed brown rancher's hat over his head. "I'm hoping to make us all one happy family."

"I should have said congratulations right away, Mr. Loveland." She hugged Boyd and breathed in the comforting smell of his Old Spice cologne.

"Katlynn, you know to call me Boyd. Could have been Pa if you two had worked out."

Tom's openmouthed expression was quickly replaced by a speculative stare. "You were engaged to him?" He pointed at Cole, who rose to his full, towering height. "I mean. That's a surprise. No judgment." He backed through the door away from the advancing giant. "I'll meet you outside, Mr. Loveland." And with that, he scurried away.

"Twitchy guy, ain't he?" Boyd observed, pulling on his gloves.

"Twitchy?" Katlynn almost laughed to hear the Hollywood power player reduced to those terms. Must be the Rocky Mountains effect. It put everything into perspective.

"Pa's got it right." Cole's boots clomped on the

wide-planked floor as he neared. "Want me to ride out with you?"

"No. Check on the heifer and calf after Katlynn's finished her coffee."

"I'm done with it." Panic rose at being alone with Cole. "I'll ride with you."

Boyd's gaze dropped to her designer heels. "You're not dressed for the climbing we'll be doing, let alone riding. Besides, you said you wanted to start interviewing family. Sierra will be in some time this morning. Daryl, too."

"Thanks, Mr.… I mean, thanks, Boyd." She turned to Cole with a sinking heart.

Great.

Just great.

Who didn't want to rehash ancient history with the man who'd shattered her once fragile heart?

COLE MANEUVERED THE ATV around another rut a few minutes later, careful not to bounce the vehicle or spew dirt up at Katie-Lynn—Katlynn— since her dress probably cost more than he made in a month. Maybe two. Or three…

What did he know about dresses?

But this one looked expensive, like every inch of the new version of her he hardly recognized. Although, he had to admit she looked fine in the fitted black dress, her legs as long and sleek as he remembered.

"I'm sorry to hear your ranch is struggling," she shouted over the roaring engine, her smooth platinum hair now wild, whipping around her flushed face in a golden-white stream.

"It's not as bad as Pa made out," his pride prompted him to holler back. Katie-Lynn was beautiful, successful and famous and who was he? A soon-to-be homeless cowboy with no prospects. Not exactly a catch by anyone's standards, let alone a star like Katie-Lynn.

Not that he was looking to get caught...

But her knowing how low his family had fallen, financially, stung him hard.

He had to turn the ranch around without selling family secrets to the highest bidder and risking his father's happiness. And he sure wasn't selling to the Cades.

Katie-Lynn turned and mouthed something to him; he caught the word, "Foreclosure."

He shook his head, keeping his eyes dead ahead in case they betrayed him, a trick he'd learned from a childhood spent keeping secrets. Katie-Lynn, on the other hand, had always lived her life out where anyone could see it, the good, the bad and the ugly, open and unafraid.

He'd admired that about her once.

Loved her for it.

Only now that trait might come back to bite him. If she revealed too much about their financial situation, shared it with the world, the Lovelands would never hold their heads up again in Carbondale, and his father's chance at happiness might vanish if Joy changed her mind. He had to convince Katie-Lynn to back off the story.

He peered at her, briefly, from the corner of his eye, taking in the delicate slope of her nose, the soft curve of her cheek, the rounded point of her chin, and his heart eased. Beneath the war paint, she was still the girl who'd held his hand at his mother's funeral, who'd kissed away his tears and listened as he'd rambled, raged and ranted during the most difficult time of his life. They used to climb up an ancient gnarled oak they'd dubbed their Say Anything tree and shout their problems to the wind, speaking everything they couldn't say to anyone else.

Would she listen and agree to kill the story? Put him and his family ahead of her ambitions and career? She hadn't before, but it was worth a shot.

A couple minutes later he parked the ATV by the calving shed, hurried around to Katie-Lynn's side and helped her out. For a moment he stared deep into her blue eyes, and his heart stopped, the birds silenced, the wind stilled, and the entire world narrowed down to just her and the feel of her soft skin against his. He breathed in her expensive perfume and recalled her clean, cottony scent that used to remind him of laundry hung on a line to dry. Fresh and full of life.

"I miss the way you used to smell."

He realized he said it out loud when her long lashes—artificial and alien-looking—blinked up at him. "You remember how I smelled?"

He forced himself to release her hand and nodded to the field behind the shed, heat stinging his cheeks. "The new calf's over there," he said gruffly.

She tilted her head and considered him for a long moment before nodding. "Let's see it."

His hand settled on the small of her back as he guided her across the uneven terrain. When they stopped at the fence, she climbed up one slat, heels and all, to lean over the top rail.

"Oh! He's beautiful, isn't he?" she breathed then turned her sparkling smile on him, full wattage. His mind seized like an overheating engine. Total meltdown. Speaking was clearly not an option. Luckily for him, Katie-Lynn had always been able to talk enough for them both.

"I love Brahmans," she babbled on, and he closed his eyes and let his ears drink in the rushing, soothing sound. "They've always been my favorite. Their gray coats. The hump in their backs. So unique. Plus, they have the best temperaments. Look how sweet his mother is being to him. He's nursing like a champ. When did you say he was born? Cole? You in there?"

His lids flew open. "A couple of hours ago."

"Were you up all night watching her?"

He nodded.

Her nails, perfect red ovals to match her lipstick, lightly scraped his hand when she patted it. "You must be exhausted. I remember pulling those all-nighters with you. Remember the time when the calf was breach, and we turned it with the rope?"

"Surprised you remember."

"There isn't much I've forgotten about us." She ducked her head and fiddled with the short zipper on the side of her dress.

He glanced at her bare ring finger, picturing the small, heart-shaped diamond he'd once placed there…the one still resting in his bedside drawer. "You're not married?"

"No. Too busy for romance. You?"

He exhaled the air stuck in his lungs. What was it to him if she dated anyone? Yet it mattered, more than it should. "Same."

They watched the nursing calf in silence. The loamy smells of fresh earth and dew-tipped grass was in the air, and a crisp wind blew down from the mountains. "You got rid of the pool."

"The year after you left." He hid his wince, recalling their first date at his sixteenth birthday party and his mother's drowning. Katie had been by his side when he'd found his mother.

Back then Katie-Lynn had chattered when he couldn't speak, held him when he couldn't stand and touched him when he couldn't feel. She'd acted as his buffer, allowing him to deal with the world from a distance, filtered through her sunshine.

"A lot has changed since then." The Brahman heifer bellowed when she spied them on the fence, protective of her newborn.

"Your freckles," he observed, watching the calf suckle.

"Freckles?"

He cocked his head and studied Katie-Lynn's smooth, flawless skin. It resembled porcelain—fragile and untouchable—so unlike the country girl-next-door he'd known. Loved. "What happened to them?"

"My plastic surgeon lasered them off." She said it like someone might say, "My dentist cleaned my teeth." As though having a plastic surgeon was no big deal, and maybe it wasn't in Hollywood.

"Why do you have a plastic surgeon?"

"To make me beautiful."

He shook his head, marveling. "You already were pretty."

He preferred pretty to beautiful the way he

liked a daisy better than an orchid. One was fresh, open and bright. The other was perfect, waxy and exotic, which was why people prized them, he guessed. He'd always been more partial to natural wonders.

"Not pretty enough. Not by Hollywood standards." She ran her hands through her tousled strands, smoothing them flat to her skull like a ribbon of golden silk.

"Why'd you dye your hair?"

"Platinum looks better on screen. You don't like it?" Her teeth appeared on her bottom lip, white against scarlet, and he had the crazy urge to kiss her lipstick off to reveal her natural rose mouth underneath.

"It's different. I liked it darker. Honey-brown."

She tilted her face to the sun and closed her eyes. "I'm different."

"I noticed." She'd changed, and he hadn't, living a hermit's life except for volunteering at Fresh Start, a local rehab and mental health facility, and working the ranch with two of his siblings, Heath and Daryl. The chasm that'd opened between him and Katie-Lynn when they'd argued over their wedding yawned again at his feet, still too wide to be spanned.

"Wow! I forgot what cold felt like!" Katie-Lynn's dress collar lifted in the wind and she hugged herself, shivering. His arm wrapped around her shoulders protectively, settling her against him, warm and snug. The remembered feel of her, the seamless fit, the sense of completeness, returned to him, sharp and sweet. Then she ducked away and slid a small distance down the fence. "I'm sorry your dad sprang me on you."

"If I'd known, I never would've let you come."

She fussed with the black-and-white concentric rings encircling her neck on a silver chain. "Why's that?"

He hesitated a second. "Because I would have asked you… Heck…I *am* asking you to stop this production before it starts."

Her perfectly shaped eyebrows came together as she frowned. "I can't."

"Yes, you can. You're the star."

"I don't have that kind of power."

His breath hissed between clenched teeth, and he forced himself to simmer down. "Who came up with this idea?"

She stiffened. "I did."

Her words knocked thought clean out of his head, so he stared at her, mute.

"I'm sorry, Cole. I am." She sighed and stuffed her hands in her pockets. "I would never have come back unless…"

"Unless what?" he managed, reeling. She'd dealt his family this blow on purpose. She'd caused it, just like the wound she'd inflicted when she walked away from him and the life he'd offered.

"Nothing." She stared straight ahead again. Overhead, barn swallows swooped and dived against a cloudless sky.

"Katie-Lynn—"

She held up a hand, interrupting him. "It's Katlynn now."

"Not for me. Because Katie-Lynn knows, better than anyone, why my family doesn't need media digging up old secrets. Tell them you did some investigating and the story's fake."

"You're in foreclosure. You need this money."

He looked down at her; she was staring at the mother and calf. "I need my pa to have a peaceful, happy wedding. Quiet and uneventful."

"Sounds like the one you wanted for us."

He pointed to Mount Sopris, where one lonely hawk circled. "On a mountaintop, just our families and the preacher. What was wrong with that?"

Their disagreements while planning the wedding had revealed fundamental differences. Katie-Lynn wanted a large affair too showy for him. Worse, he would have gone into debt funding it given his family's limited means.

"You knew how much I wanted a big wedding. Lots of people."

"Lots of strangers," he interjected. "People just coming for cake and booze. Why want them there?"

"Because I wanted them to know *I* was there. No one ever noticed me, and I wanted my wedding to be different. Just one day where I felt special, but you didn't understand that, or me."

"You wanted everyone's attention. I wasn't enough." Because of their wedding arguments, he'd sensed, deep down, she'd never be content with the quiet, humble life he was prepared to offer.

"It's the other way around," she insisted. "You didn't love me enough to move to LA when I got the job offer."

"You knew me better than anyone else. Tell me...would I have liked it in LA?"

Just weeks before their nuptials, she'd received a major network job offer she couldn't resist. When he told her he didn't feel comfortable leaving the ranch, which had hit a rough patch, they'd called off the wedding. She couldn't understand why he felt more responsible for taking care of the ranch than being with her, and he couldn't understand why she cared more about a job than him... Clearly their priorities hadn't been in sync.

Now as much as then it seemed...

They studied each other for a long moment

then she shook her head, her face an open wound. He was pretty sure he didn't look much better. "You'd hate it there."

"And you hated living here. Deep down I knew this wasn't the life you wanted. You love the spotlight and I'm..."

"Closed off," she finished for him. "We were too young to make such a big decision."

A gust of wind fluttered a strand of hair across her face, and he gently tucked it behind her ear. "We're lucky we avoided making a big mistake."

"Very lucky," she said quietly, sounding immensely sad.

"Will you talk to someone about canceling the episode?"

"I can't."

He reined in his frustration. "Then promise me this won't turn into a circus. You'll stick to the feud story and nothing else. Not my mother's suicide or the ranch's troubles."

"I'll follow wherever the story takes me, and I'll do my best to prevent anything from harming your pa's big day. I care about him, too."

"I guess we still have that in common at least."

Then she smiled, just a flash, and something moved in Cole's chest. Something warm, and something he hadn't felt in a long time. "Let's go back," she said, jumping from the fence.

He paused to study the mother and calf a moment longer, his mind on Katie-Lynn and the danger she posed…not just to his family, but to his susceptible heart if he wasn't careful.

CHAPTER THREE

LATER IN THE AFTERNOON Katlynn knocked on her parents' screen door and peered into the modest, cluttered home. Strange how small it looked. Foreign. She was the outsider looking in.

"Hello?" she called for the third time. "Anybody home?"

She paused and listened for footsteps.

In the distant kitchen, red-orange flames curled beneath a kettle set on a gas stove. Open cereal boxes, empty bottles of soda and scattered corn chips littered the counters. Flies buzzed around a thawing package of ground beef. When was the last time this place had been cleaned? She made a mental note to contact a local housekeeping service for her arthritic mother.

"It's Katlynn!" she hollered.

Steam rose from the kettle, and her nose curled at the smell of burning plastic. What was cooking? White foam frothed over the pot's lid and spilled down its sides, sizzling when it hit the grate.

"You're going to start a fire!" Katlynn dashed

inside. She leaped over children's toys as she crossed the living room's obstacle course, skidded to a stop before the stove and flicked off the burner.

The volcano of lather settled, revealing baby bottles, teething rings and, inexplicably, one warped plastic flip-flop.

"Fire? Who said fire?"

Katlynn twisted around and spied her mother. Her short hair was smashed flat against one side of her skull as if she'd been sleeping or lying down. White frizz sprung from the opposite side, fluffy as a seeded dandelion. An oversize housecoat covered all but her sharp collarbones, bony elbows and swollen ankles.

"I handled it, Ma." Katlynn bussed her mother's creased cheek. "Why are you boiling a flip-flop?"

"Frankie's teething. It's his favorite chew toy." Her mother brushed past Katlynn and poured the kettle's contents into a strainer perched atop a stack of dishes in the sink. "What are you doing home? You didn't lose your job, did you?"

"I'm taping episodes here."

Katlynn used every facial muscle trick to keep her expression neutral. Lose her job... What a crazy idea...only it wasn't, not with *Scandalous History* on the chopping block. Everyone associated with the show, from the producer down to the maintenance crew, depended on her to pull off a hit, a story brimming with intrigue and scandal, all the while not harming the Lovelands' truce with the Cades or creating a media storm.

She'd promised.

And she never went back on her word.

Except once, as Cole reminded her.

Spending time with him this morning had been like stepping into the past. She'd felt disoriented, her perspective turned upside down, her body, her feelings, her thoughts, drawn to Cole. When he'd held her, briefly, she'd wanted to lay her head on his broad shoulder and share her troubles the way she once had. But that'd be owning up to failure, something her pride wouldn't allow.

"This is a nice surprise." Her mother pulled open the fridge and stooped to rummage inside it. A moment later she produced a box of animal crackers.

"You refrigerate those?"

"Timmy likes to eat them cold."

As if on cue, Katlynn's nephew galloped past her and tugged on his grandmother's hem. "Are you gonna play with me, Grammy?"

"Hey, Timmy." Katlynn scooted down to his height and mussed his wispy brown hair. "I'm your aunt Katlynn."

The four-year-old buried his face in her

mother's housecoat then peeled back the material to peek at her, one-eyed.

"Who's that?" he whispered loudly.

"Your aunt, honey." Her mother smoothed down his cowlick. "Why don't you give her a hug?"

"No." Timmy snatched the animal crackers and bolted down the short hall to the house's three bedrooms.

"Don't mind him. He's just never seen you before." Her mother motioned for Katlynn to follow her into the living room then shoved a pile of coupon flyers off the couch, clearing a space.

The sofa sagged to the ground as Katlynn dropped into it. She hauled herself back to the edge and examined the shabby furnishings, dismayed by the conditions. Crate boxes served as a TV stand for the old set. A shadeless table lamp, its lightbulb exposed, stood on the floor beside a torn armchair. Stuffing spilled from the back of the seat and covered the matted maroon carpet as if it'd snowed.

"How are you, Ma? Did you get my check last week?"

"Keeping busy. Haven't had a chance to deposit it yet, but thank you. Though you know you don't have to do that."

"I know," Katlynn assured her mother. "It makes me feel good to help out." Since her father's work injury a couple years ago, her parents survived on his disability checks and Katlynn's contributions, which, she now saw, were woefully inadequate. She'd instruct her assistant to send three times the amount.

What would happen to them if Katlynn's show was canceled? Her determination to nail this episode rammed into a higher gear. The Cade-Loveland segment would be the show of the season...*no*...the series.

Her ma patted Katlynn's knee with a gnarled hand, the sight raising her alarm. Her crooked fingers looked worse than she remembered. "You've always been a hard worker. Had your first job when you were, what? Eleven?"

"Ten," Katlynn corrected, gripping her mother's stiff hand.

"That's right. You were cutting lawns with that old rotary push mower you found in the shed. Never knew how you had the strength to haul it around the neighborhood."

"We all pitched in back then. Pa said every bit counted. Is he here?"

"Keith ran him to Denver for an MRI." Ma pinched a couple of yellow fronds from a fern plant in a ceramic baby shoe.

"Is his back worse?"

"Same. It's just an annual checkup."

"Did you get my messages?" Katlynn glanced

around for the phone but spied only an empty jack. "I called the landline and your iPhone. You still have it, right?"

"Sorry, honey. I know it was a Christmas gift, but I couldn't figure it out. Plus, we hardly ever get reception out here so I gave it to John."

Katlynn's oldest brother—who hadn't relayed her voice mail messages. Typical. "I'll buy you another while I'm in town and show you how to use it."

Her mother shook her head. "I don't want you wasting your money on us. It's best if you keep it in the bank. You never know when you're going to need it."

Katlynn stared at her. When was the last time anyone refused her gifts? How strange to be around someone who wanted nothing from her. "Let me worry about that, Ma."

Still. Her mother had a point. If the show was canceled, she'd be out of work for who knew how long before she landed her next gig. She'd gotten lucky to even win an audition for *Scandalous History*. After her agent's mother's bridge partner mentioned her son's project, a historical investigation show, she'd sent in Katlynn's head shots and CV, which included her double major in broadcasting and history.

During the audition, Katlynn and the executive producer connected over their shared love of Wild West lore, a conversation that continued over lunch and ended in her being offered the plum job the following week.

Digging into an old-time-Western family feud was exactly the kind of story to fire her imagination and, hopefully, the audience's. Regardless of her irritating attraction to her ex, she'd savor this project, a once-in-a-lifetime opportunity to solve a historical mystery.

"Can I get you anything to eat?" Ma's deep-set eyes ran over Katlynn. "You look too thin."

Her mouth dropped open before she caught herself. "I'm good, thanks. Don't go to any bother."

When was the last time she'd eaten a home-cooked meal?

The stick-to-your-ribs kind?

Every LA restaurant seemed to be vegan, gluten-free, dairy-free places where ordering a steak felt like a felony.

Her mouth watered just thinking about juicy barbecue.

"It's no trouble. Hardly ever have time to spend with any one of my kids, so when I do, it's a treat."

Katlynn's eyes stung, and she threw her arms around her mother, pulling her close, smelling the fresh scent of the outdoors on her housecoat.

"What's that for?" Ma asked when Katlynn released her, smiling.

"I love you."

"I love you, too, honey. Wish I'd known you were coming. I'd have cleaned up the place. It's been a little crazy around here lately, plus my arthritis is acting up. The change in weather always gets me."

"I wish you'd let me fly you out to LA. I know some wonderful doctors who—"

"Dr. Walker's treated our family for generations. He knows me better than any of those fancy doctors. I'm just fine, honey. So, tell me about you. What kind of story are you doing here?"

"I'm investigating the Cade-Loveland feud."

Her ma's hands rose to cover her rounded mouth. "Have you seen Cole?" she said through her fingers.

"Yes."

"How'd it go?"

"Fine. We're both adults."

Liar. You mooned over him the moment you saw him again.

"As long as you're okay. Always hoped you made the right choice, but here you are, famous and all. Guess you got what you wanted in the end."

"Right," Katlynn agreed briskly. If she'd gotten everything she wanted, though, why did she spend thousands talking to a life coach and a therapist about her loneliness?

"I have to meet with my production team in a bit, but I wanted to stop by and ask if I could stay here while we're filming. The Holsford Hotel double-booked my suite, and they don't have any other rooms."

"Did you talk to Frank or Joanie?" her mother asked, naming the owners of the small town's only hotel. It'd been in operation for almost a hundred years and conjured up a glimpse of the Old West with its painted facade and saloon-style reception area.

"Yes, and they apologized for the mix-up and offered to boot the other people who booked it. Except it's a newlywed couple, and I can't ruin their honeymoon."

"I see." Her mother chewed on her lip a moment, and the horizontal lines cleaving her forehead deepened. "It's only… Michelle and her three kids just moved back. She caught Benny cheating on her. Again. And your brother Martin lost his job, so I put him up in the basement. Keith still hasn't moved out, so…"

"You don't have room for me."

"I'd put you up on the couch, only Keith's friend Steve is sleeping on it. They're starting up a medicinal cannabis operation."

"Cannabis?" Katlynn echoed, noticing grow lights piled in the hall along with clay pots.

Her mother nodded, pride lighting her eyes. "He's finally found something he's passionate about. Said it's his calling. Plus, it'll help lots of people. Who would have thought your brother would go into farming? Once he gets the plants started, he'll transfer them into the field behind the corn. Says they grow better in the middle of another crop."

"You realize cannabis is the scientific name for marijuana, right?"

Her mother's eyes bulged. "Like the drug?"

"Just like it."

"That bugger…" Red flamed in Ma's cheeks. "And here I told the church knitting group all about it. They're fixing to be Keith's first customers, after me, since he said it's good for arthritis. Now what'll I tell 'em?"

"Plans changed. Plus, it's legal in Colorado. Just make sure Keith has a license to sell it."

Her ma sank back into the couch. "How'd you get so smart?"

"It's genetic." Katlynn kissed her mother's cheek and rose.

A baby wailed, a startled cry as if waking from a nap. With a heave, her mother freed herself from the sofa and stood. "Shoot. That's Frankie. I watch the kids during the day while Michelle's at work. She got a promotion, you know. Heading up the bakery section at the grocery store."

Katlynn smiled at her mother. She took equal pride in her children's accomplishments, no matter what they did. How strange to be treated like everyone else. No one rushing to compliment her, fetch her favorite drink, roll out the red carpet... If she'd expected a big fuss, a celebration to welcome the returning, prodigal child, she was very mistaken.

Yet it didn't hurt like she'd imagined. Instead, the sense of being no one special, out of the limelight's glare, loosened her muscles and made her breathe easier, despite her evil shapewear. "Michelle was always the best at birthday cakes."

The baby's wails escalated into a screech.

"I'll be by tomorrow, if that's okay."

"Anytime, honey, you know that. Only, your brother John's working a double, so I'll have his four kids. And your aunt Betty's dropping by because her grandchildren like to play with two of John's boys so—"

"It'll be busy," Katlynn finished for her, resigned to the fact that her mother's schedule was, as always, too full to fit her. "How about you call me when things are a little less crazy. You have my number."

Her ma pointed at a scrap of paper stuck to the cluttered refrigerator by a marijuana leaf magnet. "I'll fix your favorite meal. Chicken and biscuits."

"Thanks, Ma. That'd mean a lot," Katlynn said, even though Michelle was partial to the meal, not her. "And you know the magnet's a marijuana leaf, right?"

"Keith got them at some convention in Denver…" Her mother's eyes widened. "And I gave some out at the church group. What'll they think of me?"

"That you're a sinner in need of penance."

"Glory be." Her mother sighed. "You sure you'll find a place to stay?"

Katlynn opened the screen door, stepped outside and turned. "I'll be just fine. No need to worry about me."

Her mother patted her on the cheek. "Nope. Could always count on you to never give us a moment's worry. It's what made you special." And with that, she hurried after the baby, leaving Katlynn staring after her, mouth agape.

Not needing her parents' attention, not causing them concern, had made her stand out? She'd always done her best not to add herself to their list of things "to handle," but it'd never occurred to her they'd noticed.

Inside her rented sedan, she reviewed her housing choices.

Staying in a Denver hotel meant an hour-plus

commute every day, not to mention her hair and makeup team remained at the Holsford Hotel.

Tom had offered to share his suite with her, but he had a reputation, as well as two ex-wives. She'd been in the business long enough to understand offers like his also came with expectations and gossip-rag headlines.

Which left Boyd's offer to stay at Loveland Hills. Eyes on her back-up monitor, she reversed out of the twisting driveway and onto the gravel road. The powerful engine purred as she pressed on the gas and zipped around the shoulderless curves.

If she accepted, she'd have greater access to the story—a plus. On the other hand, she'd also be near Cole, and the show demanded all her focus—a big negative.

Could she stay at Cole's house and keep her professional distance?

She met her eyes in the car mirror, her nerves jumping in her stomach. She'd worked too hard, on herself and her career, to be swayed by an old flame. Whatever feelings she'd experienced today were just echoes from the past. They had no bearing on her life now…she wouldn't let them.

She blew out a long breath then spoke to the car's AI system.

"Siri, dial Loveland Hills Ranch."

"KATIE-LYNN'S STAYING HERE?" Cole paced in his family's kitchen, clenched hands shoved in his pockets.

"Her mother doesn't have room for her." Boyd swiped a washed plate with a towel and slid it into the rack above the sink.

Cole grabbed a dish towel and thrust it inside a glass, swirling it as he imagined Katie-Lynn sniffing around the place, exposing all their secrets. "I don't like it."

"I think it's awesome!" Sierra breezed into the kitchen in a cloud of her orange-blossom scent, her blond hair wet from her shower, her red cowboy boots matching the sleeveless blouse topping her floral, ruffled skirt. She plucked the dried cup from Cole's hand and stowed it in a glass-fronted cabinet. "Finally, another female to balance things out around here. Plus, she was my friend before you stole her, Cole."

"What's your objection?" Boyd slid another plate into its slot on the drying rack. "Do you still have feelings for her?"

"No!" He choked out his response, his throat tightening around the automatic denial.

Sierra thumped him on the back. "Not buying that, big brother."

"I haven't thought about her since she left." He swiped at his stinging eyes, filled a glass of water and drained it.

"Then why haven't you dated anyone else?" asked his younger brother Heath, joining them. He carried his six-string slung across his back, one of the guitars he handcrafted as a hobby when he wasn't ranching or gigging at local honky-tonks.

"Too busy keeping track of you troublemakers."

Heath shook longish bangs out of his purple-blue eyes. "That's your story?"

"Yep. And I'm sticking to it." Cole caught Sierra's eye-roll. Why did they think he pined for Katie-Lynn all these years?

Because you have been...

The heart-shaped diamond engagement ring still in his nightstand called him out—just as loudly as Sierra and Heath.

But seeing her today, noticing how much she'd changed, proved that even if he had carried a torch, it'd been for a girl who no longer existed. *Katlynn* was someone he didn't know.

"I'm heading out for my sound check." Heath donned a brown cowboy hat and curved its brim. "See you two there?"

"We wouldn't miss it. You're doing the new set, right?" Sierra placed the last glass in the cabinet and shut its door.

"Classics and originals." Heath shot them a quick smile then ducked outside.

"He's nervous," Sierra observed, hooking a pot on the rack above their table.

"Don't know why he wastes his time with those songs," Pa grumped. "Ain't like he's going to Nashville or getting famous."

"He's not trying to be a country star, Pa." Cole sprayed cleaning fluid over the cleared table and rubbed a paper towel over it, gathering crumbs.

"And what if he was? What's so wrong about that?" Sierra huffed, one fist on her hip.

"It's a road full of disappointment," Pa observed quietly.

Silence swelled, heavy enough to ache, as they finished the after-dinner cleaning. Cole supposed they all thought of Ma and how her unfulfilled dream to sing professionally drove her to drink. She'd taught Heath to play guitar and fiddle, the only one of her children interested in music… or who'd shown any talent for it. The rare times Cole saw her smiling, heard her laughing, was when she and Heath played together, those music sessions usually followed by even heavier drinking.

"You kids ruined my life!" she'd scream, stumbling around the ranch, searching for her stash of booze. "I wish you'd never been born."

Or…

"You trapped me!" She'd sometimes hit his father while hurling accusations. "Got me pregnant so I'd be stuck on this miserable ranch."

Cole must have made a noise because Sierra's hand pressed his, yanking him back to the present, away from the mother who'd blamed him, her oldest child, for all her woes, for holding her back from her dreams. "Cole? You okay?"

"Fine."

"Anybody home?" called a familiar, beautiful voice.

His body clenched as if bracing for a blow.

"In here, Katie-Lynn!" shouted Sierra, still staring up into his face. "Sure you're okay?"

"I'm fine," he muttered under his breath, needing his sister to move her eagle eye off him. "And she's Katlynn now."

When Katie-Lynn appeared in the kitchen, Sierra flung herself across the space and hugged her old friend tight. "Good to see you, girl!"

"You, too." Katie-Lynn's eyes met Cole's over his sister's shoulder, and he ducked his head and draped his damp towel over the drying rack. "Thanks for letting me stay, Mr. Love—"

She broke off when Boyd waved a spatula at her.

"Boyd," she amended with a slight catch in her voice. Cole glanced up and caught the pretty flush rising in her cheeks, her eyes still on him.

"Want to come line-dancing with us? Heath's playing, and he's doing some originals, too."

"Oh—uh—I'm not sure," Katie-Lynn wavered, her gaze now shadowed by her long, lowered lashes.

"It'll be fun," Sierra implored.

Katie-Lynn smoothed a hand over her sleek black dress, drawing his attention to the lush curves beneath the expensive fabric. Unwelcome heat flared inside him. "I'm not exactly dressed for the Hoedown Throwdown."

"I'll loan you something. We're probably still the same size." Sierra stepped back, sizing Katlynn up. "Give or take."

"Um. I have interviews set up in the morning, so I should probably just go on up to bed."

"At eight o'clock?" Sierra scoffed, ever the dog on a bone when she wanted something bad enough. As the only girl among five brothers, she'd learned fast how to assert herself.

"She's too fancy for country line-dancing," Cole heard himself say, the words flying from his tongue without his permission.

"Excuse me?" A slight twang entered Katie-Lynn's voice as it rose a half octave. "I've probably forgotten more steps than you'll ever know."

"Those sound like fighting words," Boyd observed, leaning against the counter.

Cole stepped close and Katie-Lynn angled her

face up to his, her chin jutting. "I don't believe you."

"Want to bet?" Katie-Lynn challenged, her cool, controlled mask slipping. Before him stood the competitive country girl who used to dare him to climb trees as high as her, race horses as fast, catch as many trout. And he'd lost almost as often as he'd won. Not that he'd cared. Then.

"You're on," he said, unable to resist her sparkling eyes.

"It's a dance-off!" Sierra rubbed her hands together. "And I'll be the judge. Cole, what are you betting?"

"If I win, Katie-Lynn finds another place to stay."

Katie-Lynn's head shake silenced his father's and Sierra's protests. "No need to worry. I'm not planning on losing." Her nose flared, and her left eyebrow twitched up.

"What'll you get if you win?" Sierra smacked Cole with a death-by-glare look.

"TBD," Katie-Lynn announced, her radiant expression mischievous and daring. His breath caught at the glimpse of the gutsy girl he'd fallen for years ago. "Come on, Sierra. Show me some jeans. The real kind without a designer label."

And with that, the two women disappeared up the stairs, leaving Cole to stare after them.

"What's TBD mean?" his father asked.

TBD. To be determined. Which could mean anything. He had to win this dance-off and get the intriguing Katlynn Brennon as far from him as possible. She'd already messed with his head and his heart enough for one lifetime.

He hung his head and peered up at his pa.

"It means I'm a dang fool."

CHAPTER FOUR

"COLE LOVELAND?"

At his name, Cole stopped inside the Silver Spurs' entrance and peered into the throng of country-western-dressed locals. The dim, one-room honky-tonk was packed. Overhead fans stirred humid air reeking of beer, sweat and peanuts while cowboys and cowgirls jammed the old-time wooden bar. In the far corner, his brother Heath, wearing a black T-shirt with sleeves shoved up to his shoulders, ripped through a guitar solo, sending his hovering female fans into a tizzy of squeals and shrieks.

"Is that you?" Ted Jansen, an old high school buddy, stomped up and clapped Cole on the back.

"Unfortunately," Cole muttered under his breath. Nothing against Ted. He just wasn't much for talking to people. Or just plain talking.

"Haven't seen you in so long—thought you were dead or something." Ted's whiskey-scented laugh blasted Cole. Beside him, Katie-Lynn coughed into her hand.

"Or something," Sierra drawled, elbowing Cole. "My brother isn't much for socializing."

"That's an understatement," Travis spoke up, joining them with their adopted brother Daryl. Travis hooked his thumbs into his belt loops and planted his boots wide on the scuffed wooden floor. "Cole only leaves home to volunteer at Fresh Start. Otherwise, he's a hermit."

"*Recluse* has a nobler ring to it." Sierra shot Cole a sideways smile beneath the lantern lights dangling from an exposed-beam ceiling.

He could feel Katie-Lynn studying him, sensed the warm blue of her eyes touching his jaw like a caress. Slipping a finger into his shirt collar, he pulled it from his heated neck.

"Walking dead's closer to it." Daryl lifted his black cowboy hat to reveal brown curls plastered against his forehead before settling it on again. "Just barely alive."

"Knock it off," Cole growled, accepting a beer from Ted. He tossed back a long drink.

"You can dish it out, but you can't take it," Katie-Lynn teased.

The Western twang creeping into her voice again made him bite back the smile he'd been fighting since she'd emerged from his sister's room dressed in faded Wranglers, dusty boots and a plaid shirt with fringe piping on the sleeves. She looked downhome and pretty, her hair back in a French braid, her red lipstick swapped for clear gloss over naturally rosy lips.

"When do I dish it out?" he protested, dragging his eyes off her pretty mouth.

"Puh-lease," guffawed Travis.

"All. The. Time!" exclaimed Sierra.

"Like I said, no sense of humor." Daryl turned slightly and whistled. "Katie-Lynn? You're looking good, girl!"

"So are you. Congratulations. Heard you got married. Is your wife here?"

Katie-Lynn bestowed one of her killer smiles on Daryl. Cole pinned his eyes on the rollicking band, trying—and failing—to tune her out.

"No… I…uh…she's not feelin' herself tonight." At the note of sadness creeping into Daryl's voice, Cole turned to study his brother. Daryl and his wife's marital troubles weren't hard to miss given she alternated between sulky pouts and sharp put-downs on the few occasions she accompanied Daryl anywhere. But it wasn't Cole's business to stick his nose in, so he kept quiet. Didn't stop him from worrying about his brother, though.

Not one bit.

"Now I see why you came out tonight, Cole." Ted half mauled, half hugged Katie-Lynn, stumbling slightly when Cole pulled her from the man's grip. "You two, together again. Never would have believed it."

Travis's eyes dropped to the arm Cole wrapped around Katie-Lynn, then rose to meet Cole's gaze.

Katie-Lynn jerked free. "I'm here on business."

"What kind of business?" Ted leered, winking.

"Easy." Cole glared at Ted.

"Hey, she's your lady." Ted backed off. "I get it."

"No, she's not!" Cole hollered at Ted's retreating back.

"Sure about that?" Travis grabbed Cole's arm, stopping him, when the rest of the group departed for the dance floor. Katie-Lynn shot him an inscrutable, over-the-shoulder look before disappearing into the crowd.

"What's that supposed to mean?"

"I see the way you've been looking at Katie-Lynn."

"What way's that?"

"Like you've still got feelings for her."

"Dead wrong." Cole raised his bottle for a drink to shield his expression. Travis was as sharp-eyed as a hawk, reading people and situations in an instant. A good trait for a sheriff. Not so good in a brother when you were hiding something...

Was he covering up feelings for Katie-Lynn?

Attraction—yes. But emotions?

No.

Not a chance.

"I hope so." Travis's jaw squared. "Just remember what happened after she left you."

"Nothing happened."

"Except you disappearing for three months."

"I was driving cattle."

"Sleeping out on the range, never coming home…"

Cole drained the last of his dark malt and handed it to a passing waitress. "Are we done here, *Sheriff*?"

Travis pinned him with a steady, hard look before nodding. "You're free to go…with a warning."

"Which is?"

"Don't repeat a mistake you already learned from. Anyone messes up once. Doing it twice is just plain stupid."

"Stupid I'm not," Cole said, eyeing Katie-Lynn's animated face as she smiled up at another one of their old high-school friends, her hand on Lyle Carter's arm.

It didn't bother him. Not one bit. Yet he found himself closing the distance between them in fast, long strides. "Don't mean to interrupt. Katie-Lynn, I believe this is our dance?"

Lyle tipped his head, returned another friend's wave and headed to a crowded pool table.

"Hey… I was talking to him…" Katie-Lynn

protested as Cole snagged her around the waist and guided her onto the dance floor.

"Who?" he asked, the side of his mouth hitching up when her expression went blank. "You don't remember his name."

"Of course I do."

"Yeah? What is it?"

"It'll come to me," she grumbled.

"Thought you would have forgotten everything about Carbondale."

"Not everything," she said obliquely then lined up with the other dancers as Heath's band swung into "Boot Scootin' Boogie." "In fact," she shouted over the driving song, "I'm about to prove I remember more than you by winning our dance-off."

"Good luck, darlin'," Cole said in her ear. He tapped the floor with the heel of his left boot twice, then the right along with the hooting, clapping group on the dance floor. "You'll need it."

"Don't think so," Katie-Lynn hollered back, kicking her left heel up before turning with him, their bodies in sync.

"Not half bad." They did a grapevine to the right, stopped and clapped. "For a Hollywood-type."

Katie-Lynn rocked forward four steps, lassoing an invisible rope overhead. "What's a Hollywood-type according to you?" she asked directly into his ear before they pivoted again.

"All about money. Fame."

"Nothing wrong with being ambitious," she shouted as they hopped backward. "You never got that."

"What about fake?" he challenged once Heath strummed the last note on his six-string. "You changed who you were."

"For the better."

"That's one opinion. Your freckles are scraped off."

"Lasered." She shoved loose strands of her white-blond hair off her glistening forehead and squared off against him. "And they're not gone-gone. If I'm out in the sun without protection, they'll come back." She mock-shuddered.

"'Cause looking like your real self would be a fate worse than death, I'm supposing," he drawled.

"Almost as bad as having to socialize with people instead of cows and cattle dogs," she countered, her eyes glittering bright blue beneath a black fringe of lashes. "Right?"

"Guess we understand each other."

A short, humorless laugh escaped her. "Doubtful."

"Seein' as we never did."

"Except at our Say Anything tree," she added.

Their gazes locked for a brief, heart-pounding moment before she suddenly got engrossed smoothing her shirt fringe.

Sierra gave them both a thumbs-up as Heath strummed the opening counts to "Achy Breaky Heart." Cole clamped his jaw. He had to beat Katie-Lynn. Otherwise, he'd spend the next couple of weeks up close and personal with her while she bunked on his ranch.

Worse, he'd owe her some sort of favor.

TBD, she'd said.

To be determined...

As they slid, twirled and stomped through the Billy Ray Cyrus tune, his body was acutely conscious of her curvy form beside him. If he closed his eyes, he'd picture them doing these exact steps ten years ago, a couple in love and altar-bound. But love didn't always guarantee happiness. His pa was a case in point. Close to the band, Boyd ushered Joy Cade through the song, repeating every step while keeping one protective hand on the small of her back.

Cole smiled at the sight of his father's open, happy expression. It'd been a long time—if ever—since he'd seen Pa smile like that, no worry darkening his eyes, no concern deepening the lines on his face. He'd been miserable married to Cole's mother, and deserved happiness at long last.

By reopening wounds and stirring up controversy, Katie-Lynn might mess up the former high school sweethearts' second chance. She'd promised Pa to keep things aboveboard, but Cole wasn't so trusting.

"You two can dance," Sierra shouted once the song ended, fingers cupped around her mouth. "Too close to call yet."

"Do I get extra points for style?" Katie-Lynn angled her borrowed, black, leather-tooled boots. "These feel like walking on clouds. I'm always in heels."

Sierra laughed. "I don't even own a pair."

"Count yourself lucky," Katie-Lynn insisted, sounding sincere. Cole's forehead scrunched in confusion. Wasn't wearing fancy clothes, looking like a star, why she'd left Carbondale? Him?

"Okay," Heath hollered into his microphone. "This one's for everybody who wants to be country for just one day!"

A roar practically lifted Silver Spurs' tin roof. Katie-Lynn pressed close as people shoved by onto the dance floor. Instinctively, his arm clamped around her waist. His eyes nearly closed at the heavenly softness of her against his hard angles. How long since he'd held a woman?

Too darn long…

Not since Katie-Lynn, years ago.

A lifetime ago, it seemed.

His fingers strummed the length of her back, and she shivered, angling her face up to his, her eyes wide and hazy. The need to get her alone, to undo her braid, to kiss those lips, to smudge her polish, seized him hard.

Katie-Lynn slid left and flowed into the dance's next move. Mind blank, Cole struggled to match her steps. Since he rarely went out, he'd never danced this newer song before.

Did that make him a hermit?

He jerked right then turned in the wrong direction, bumping into Travis, who shook his head and shot Cole an amused grin.

No. Cole was just private.

His family could tease all they wanted, but he was happy with his life.

An ache twisted through his heart as he eyed Katie-Lynn.

Happy, dang it.

"Wrong way!" His former principal, Miss Groover-Woodhouse, frowned and pointed him in the opposite direction.

When he whirled, he smacked into Katie-Lynn.

"Hey!" she protested, rubbing her nose as she glided away then back while his feet stuck to the floor. "Why aren't you dancing?"

"I'm dancing in here." He pointed to his heart, calling up one of her gorgeous smiles.

"That's a fifty-yard penalty for corniness. You really need to work on your sense of humor."

When she danced away, crooked finger beckoning him, lips curving in a coy smile, he froze, mouth slack. The dancing line barreled down on him, and he careened into Jewel Cade, the youngest of the Cade clan, to dodge it.

"Sorry," he apologized loudly. She didn't seem to hear. Heath captivated the cowgirl as she stood motionless on the dance floor's edge, watching him sing.

Cole wanted to warn her not to bother mooning over his younger brother, seeing she wasn't Heath's girly-girl type. Plus, he was practically engaged to Mandy Baker, whom he'd been seeing on and off since high school. If Jewel pined after Heath, she'd learn fast he was a one-woman man... Not to mention she'd be their stepsister in a couple of weeks. A relationship between her and Heath was every kind of wrong, especially since the families had only called a temporary truce for the wedding.

Not that Cole approved of entitled, snobbish Mandy, only daughter of a ranching supply company tycoon, for his humble, sensitive brother, either. But to each his own...

The music ended with a laughing, magnetic Katie-Lynn in the dance floor's center, soaking up the admiring attention shining down on her from every angle. It was like she wanted everyone's glance, every thought, every feeling—not just Cole's—since his admiration had never been enough.

And now he'd be seeing her nonstop at the ranch, day in and day out.

"You lose, big brother." Sierra clapped Cole on the back. "What will Katlynn make you do now that she won? She said TBD…"

"I don't know." Katie-Lynn's face sobered when she caught him staring. He ripped his eyes away.

Busted.

"Guess I'll just have to wait and find out."

And avoid her at every chance possible.

Travis warned him only stupid people repeated mistakes.

This time he wouldn't be the lovestruck idiot he'd once been for Katie-Lynn. He was older. Wiser. Not a young man full of faith and fancies…

So why did he sense, deep down, he might be just the tiniest bit happy she was staying at Loveland Hills?

'Cause you are that stupid, Stupid…

KATLYNN ROLLED HER stiff shoulders, wincing as she eased into the porch swing's soft cushion. Overhead, morning light streamed from a cloudless sky. She pulled on a pair of sunglasses against its glare and buttoned up the sweater she'd tossed over her dress shirt. Was she thirty-two or ninety-two? Grueling daily workouts, overseen by a personal trainer, hadn't prepared her for the rigors of "Boot Scootin' Boogie," apparently.

Go figure.

Nor had hours of "mindfulness" coaching armored her against Cole Loveland's sapphire eyes or the wistful smile he wore when he didn't think anyone watched.

And she'd been looking plenty.

Way too much for an enlightened, successful, evolved woman who knew better. She needed to focus on taping the show of her life, not mooning over a gruff, withdrawn cowboy. Her eyes drifted shut, and her head tipped back to rest on the seat.

But she could indulge herself for just one moment.

Dancing with Cole, spending time with his family, had been fun. By the end of the night, her cheeks had hurt from smiling. Very different than the posh parties she usually attended where "coolly amused" was as wild as she got. After years listening to the same conversations about yachting vacations in St. Barts, fashion shows in Milan or speculations about who had what plastic surgery, it all blurred, leaving her numb. Last night, though, she'd felt alive, interested, electric.

Being part of a group rather than its star lightened her somehow. It challenged her belief that her authentic self was something to hide. Just being her old self had felt *so* good. No doubt it was the newness of coming home. Soon she'd grow bored as she had years ago, feeling marginalized, invisible and itching to leave. Best she remember the feeling when her thoughts strayed to the man who'd tempted her to stay once upon a time.

So. Work.

Today she hoped to meet with Cole's great-great-aunt, Susanna Loveland, if the woman would ever return Katlynn's phone calls. She seemed as reclusive as her nephew. Katlynn rose in the seat to head inside and call Susanna again, then sat when a black town car rolled to a stop. A suited man stepped from it and slammed the door.

"Morning, beautiful!"

She returned Tom's double cheek air kiss when he joined her. "How'd you sleep?"

"Terribly. It took three Ambiens and a bottle of cheap Zinfandel to knock me out. Now I have a pounding headache." Tom brought his phone to his mouth to dictate. "Reminder. Have Sara overnight me a case of Scharzhofberger Riesling." He lowered his cell. "Any requests? Sparkling water? A facialist?"

Katlynn's hands rose to her cheeks. Did she look sallow? Corpse-like as Gabe, the director, had said? And had she applied sunscreen? The delicious sound of twittering birds and frying bacon hustled her out of bed this morning without much thought to her appearance.

Strange, considering how she obsessed about it in LA.

"I'm good, thanks."

"Of course you are. Our star's no diva." Tom's smile fell when he considered her somber face. "I mean, not that demanding women are all divas or…or…"

She held up a hand. "It's okay, Tom."

His shoulders lowered, and he dropped onto the porch swing beside her. "Just feeling the pressure, I guess. Heard from headquarters the higher-ups are meeting with writers pitching a reality show called *Millennial Millionaires*. It's being workshopped for our slot if our numbers don't improve."

"They're already considering our replacement?" she asked when she trusted her voice.

"They're always considering replacements. It's the biz. With our network's takeover, and TV viewership down, we've got to take this seriously."

"I am." Katlynn's lungs inflated in a long, steady intake of air. When she exhaled, she tried pushing out her anxiety. *Tried* being the operative word; it clung to the back of her neck, squeezing. "A lot's planned. I'm meeting with Loveland family members this morning and then heading to County Records to look up survey maps of the families' properties."

Tom smothered a yawn. "Sounds dead boring. Survey maps?"

"Water rights is a major component of the feud. If I can prove, definitively, who has legal access to the Crystal River—"

"Katlynn," Tom cut her off. "Legal mumbo jumbo doesn't grab ratings. Rumor has it the first episode of *Millennial Millionaires* is about a twentysomething who made her first million as a preteen by selling virtual real estate."

"How can you sell something that's not real?"

"It's part of an online game. Wish I'd thought of it. You know, a show with that kind of potential might need an experienced producer like me…"

She peered at him steadily. "Are you jumping ship?"

"No…just preparing myself…in case…"

"We'll nail this. Without shortcuts or virtual whatever. And investigative reporting is part of my job, by the way."

"Let's not kid ourselves." Tom's hand dropped to her knee, and his thumb stroked the bare flesh below her hemline. "You're gorgeous, smart, articulate and more important, people *like* you. It's great you have a history degree, but that beautiful smile's the draw, not your brain."

She jerked her leg away. "Are you asking for a sexual harassment suit?"

Tom shrugged. "Okay. Touchy. But leave the fact-checking to our team and focus on finding skeletons in closets. We need scandal. Intrigue. Sex. Maybe throw in something about your breakup with that bull in a cowboy hat. What's his name? Propane?"

"Cole," she said through gritted teeth. "And personal stuff is off-limits."

"Why'd you two break up?" Tom sprawled back in the swing, undeterred. "Can't see how you were ever a couple."

"It was a long time ago."

"He called you Katie-Lynn."

"Don't use that name." Hearing Tom say it rubbed her every kind of wrong way.

"Just when I want to get your attention, then?" *"Really?"*

Tom held up his moisturized hand, his buffed nails gleaming in the strengthening light. "I get it. You don't like being reminded of where you come from."

She dropped her gaze, and Tom ducked his head to catch her eye. "Hey. None of us do. That's why we all came to Hollywood. Land of pretense, right? Who wants to be real when illusion is much more civilized?"

"Why'd you come over this morning?"

"Since I'm scouting locations down the road at Cade Ranch, I thought I'd drop by. One of our interns dug up something about the Cade girl who died. Said she might have been betrothed."

"Maggie Cade?"

Her producer nodded. "And not to the Loveland man they think killed her and stole the family jewel."

"Interesting…"

"Find out what you can about that. Was she a runaway bride? Was Everett Loveland a jilted, murderous lover? I want you to question everything and everyone. Overhype even the slightest rumor, whether you can verify it or not. Lots of drama."

Katlynn folded her arms and glared at Tom. "The Lovelands aren't those kinds of people."

"They're the subject of a make-or-break episode for us… *Make* them those people."

"The hell she will."

Tom jumped to his feet at the sound of Cole's growling bass and scuttled to the porch steps. "Our contract allows us full coverage. Ask your father. He signed it."

Cole advanced, a muscle jumping in his jaw. In dark jeans and a black cowboy hat, he looked like an avenging angel, otherworldly handsome and deadly. "No drama."

"Talk to him, Katlynn," Tom called before scrambling into his car. "Remember where your loyalties lie." The door slammed, and the sedan roared down the drive, tires kicking up dirt.

Loyalty... She owed the show hers, yet she wouldn't go against her principles, or this fine family she might have called her own once.

"The show *is* called *Scandalous History*." Katlynn joined Cole at the porch's railing and stared out at Loveland Hills. Tiny green leaves colored the twisted limbs of distant apple trees. Farther still, gray Brahmans milled in a pasture, calves nursing and frolicking in the cool spring sunshine. For such a peaceful spot, it'd witnessed its share of heartache, even hers.

"You gave Pa your word." Cole spoke without taking his eyes off the distant, snowcapped mountains.

"And I'll keep it. Your mother won't be in the episode. What happened to her—" Katlynn's voice broke slightly as ghastly images from that night returned. "It has no bearing on the story."

"It's scandalous. And it's history."

"But it didn't cause the feud. It's not relevant."

"The feud's more about people than water rights access. Thirty odd years ago, a Loveland lost the woman he loved to a Cade. Now he's marrying her. It's connected."

She slid her hand over the one he wrapped tight around the banister. "I won't connect them. Don't you trust me?"

He flipped his hand and laced his calloused fingers in hers. The spot where his warm, hard palm rubbed against hers ignited a shivering awareness. The tiny hairs on her arm rose. "I used to."

"We never lied to each other."

"We lied to ourselves."

"True. But we're older now."

Cole leveled his deep blue eyes on hers. "Maybe I don't trust myself with you."

"Oh." Her tongue darted out to lick her dry lips. "I—I—"

He jerked his hand free and raked it over his hair. "Forget I said that."

She nodded, her throat tight. "Forgotten." Did he still have feelings for her? Did she return them?

Good thing her life coach was on speed dial. Now all she needed was a cell phone signal... something she hadn't considered when she'd marooned herself out on Loveland Hills.

Cole leaned one shoulder against a newel post. "What's this about the episode being make-or-break?"

"Nothing."

"Thought you said we never lied to each other." He peered at her steadily. "Say anything, Katie-Lynn."

An exclamation of air escaped her. He'd invoked their sacred credo. "Say Anything" was shorthand for "Tell the truth," a rule they'd created when they'd begun meeting at the tree that'd been remote enough, and big enough, to hold all their secrets and fears.

"Fine," she said. "The show's been flagged for possible cancelation. We need big ratings to impress the higher-ups."

"And if you don't?"

"Then I'm out of a job."

"You'll find something else."

"Starring roles don't grow on trees." She gestured to the orchard. "I worked hard to get where I am. Made a lot of sacrifices."

"I'm aware," he said, his voice dark. Hushed.

She swallowed hard. "I'll be a nobody again."

Cole lifted her chin with strong, gentle fingers. "You'll never be a nobody, Katie-Lynn. Not to me." He dropped his hand. "You saw my pa and Joy last night. He's happy. I don't want you to ruin it by digging up old hurts."

"History isn't easily erased."

Their eyes clung for a long, charged moment. A bawling calf echoed in the quiet.

"You need to save your job. I need to save the ranch and keep old animosities from threatening Pa's wedding."

She nodded. "We both have a lot at stake."

"We have that in common at least."

"We can help each other," she speculated out loud.

Despite their thorny past, Cole would be an asset. At the very least, he'd help get his eccentric great-great-aunt Susanna to return her call. Sierra had told her that Susanna, a bit of a hoarder, had many Loveland artifacts.

Cole shook his head. "Your boss wants scandals, and I want to prevent them."

"So do I. Join me. I need someone who knows this land, your family, intimately to guide me."

One thick brow lifted. She nearly squirmed under his intense, speculative stare. "What do I get out of it?"

"My investigative expertise and know-how in examining historical documents. Plus, you'll get to keep an eye on me."

"You had me until that last part."

"Come on, Cole. We used to work well together. Maybe we're on different sides, but we both want the truth."

When his wary expression didn't budge, she added, "Plus, you owe me."

"Owe you?"

The screen door creaked open behind them.

"I won the dance-off last night. I'm calling in the bet."

"If I'd known you'd ask me to work with you, I wouldn't have agreed."

Katlynn stiffened her spine to keep from flinching. She was a red-carpet darling. America's sweetheart, according to *US* magazine. But to Cole, she was a nobody. No one he wanted to be around, anyway.

"Katlynn said 'to be determined,'" Sierra pointed out, joining them. She'd donned kitten-print scrubs over jeans tucked into heavy work boots, her blond hair scraped into a low ponytail. "And you gave your word. And Lovelands—"

"Always keep their word," he finished for his sister. A look of resignation pulled down the corners of his mouth. He hesitated then stuck out his hand and clasped Katlynn's. "Looks like you got a partner."

Katlynn flashed her trademark smile, despite the unease rattling inside.

She'd liked the sound of "partner."

Way too much.

She'd come to uncover the truth of a story seeped in murder, betrayal and theft.

Would her heart betray her, too? Cole had stolen it once before…and if she wasn't careful, he might succeed again.

CHAPTER FIVE

"AUNT SUSANNA? IT'S COLE."

Cole knocked on the front door of a ramshackle, two-story house smothered in ivy. Scattered pines filtered the afternoon sun and cast a cool pall over an unkempt front yard.

"Are you sure she's home?"

His nose curled at the dank smell rising from a moss-covered wood stack beside the stairs. "It's Monday—she's home."

Katie-Lynn peered up at him through oversize sunglasses. In a gray fitted suit and dark heels, her hair stiffly molded to frame her made-up face, he hardly recognized her from the laughing, flushed, disheveled woman who'd ensnared his attention last night. "How do you know?"

"Because she only goes out on Sundays for church." The front door's glass panes rattled as he knocked again.

"How come I've never met her?"

"If we'd made it down the aisle, you would have."

"Better late than never." The slightest hint of

sadness tinged her voice. He wished he could read her eyes behind those dark lenses.

"Might think differently once you've met her." He eyed the curtains in his aunt's second-floor bedroom. The edge of a panel fluttered.

Cole stepped off the porch and cupped his hands around his mouth. "Aunt Susanna! It's Cole. Your favorite nephew. The one who doesn't talk much or bother you."

Katie-Lynn snorted.

With a swish, the window sash rose. Aunt Susanna poked out her permed head of gray hair. "You're bothering me now."

"It's one-thirty."

"Time for my afternoon nap," she snapped.

"Only plan on taking a bit of your time."

His aunt held up a hand and wagged her fingers. "Five minutes."

"Thirty and I'll bring you fresh strawberries when they're ready for picking," Cole promised.

The window slammed shut.

"You sure know how to sweet-talk a lady." Katie-Lynn's arched brow appeared above her sunglasses' frame, the same sassy expression he'd always found so attractive.

"It ain't hard if the lady's sweet already." He placed his hand on the wall beside her face and breathed in the fresh, clean cotton scent of her skin. He preferred it to the insect repellant masquerading as designer perfume she'd worn yesterday.

She pulled off her sunglasses and narrowed her eyes. "Am I sweet?"

"Nah." He cupped her cheek. "You're tart as unripe raspberries."

He watched, fascinated, as she chewed off a bit of her bright lipstick, revealing the rose beneath it. "Those used to be your favorite."

"Still are."

Her mouth dropped open, and he leaned closer, tempted to see if she still tasted like tart raspberries. The door beside them creaked open.

"If you two lovebirds are finished canoodling, come on inside," Aunt Susanna groused. Her housecoat billowed as she pivoted and stomped away.

Katie-Lynn ducked under Cole's arm, her face aflame, and fled indoors. He shoved his hands in his pockets and followed.

He'd almost kissed Katie-Lynn...

Keeping his distance was going to be harder than he thought.

Turning sideways, he edged through a hallway narrowed by stacks of boxes overflowing with knickknacks, electrical cords and unopened mail. When he emerged into the living room, it only got worse. Clothes, broken electronics, abandoned home improvement projects, trash bags and old newspapers piled around the room in four- to five-foot mounds.

A dozen cats stared balefully from atop a frayed couch. Or he guessed it was a sofa since books, record albums, an empty violin case and pictures covered it. Nearby, a dachshund chewed on a stained pillow's stuffing. It lifted his head and woofed halfheartedly before returning to his task.

"If I'd known you was coming, I would've fixed you some lemon bars," Aunt Susanna called from the kitchen. Through a large archway, he glimpsed her at a sink filled with empty cartons of juice and soda bottles. "You want something to drink?"

"Don't go to any fuss." Cole watched as Katie-Lynn turned slowly, her wide eyes cataloging the space, her horror mirroring his. It'd been a long time since he'd been inside his aunt's house. Did his pa know his great-aunt was hoarding? They needed to help her. Immediately.

"How long have you lived here?" Katie-Lynn asked when Aunt Susanna returned, carrying a jug of sweet tea and red Solo cups.

"Since I moved off the ranch." Aunt Susanna poured them each a glass, then tossed the empty jug onto a stack of magazines. "About fifty years ago when our aunt Gemmy left it to me. Boyd inherited the ranch, so I got this house."

"How long's it been in your family?"

"One hundred and fifteen years," Cole supplied.

Aunt Susanna's eyes gleamed beneath drooping eyelids. "Was built by Theodore and Reginald Loveland, a couple of bachelors who'd left the family ranch to work at John Osgood's marble quarry in Yule Valley. As younger sons, they didn't stand to inherit, so they made their own way."

Katie-Lynn cocked her head. "I didn't know marble was quarried here."

Aunt Susanna's shoulders lifted and fell beneath her housecoat. "You're not from around here."

"She used to be." Cole struggled not to make a face as he downed a gulp of the lukewarm, bitter tea.

"That right?" Aunt Susanna's raised eyebrows communicated her disbelief. "Well, Yule Marble's the best in the world. Look at any government building or bank and you'll see it—white and smooth, polished like glass. Was even used to create the Tomb of the Unknown Soldier in Arlington Cemetery."

Katie-Lynn sipped her tea, her expression serene. If her drink tasted as nasty as his, she hid it well. "You know quite a bit of history."

Aunt Susanna's chin wobbled in a jerky nod.

"I was the local historian at Carbondale Museum for over forty-five years."

Katie-Lynn flashed her trademark warm smile. It said, "I like you. We're going to be friends." It drew others to her...had drawn him, once.

Still did.

"We've got a lot in common, then. I'm the host of a history show and—"

Aunt Susanna's raised hand forestalled the rest of Katie-Lynn's words. "Heard it in your messages. You're a pushy thing, aren't you?"

"I'll take that as a compliment?"

Cole's lips twisted into a smile. Katie-Lynn had pluck, as his grandma used to say.

"It is," Aunt Susanna said firmly, approvingly.

"She's Gary and Brenda Brennon's daughter," Cole said. Everyone feared and avoided formidable Aunt Susanna. Yet Katie-Lynn thawed her with ease.

She could charm the birds out of the trees... Another one of his grandma's expressions that fit Katie-Lynn.

"Of course!" Aunt Susanna clapped a hand on top of Katie-Lynn's. "Didn't recognize you. You used to cut my lawn with an engineless mower. Could never figure out how a scrawny little thing could push that metal contraption, but you never quit."

Katie-Lynn nodded. "I never do."

Except on me. Cole forced down the last of the tea and gagged as a few unidentifiable bits hit the back of his throat. Katie-Lynn was persistent when going after something she wanted. She didn't wait for things to happen like he did; she *made* them happen. And he still liked that quality about her. A lot.

"Your ma gave me that magnet on my fridge. Your brother Keith's got some miracle cure for arthritis."

Cole followed his aunt's finger point and spied a marijuana leaf cutout. Beside him, Katie-Lynn made a choking sound, cheeks bulging as she held in a laugh. When her dancing eyes met his, he clamped his lips shut to keep from chuckling.

"We're all so proud of him," Katie-Lynn intoned a moment later, shooting Cole a quick sideways glance, communicating a private joke. His brief frown expressed mock-outrage.

Aunt Susanna's eyes swung from Katie-Lynn to him. "And you two were engaged. How could I have forgotten? I still have your save-the-date picture."

"Where?" Cole's heart tapped a strange beat. He'd thrown out everything that reminded him of Katie-Lynn long ago.

"It's on the fridge."

Cole strode through the path to the kitchen and stopped in front of the refrigerator. The photograph of him nuzzling a laughing Katie-Lynn beside a slatted wooden fence struck him like a blow. He'd looked so…happy. In love. At peace.

Who was that young man with hope in his eyes? Such faith?

He was gone now.

Long gone.

Cole tugged the picture free and cupped it in his palm. He read the "Save the Date" he'd painted on the fence. He glanced over his shoulder, pocketed the picture, then strolled back to the living room.

"You come from good people, Ms. Brennon," his aunt said. "How can I help you?"

"Please call me Katlynn. And I'm hoping you might help me with the Loveland-Cade feud. I'm investigating its origins and what happened to Cora's Tear."

"Whistling Dixie, that be quite a find. A fifty-carat sapphire. Be worth millions today."

"What can you tell me about it?" Katlynn pulled her cell phone from her pocket. "May I record you?"

Aunt Susanna nodded, drawing in a deep breath. "Jeb Cade, a prospector, hit a lucky streak in 1887. Lots of silver and a fifty-carat sapphire. He used the funds to buy land for his ranch and sent the stone to Oberstein, Germany, a famed gem-cutting city. They created a tear-shaped brooch for his mother, Cora."

A keen light gleamed in Katie-Lynn's eyes. "Quite a history."

"I'm just getting started. How about we sit outside?"

Cole followed the jabbering pair. They stopped beneath a large oak where Aunt Susanna lowered herself onto a wooden bench encircling the trunk. Katie-Lynn perched beside her on the worn seat. Cole's gaze wandered back to the dilapidated house. They had to gut the place. Raze it possibly, though it'd be a shame given its age and importance to his family.

Katie-Lynn primly crossed her ankles and placed her phone on her lap. "Who was the first Loveland settler in the area?"

"Wyatt Loveland." Cole tested the bench's soft wood before lowering himself to it. "A cavalry man who fought in the Colorado War. He deserted rather than take part in the Sand Creek Massacre."

Katie-Lynn shuddered. "An entire village of Cheyenne and Arapaho were ambushed and killed."

"No glory there," Aunt Susanna observed, picking up the story. "Just a plain tragedy. Anyways, Wyatt was a loner. Bucked the system. Did things his own way."

"Apples don't fall far from their trees, do they?" Katie-Lynn asked, her eyes on Cole. The pocketed photograph crinkled as he moved, restless, under her stare.

Aunt Susanna chuckled. "Nope. Lovelands keep to themselves unless there's help needed. Then we're first to arrive."

"Speaking of help, Aunt Susanna, I'd like to—"

"Shush, boy." She cut Cole off with a wave of her hand. "Wyatt fell for a Cheyenne gal, Ayiana, who was Chief Black Kettle's daughter. He rescued her from Sand Creek, married her and brought her to Carbondale, where he used his pension and savings to buy Loveland Hills. Was quite the scandal."

"Seems to be a theme for the Lovelands."

"We don't go looking for drama, but it finds us. That there's the truth," Aunt Susanna avowed. "Unlucky in love, too. Ayiana died giving birth to their one and only son, Terrance."

"Such a shame."

"Lots of sad stories when it comes to the Lovelands."

The save-the-date picture burned in Cole's pocket.

"What can you tell me about Everett Loveland?"

Overhead, leaves rustled in the slight breeze.

Cole yanked his gaze off Katie-Lynn and peered upward, ignoring a familiar pang, his weakness for her friendly, determined, persistent nature. Backlit by the sun, the leaves glowed neon green.

"Not much other than what was passed down from my grandmother." Aunt Susanna's house slippers scuffed the dirt. "Everett was Terrance's youngest boy. Didn't stand to inherit anything. Had no prospects. Certainly not the kind of man able to go courting, especially not the sheltered daughter of a prosperous rancher. It's a mystery why he was holding Maggie Cade's body at the bottom of McClure Pass."

"What's your theory?"

"Hard to say." Aunt Susanna toyed with a tarnished silver locket hanging from her neck. "I don't think he murdered her or stole the gem. If he did, they would have found it on him."

"Didn't make any difference to the Cades." Cole waved away a hovering cloud of gnats. "They hanged Everett from the nearest tree when they discovered him with Maggie. But that's the Cades for you…hot-tempered, impulsive outlaws."

Katie-Lynn's eyes flicked to his. "Travis mentioned some of them had hid out and harassed the Lovelands."

"Two of Maggie's brothers. The sheriff, Everett Loveland's brother Earl, arrested them, but relatives broke them out of jail." Aunt Susanna rose from the bench and brushed off the back of her housecoat.

"Typical," Cole muttered, thinking of all the skirmishes between his family and the Cades. It'd be a flat-out miracle if the wedding went off without a hitch, no one hurt or worse.

"Was Maggie betrothed at the time of her death?"

Aunt Susanna dropped back to the bench at Katie-Lynn's follow-up question. She sure knew how to coax people into talking. Most important, she was an excellent listener.

The thought wrenched him back to their Say Anything tree after his mother's suicide. Her soft hand had curled in his as they'd perched on a branch. The horror of discovering his ma had struck him mute. They'd simply sat for hours. Days. Until eventually, he'd begun to speak. The secrets, the anguish, the shame he'd bottled up as an alcoholic's child, had poured out.

And she'd listened.

It'd meant everything.

Aunt Susanna rubbed her chin then snapped her fingers. "Came across an engagement announcement with Maggie's name when I was archiving old newspapers."

"Who was her fiancé?"

"Name slips my mind, but it'd be on file at

the museum." Aunt Susanna supplied them with dates to check.

"Would you have any old family records, pictures, maybe the family bible?"

Aunt Susanna nodded. "Might be hard to get to them. I've been meaning to organize…"

Cole saw his opportunity and jumped at it. "We'll help."

His aunt's face paled. "Oh. I don't know. It'd be an awful lot of work. Wouldn't want to put anyone out."

"It'd be no trouble," he insisted. "Plus, it'd help solve an old mystery."

"Which would bring a lot of attention to the rich history of this area," coaxed Katie-Lynn, reading his aunt with spot-on accuracy.

Aunt Susanna's head whipped between them. "No throwing anything out."

"We'll sort it and let you decide," Cole assured her, taking her veined hand in his. "You have my word."

Aunt Susanna's shoulders lowered. "Well, then…" She brushed at her eyes. "Don't want any strangers in here. Just family."

"You got it. What about Katie-Lynn?" His eyes lingered on her earnest expression. As much as he wanted to keep his family's secrets private, she deserved to be here.

"She's practically family, ain't she? Or was…

maybe I should ask you some questions." Aunt Susanna tapped him on the knee. "How'd you let a gem like Katlynn get away?"

"I'm beginning to wonder that myself."

"THERE IT IS!" Katlynn exclaimed when the grainy image of a newspaper engagement announcement filled one of Carbondale Museum's computer screens. "Mr. and Mrs. Jeb Cade, of Carbondale, Colorado, announce the engagement of their daughter Maggie Elizabeth Cade to Clyde William Farthington, previously of Chicago, Illinois," she read aloud. "He is the only son of the late Mr. and Mrs. Prescott Farthington. Mr. Farthington is a graduate of Harvard University and owns the Crystal River Railroad Company. The wedding will take place June 1, 1907."

Cole placed a hand on the back of Katlynn's chair and leaned down for a closer look. Her eyes closed as she breathed in his clean, masculine scent: pine, leather and sandalwood. Delicious. And forbidden. She snapped her eyes open. *Focus*.

"He looks a lot older than her." Cole's deep voice rumbled by her ear.

"At least twice her age or more. He could be her father. Grandfather, even." Katlynn scanned their faces, looking for hints of the story behind their stern expressions. "She doesn't look happy, either."

"How can you tell? Nobody smiled in pictures back then."

"Her eyes. They're sad." Katlynn studied the young woman's pretty face, noting her drooping bow-shaped mouth and the despair in her large brown eyes. Thick, honey-colored hair swept upward into a top knot, and she wore a blousy white shirt with lace edging the high-neck collar. "She doesn't like him."

"Now you're making stuff up."

"I'm serious. Look at how she's sitting. She's on the edge of the chair, as far from Clyde as possible. And see how he's kind of looming over her, standing behind the chair?"

Out of the corner of her eye, she caught Cole's slow nod.

"He's possessive," Cole observed.

"Yes. You can see it in the way he's gripping her shoulder." Katlynn peered at the pinch-faced, mustached man who wore a three-piece suit and a derby hat over clipped white hair. "His fingers are denting her shirt. It looks almost painful. Like he's forcing her to sit and take the picture."

"Arranged marriages were common. He was a wealthy man. It would have been considered a good match."

"For him," Katlynn countered. "He was getting a young, beautiful woman."

Cole pulled up a chair. "And she'd be marrying a man of means and gaining a privileged life. Isn't that what women want? Fame and fortune?"

Katlynn turned and sucked in a fast breath when their noses almost touched. "What about love?"

Cole blinked. "For some, it's not enough."

Her heart seized. "Are we still just talking about Maggie and Clyde?"

"Depends."

"On?"

"What *you* want to talk about."

"Oh. Well," she faltered. "Let's stick to Maggie, Clyde and Everett for now."

Cole's steady blue eyes bored into hers. "If that's what you want."

"I don't think she wanted to marry him."

Cole shrugged. "Maybe not. But people were practical then."

"No, they weren't," she insisted, fierce. "Everyone wants to find their special someone."

"Maybe it's not possible for everyone." A sad note entered Cole's voice as he stared at the picture once more.

Her pulse stumbled in her veins. Was Cole right? Her focus on her career left her little time for love. Would she end her life without ever finding it again? What a depressing thought... worse than losing her show. What good was success if you had no one to share it with?

"Is that Cora's Tear?" Cole pointed to the brooch pinned to Maggie's collar.

"Let's enlarge the shot."

She zoomed in and the teardrop shape of the large, dark stone emerged. "That's it!"

For some crazy reason, her eyes stung as she studied the infamous gem causing over a hundred years of strife.

What happened to you? she thought, staring into Maggie's forlorn eyes, the familiar urge to unlock long-held secrets, to unravel a mystery, coursing through her. *And where's the jewel?*

Cole whistled. "That's something."

"Worth killing for?"

Before Cole answered, the museum's curator joined them. She was a tall, thin, middle-aged woman, with short white hair tucked behind her ears. "Excuse me," she whispered, despite the otherwise empty, two-story building. "We'll be closing in five minutes."

"May I print this?"

The curator nodded at Katlynn, smiling. "The printer is by the front desk. Is there anything else I can help with?"

"Have you got anything on the Crystal River

Railroad Company?" Cole asked. "Or its owner, Clyde William Farthington?"

"We have an entire room devoted to the railroad company, if you'd like to head upstairs."

"I wouldn't want to put you out." Katlynn eyed an old-fashioned grandfather clock keeping time in the corner. "We can come back tomorrow."

"May I just ask—" The curator bounced on the balls of her feet. "Are you Katlynn Brennon from *Scandalous History*?"

Cole's muffled scoff ended when Katlynn elbowed his side as she stood. *Honestly.*

"Yes, I am."

The woman clapped her hands. "I thought so. I never miss an episode and neither does my husband. It's the only thing we watch together, besides baseball."

"I'm flattered."

Again…with the scoffing. She shot Cole a death glare. He was ruining her moment.

"He'll be so excited when I tell him I met Katlynn Brennon," gushed the curator. "If it's not too much to ask…would you sign something 'scandalous' to him? It's his birthday tomorrow and…"

"I'd be happy to."

"Thank you!" The curator called over her shoulder as she hurried away to her desk.

"How often does that happen?"

"What?" Katlynn asked as she scrolled the computer mouse to the print icon and clicked.

"Getting recognized. People bothering you."

She closed out the screen, powered down the computer and straightened. "It's no bother. Plus, it goes with the job."

"No privacy. No downtime…"

"Growing up, I never had any privacy, and no one noticed me. I guess that's why when you…"

He stepped closer until they stood toe-to-toe. "When I?" His voice deepened. "Say anything, Katie-Lynn."

She studied his handsome face for a breathless moment, then blurted, "When you noticed me, it was the first time I felt like I mattered to someone. Like I was special."

"Katie-Lynn," Cole half sighed, half groaned, sliding a finger down the side of her jaw. His gaze had a hypnotic, almost paralyzing effect.

When the returning curator's boots clomped on the wooden floor, Cole dropped his hand and jerked back. Katlynn released a long, shaky stream of air.

"Would you make it out to Honey Cheeks?" She thrust a book titled *History of Carbondale* at Katlynn.

Sensing an imminent chuckle, she stepped preemptively on Cole's foot. "Of course." With a swift, practiced hand, she inscribed:

To Honey Cheeks,
Live a scandalous life...make history!
Katlynn Brennon

"I'm not sure I'm okay with you calling another man Honey Cheeks," Cole teased after the effusive curator pointed them toward the railroad room, promising them an extra half hour.

"You wouldn't believe the crazy things people ask for." She strolled to the first glass case and studied maps laying out the railroad's track.

"Is it worth it?" Cole asked, joining her.

She caught sight of her frowning reflection. "I think so." She bit her lip then added, "Yes."

"You think so...yes? That doesn't sound certain."

A sigh escaped her as they moved onto a collection of tools used to build the railroad. "I'd be lying if I said it was everything I dreamed of."

"What's your biggest complaint?"

"Shapewear."

"Shapewear?" Her body tingled when his eyes dropped to her toes and rose slowly to her face. "Your shape's just fine."

"Because I'm wearing spandex."

Speaking of which, she hung back when they strolled to another display, and eased the cursed elastic off her spleen.

"You looked good wearing jeans and a shirt last night."

His compliment set her body alight. "It's different in Hollywood." She crouched to examine old documents, including bills of sale and land surveys. "Everyone's a size zero and I'm—" her voice sank to a whisper "—a six."

"A size six in Carbondale might earn you a muffin basket from well-meaning neighbors worried you're sick."

She cast him a quick sideways glance. "Not sure if that's a compliment. And I couldn't eat the muffins."

"Why?"

"Carbs. I'm on a strict diet."

"Let's get this straight. You have no privacy, have to write salacious notes to strangers' husbands and you're always hungry and judged for still not being thin enough?"

She grinned, rueful. "Sounds awesome, right?"

"Well. No wonder."

"No wonder what?"

"No wonder you wanted to come home."

She stared at him, mouth agape.

"I don't know much about clothes sizes," Cole continued, blue eyes squinted at her, "but you look perfect to me."

Nothing in the world could stop the warmth building in her chest. "If only everyone was that easy to please."

"You think I'm easy to please?" Cole protested. "There hasn't been anyone since you."

Her sharp intake of air cracked in the sudden silence.

"Forget I said that." Cole stomped to a glass case containing black-and-white pictures.

"The heck I will. You haven't dated since we broke up?"

His chest rose and fell with the force of his exhale. "No. I haven't."

"Why?"

"Have you?" he countered, dodging her question.

"Not seriously."

"How come?"

The truth weighed down her tongue: because she was too busy, because she didn't want to feed the gossip rags material, because…because no one could ever compare to Cole.

She tore her eyes from his, afraid they'd see too much, and stared at a trio of men posing by a stack of rail ties. The photo was faded sepia and grainy. The edges ragged. Yet a distinctive face jumped from the image. He may as well have been Cole's twin.

"Look!" She pointed at the man in the middle. "That's a Loveland."

Cole peered at the photo. "How can you be sure?"

"Take off the beard and the grime and that's your face."

He rubbed the back of his neck. "Everett Loveland?"

"Possibly. Only one way to know. We need to see the company's payroll ledger. Wonder if the museum has it?"

"Perhaps I can help?"

They turned at the trembling voice behind them and spied a bent, white-haired man leaning on a cane. A door marked Staff Only yawned open behind him.

"Hello." Katlynn extended a hand. "We'd appreciate any help we can get. And you are?"

"Clyde William Farthington, the fourth."

CHAPTER SIX

"YOU'RE IN TIME for tea." Clyde William Farthington, the fourth, lifted a small, silver bell from a mahogany side table and rang it a half hour later. "I'd be honored to have you join me."

"Pleased to." Cole perched on the edge of a high-backed chair, a pool of sweat gathering at the base of his neck. In the corner, a fire roared in a marble fireplace, despite the warm spring day. It was hotter than a two-dollar bill in Clyde's lavish Victorian mansion. Near a hundred degrees, he'd wager.

"We're grateful for the invitation." Katie-Lynn looked right at home in this posh front room. Her platinum hair glowed beneath scrolled sconces hanging from burgundy velvet wallpaper. Her expensive suit matched the elaborate, claw-footed furniture resting on Oriental rugs. Despite the early hour, heavy drapes shrouded a large window combination, leaving the room dim and smelling like his grandmother's potpourri.

A woman in a black-and-white maid's uniform pushed a metal cart through an open pocket door.

It held a floral-patterned teapot with matching cups and a three-tiered stand filled with miniature sandwiches and cookies too fancy to eat.

What he'd give for black coffee and beef jerky.

Mr. Farthington clasped his hands. "This looks delicious, Renata."

"May I get you or your guests anything else, sir?"

Mr. Farthington's teeth appeared in a reserved smile. "That will be all, thank you." He lifted the porcelain teapot. "How do you take your tea?"

After fixing them each a cup, Mr. Farthington settled back in his chair with a sigh. "It's a treat to have company." He lifted his cup and regarded them over the brim as he sipped.

Cole struggled to grip his cup's fragile handle without breaking it. Even his pinky was too big to slip through. Fussy places like this made him feel like a bull in a china shop. And claustrophobic. His neck strained against his shirt collar.

"I believe I've seen you before." Mr. Farthington settled his cup in its saucer with enviable finesse while Katie-Lynn held hers as delicately as a newborn chick. Cole downed his tepid tea in one gulp. The cup rattled when he placed it—gently, he thought—back down, earning him a sharp glance from his host.

He stopped himself from apologizing like a schoolboy.

"Have you seen my show, *Scandalous History*?"

"I only read books." Mr. Farthington gestured to a glass cabinet filled with leather-bound tomes. "Though I am a bit of a history buff. I believe I saw you at a yacht party... St. Tropez?"

"St. Barts?" Katie-Lynn queried after a dainty sip.

When Cole reached for a cookie, she subtly shook her head then pointed her chin at a pair of tongs.

Tongs.

Sheesh.

Despite taking care, he left a trail of crumbs as he deposited shortbread on a scalloped plate no bigger than Sierra's old toy set.

After a pointed look, Mr. Farthington continued. "Yes. I believe you were with Seth Rutherford. Owner of Ultima Productions? He's quite a catch."

Cole swallowed a bite of cookie wrong and choked.

Katie-Lynn peered at him, eyes wide. "Are you okay?"

He nodded once the coughing fit subsided, although he wasn't okay. He considered himself a mild-mannered person unless provoked. And it was uncomfortably provoking to imagine Katie-

Lynn out with some big-shot yacht guy who owned a company.

Earlier, she'd insisted love mattered most and everyone wanted to find a special someone. Yet this proved she spent time with rich men who enjoyed the lifestyle a broke, soon-to-be home-less cowboy like him couldn't provide. It burned his chaps, no denying it. Proof he still carried a torch for Katie-Lynn?

Darn straight. And stupid as all get out.

"Mind if I smoke?" Mr. Farthington flipped open a thin gold case and extracted a cigar.

"Not at all." Katie-Lynn reached for the cookie tongs, hesitated then lifted her teacup again in-stead.

What kind of place made beautiful women insecure about their weight? That quarter-size cookie couldn't contain more than fifty calories tops, and that was being generous considering it tasted like nut-flavored cardboard. Next chance he got, he'd grill her a thick rib-eye with foil-wrapped potatoes, extra butter and two dollops of sour cream.

"Mr. Loveland?" Mr. Farthington extended the cigar box.

"No, thanks." Cole shifted in his chair. Sitting so still made his legs grow numb. "You said you'd help us find the whereabouts of a relative of mine. Everett Loveland."

Mr. Farthington nodded as he struck a match and held it to the tip of a cigar clamped in his mouth. A couple of quick puffs, followed by a white, cherry-scented exhale, then—"I have payroll records from the Crystal River Railroad Company. When did he work for the company?"

Cole swallowed a dry mouthful of almond-flavored shortbread. "Not sure, but it'd be no later than May 31, 1907." The date of Maggie's death and Everett's hanging.

Mr. Farthington tapped ash into a yellow-glass ashtray. "He would have been laying track from Placita on to Marble." After another long inhale, he continued. "The route hauled marble out to market, as well as supplies into town."

Katie-Lynn leaned forward. "What happened to the line?"

"Scrapped it in 1943 when Yule Marble shut down."

"Sorry to hear that."

Mr. Farthington waved his cigar. "No matter. My family always lands on its feet."

Cole glanced at the room's thick crown molding and the gilded light fixture hanging from a coffered ceiling. The Farthingtons were in tall cotton, no mistaking. "The first Clyde Farthington was engaged to a local woman, Maggie Cade."

Mr. Farthington dragged on his cigar again

before resting it in the ashtray. "Indeed, though such a match was quite out of character and would have been most unfortunate. Farthingtons have married distant New England relatives for generations."

"Here's their engagement announcement. Maggie died the day before their wedding day." Katie-Lynn passed over the paper.

After donning a pair of reading glasses, Mr. Farthington scanned the piece. The printout trembled slightly as he lowered it. "She looks decently respectable, for a frontier woman." Mr. Farthington sniffed. "I believe she was at the root of some sort of family feud or local kerfuffle."

Cole and Katie-Lynn's eyes met briefly. Disbelief drove light furrows into her brows. Mr. Farthington may not watch television, but he didn't live under a rock. Everyone knew about the Cade-Loveland feud. Especially locals. Why act as though he wasn't familiar with it?

Katie-Lynn cleared her throat. "I'm investigating the Cade-Loveland feud for *Scandalous History*."

Mr. Farthington paled. "And you're connecting it with my family?"

"Should we?" Cole asked, bristling for no good reason except something felt off.

"We'd only reference your ancestor in terms

of his engagement to Maggie. What can you tell us about him?"

Mr. Farthington snatched up his cigar and inhaled so deeply a half inch of ash formed on its tip. White rings of smoke peeled from his mouth before he spoke again. "His father squandered the family shipping fortune with bad investments and gambling debts. After marrying Amelia Griswold, heiress to a banking empire, he invested in railroads and built this home for her. Sadly, Amelia died when she tumbled down those stairs and broke her neck."

Cole followed Mr. Farthington's finger point and a chill ran down his back when he glimpsed a scrolled, mahogany balustrade through the pocket door.

"His second marriage also ended tragically. He lost his second bride, Rose Webster, heiress to her family's gunpowder fortune, during a picnic outing. While rowing her across a pond, the boat tipped, and Rose fell overboard and drowned. Clyde was left bereft."

"And loaded," Cole added.

Katie-Lynn shot him a quelling look. "It makes sense he'd want another bride, like Maggie Cade."

Clyde tapped his cigar against the side of the ashtray. "He would have had his pick of pedigreed ladies. This engagement may have been coerced."

"Forced?" Katie-Lynn gasped.

Mr. Farthington coughed lightly into his hand. "Miss Cade may have been in the family way. It wasn't uncommon for women to target men of means."

"Or older men to prey on vulnerable young women." Cole recalled Clyde William Farthington's possessive grip in the old-time engagement photo, the sadness in Maggie's eyes. If coercion had been at play, his money was on Clyde doing the forcing.

"This tea is delicious," blurted Katie-Lynn, breaking the sudden tense silence. She settled her empty teacup in its saucer and set them back on the tray. "If you have time, would you kindly show us the railroad's logbooks?"

Mr. Farthington stubbed out his cigar, rang the bell and stood. "Follow me."

They trekked down a long hall. Mr. Farthington's cane thumped against black-and-white diamond-patterned tiles. Gleaming side tables, set with lavish flower arrangements, stood beneath mirrors ornately framed in gold leaf.

Cole glimpsed his ragtag appearance in them. Faded Wranglers, scuffed boots and a plaid shirt, his hair flattened by his hat. He resembled a hayseed ranch hand, which he was…and proud of it… Yet seeing himself this way reminded him that he didn't belong in Katie-Lynn's world. Never had. Never would.

She was as untouchable as the marble bust Mr. Farthington paused beside.

"This is Clyde William Farthington, the first."

Cole squinted at the writing engraved in a gold plaque and noted the dates 1860 to 1931. "He lived a long life."

Mr. Farthington leaned on his cane and peered up at him. "But not a happy one. He lost his third wife in childbirth when he was forced to choose between his unborn heir and his wife."

Katlynn hugged herself with her arms. "As in perform a Caesarean section?"

"Yes. Luckily the child was a male, Clyde William, the second, so all wasn't in vain."

"Luckily?" Cole didn't bother hiding his scorn. How could any man make such a choice? Seemed no task at all for a Farthington.

"He's certainly had his share of tragedies." Katie-Lynn squatted and peered eye to eye with the statue as if she could glean some hidden information in the cold marble facade.

Mr. Farthington's expression shuttered. "Every family has its legends, a story, as do we."

They resumed their walk and stepped inside a library filled with jammed, floor-to-ceiling bookshelves. "Our oldest records are kept here." Mr. Farthington unlocked a glass-doored bookcase and retrieved a faded, green, velum-covered logbook.

At a wooden table, they examined the payroll.

"There he is!" Katie-Lynn exclaimed, pointing at a handwritten line with "Everett J. Loveland, paid $3.50, on April 27."

A strange rushing sensation swept through Cole, nearly lifting him off his feet. Seeing his infamous ancestor's name in black-and-white made Katie-Lynn's quest real. This wasn't just a legend, but a real person, someone's actual life. Cole's plan to assist Katie-Lynn to ensure she didn't stir up old scandals was even more personal now. He wanted to vindicate Everett, too. He might not have been famous or rich, but he still deserved justice. Like Cole, Everett had little but his pride. And he'd restore it to Everett, a man wrongly accused and shamed by a dishonorable death.

"What does 'WO' mean?" Katie-Lynn pointed to the letters entered next to Everett's name on May 31.

"Wages owed," Mr. Farthington supplied. "Presumably, he'd left the job before payday."

"Why?" Cole flipped a few pages back and noted Everett had been collecting his weekly pay until then. As a younger son with no prospects, seemed unlikely he'd walk away from steady wages.

"Any number of reasons." Mr. Farthington closed the book, returned it to the glass case and led them out. "Injury. Illness. Bad news calling him home. It would have been a significant reason since reliable, well-compensated jobs were few and far between in Everett's day."

"You've been a big help." Katie-Lynn stopped at the front door and gifted the older man with her winsome smile. "Thank you, Mr. Farthington."

"Much appreciated, sir." Cole clasped the other man's frail hand.

"If I can be of any further help, please let me know," Mr. Farthington called after them.

Cole opened his truck's passenger door and helped Katie-Lynn up into her seat. "There's never been any mention of Everett being sick."

"Or injured." Katie-Lynn peered down at him. "Though we should probably look at medical records to be sure."

Cole donned his cowboy hat and pulled the brim low against the sunshine. "Why leave a lucrative job to come home? Had to be something important."

"It usually is." Katie-Lynn's eyes darkened slightly before her lashes lowered, obscuring her expression.

Was she thinking about her job? Him? Both?

"According to the story, the family was surprised he was home. If they didn't summon him, who did?"

Katie-Lynn's brow furrowed. "We need to find out."

Cole jumped behind the wheel of his truck and tore off down the road.

He liked the sound of "we" too much for his own good.

"THANK YOU FOR seeing us on such short notice." Katlynn eyed the fluffy chocolate chip cookies Joy Cade transferred from a baking sheet to a cooling rack later that night. She clenched her gut to keep it from rumbling. This morning's weigh-in showed she'd lost a pound...so only four more to go.

Only.

Four pounds seemed insurmountable when faced with gooey, homemade cookies. The rich, chocolaty smell filled her nose, and her mouth watered. Who could resist? Not Cole.

"Mind if I?" he asked, then grabbed a couple of the treats at Joy's smiling nod.

"How about some milk for dunking?" Joy cocked her head and the blunt ends of her thick, silver bob swung.

"Thank you," Cole mumbled through a bite.

Joy's hazel eyes, bright behind frameless

glasses, peered at Katlynn. "How about you, honey?"

Before Katlynn managed a polite refusal, Cole said, "She'd like a glass, too," and passed over a stack of cookies.

Diet sabotage!

Her mouth opened and closed, thoughts tumbling. An inner war waged, a battle between being polite to her hostess and capitulating to her merciless shapewear and bodycon dresses.

"Are you trying to ruin my diet?" she said beneath her breath once Joy rummaged inside the refrigerator.

"Nope." Cole bit off half a cookie, chewing, lips twisted in a smirk. "I'm just trying to get you to eat."

She sighed. Strange how the trait you admired in a person was just as likely to drive you crazy. Cole always looked out for others. Case in point. He'd leaped in to offer Aunt Susanna help while being respectful of her fears. Loyal and devoted as ever. Never out for himself.

His opposition to her investigation and his involvement to safeguard his family only underscored his protectiveness. It'd been a long time since she'd been around a selfless person. He was hardly a saint, though. The twinkle in his eye as he waved a cookie beneath her nose was one hundred percent pure, unadulterated evil.

"Fine," she mumbled, relenting, then bit into the soft, warm cookie.

Manners 1, Willpower 0.

Fireworks exploded on her tongue. Whistlers streaked straight to her brain and popped. The sweet chocolate melted on her tongue, and she closed her eyes in deep appreciation. No gluten-free, sugar-free, soy-free Hollywood patisserie held a candle to simple, made-from-scratch cookies.

"Would you like more?"

At Joy's gentle question, Katlynn opened her eyes and peered down at her empty napkin, dumbfounded. She'd eaten all the cookies? A quick glance at a grinning Cole confirmed the horrible truth.

Joy hurried off to answer a ringing phone.

"You." Katlynn pointed another cookie at him before dunking it in her milk. "You made me do this."

"You can bring a starving woman a cookie, but you cannot make her eat," he intoned, mock-serious.

She nearly choked on her soggy, milk-laden treat, laughing. Cole's deep chuckle mingled with hers in the homey kitchen, the moment suddenly intimate. Eventually, their merriment subsided and smiles disappeared as their eyes locked. Cole, sitting on a stool beside her at the granite-topped counter, leaned closer. Drawn by forces nearly as strong as the cookie, Katlynn's mouth puckered. Her eyes closed. In her eardrums, her heart banged a fast rhythm.

"You have chocolate on your cheek," Cole whispered in her ear before brushing his lips to her skin with a kiss so soft, so brief, it felt like a child's dream. When he withdrew, she almost wept with a new craving altogether. And she wasn't exactly known for her willpower.

"That was your father." Joy turned from the phone, blushing and beaming. "Says Aunt Susanna's agreed to let the family come over and work at her place tomorrow. She thinks she might have some information for you."

"What kind of information?" Cole asked.

"About the feud?" asked Jewel Cade, Joy's only daughter, joining them. A tight braid revealed her pretty, freckled face and enormous brown eyes. "Hey, Katie-Lynn. Saw you at Silver Spurs."

"Hats off in the house," Joy said without turning from the oven.

"Oops. The cookies smelled so good, I forgot." Jewel hung up her black Stetson and sauntered back to the granite island. She shoved half of one in her mouth and swallowed with barely a chew.

"She goes by Katlynn now," Cole said.

Jewel crossed to the fridge and grabbed some milk. "Is that right."

"It's for professional reasons," Katlynn clarified.

"So she doesn't sound like a hayseed," Cole contended, one eyebrow cocked.

"And no drinking straight from the carton," Joy said without looking away from the stove as she slid in another sheet of unbaked cookies.

"Dang it." Jewel lowered the carton. "Do all mothers have eyes in the back of their head, or just mine?"

"Or cussing."

Jewel, Cole and Katlynn burst out laughing.

"What's a Loveland doing here?" asked someone with a raspy male voice. Justin Cade, clad in head-to-toe black, ambled into the kitchen then halted.

"Cade," Cole growled, sizing Justin up through narrowed eyes. The air in the room morphed from lighthearted to tense in half a heartbeat.

Justin filched a cookie from his sister's plate. "Howdy, Katie-Lynn. Good seeing you. Would be better if you weren't with this guy." At Jewel's lightning-quick shoulder jab, he dropped the treat and backed away, rubbing his upper arm.

"She goes by Katlynn now." Jewel lowered her balled hand.

"Your sister's got a nice cross punch," Cole drawled.

"You wouldn't think so if you were on the receiving end of it," Justin said, rueful. He kissed his ma on the cheek when she fixed him a plate.

Jewel, a tough cowgirl through and through, stopped scowling at her brother and bestowed a smile on Cole. "Least someone's got some manners around here."

"What are you doing back home, Katie—Katlynn?" Justin asked. "Not taking up with Cole again, are you?"

"I'm investigating the family feud for my show."

"Heard about that now as you mention it."

"A Loveland in our kitchen... Is it the apocalypse?" James Cade entered the room with his adopted son, Javi.

"Will he bite me?" Javi whispered, eyes wide as he hid behind his father's legs.

"I'll protect you." Jewel scooped up Javi and snuggled him on her lap, tickling his belly.

"Katie-Lynn?" James, an old classmate, swept her off her feet in a tight hug that left her breathless. "What a nice surprise. Ma said you were doing a show here about our family."

Cole shot to his feet. "She goes by Katlynn."

James took his time releasing her in the face of Cole's scowl.

"Funny how you keep reminding everyone of that," Katlynn said to Cole. "Yet you can't remember it yourself."

Jewel and Justin guffawed, and red stained Cole's handsome face.

"Are Lovelands really snakes?" Javi asked. "Uncle Jack says so."

"Only on a full moon," Cole said with a wink, as James, Justin and Jewel suddenly got busy cleaning up the baking pans.

"Is he funning me?" Javi's large eyes grew so big they nearly swallowed his small face.

"Yes, he is. He's a regular person same as you and me." Joy frowned over Javi's head at her offspring. "And a guest in this house."

Everyone jumped slightly when she set a fresh platter of cookies down with a bang.

"Will he be my uncle?" Javi grabbed a cookie.

Cole nodded. "And you'll be my nephew."

Jewel, James and Justin exchanged frowns. Despite the temporary truce, it seemed the about-to-be blended family was on shaky ground. No wonder Cole worried the investigation might open old wounds. They hardly seemed healed at all, despite their parents' upcoming wedding. The full consequence of her investigation hit her. She needed to take every precaution to do no harm to the fragile peace.

"Are you poor?" Javi asked Cole as he chewed, openmouthed. "Me and mama were poor once. Do you get your clothes from the shelter?"

"Javi, that's not polite." Joy turned to a stone-faced Cole. "Please accept my apologies."

He shook his head. "The boy only says what he's been taught."

"I was apologizing for my children," Joy clarified, glowering at them. "And I'm sure they will, too."

After a chorus of hurried *sorry*s, Justin turned to Cole, "Are we set for the softball fund-raiser this weekend?"

"Got things covered on my end. The Lovelands are ready to kick some Cade—" He broke off when he glimpsed a rapt Javi. "Tires," he finished lamely.

Bitten-back grins circled the group.

"Why's he going to kick our tires?" Javi's face scrunched.

"It's just a figure of speech." Joy ruffled Javi's hair.

"We're planning on kicking your—" Jewel cleared her throat "—tires, too. Into next week."

"Guess we'll see." Cole shrugged. "May the best family win."

"And we know who that is," James growled.

"This is for charity, right?" Katlynn asked. Given the tension, it might have been a fight-to-the-death match.

"Yes." Joy nodded. "We're raising money for Fresh Start, a rehabilitation clinic in town. Justin works there part-time doing ranching workshops. Cole runs their Al-Anon meetings."

Katlynn stared at Cole, amazed he'd oversee anything involving talking, let alone about his painful past. Knowing how much it must cost him to open up, to help others, touched her.

Her reasons for leaving him so long ago were growing harder to remember by the day…

"I help out at those meetings, too." Justin clamped his mouth tight for a quiet moment then said, "For Jesse."

Sympathy welled for Justin, who'd lost his identical twin. She'd heard Jesse became addicted to opioids after a sports injury, a dangerous habit leading to his death at the hands of dealers calling in his debt.

"I meant to say earlier, I'm sorry for your loss," Katlynn said. "Jesse was sweet. And caring. He always found me in the library at lunch and shared his food when I didn't have any."

Joy dabbed at her eyes, and her kids crowded around her, holding her tight. "That—that—sounds like our Jesse." After returning her children's hugs, she waved them off. "We're starting to move on, thanks to Javi and Sofia."

"Jesse was my daddy, but now James is, right, Pa?"

James clasped the child in his arms. "That's right."

"Jack and Jared are married with kids, too. And Justin's engaged." Jewel made a gagging sound. "To a pastor, if you can believe it. Fresh Start's manager, Brielle Thompson. She'll have her hands full keeping this sinner in line."

"You'll be the only single one in the family, Jewel," James observed.

"No surprise. She's as approachable as a cactus," Justin teased.

"You're one to talk!" Jewel rejoined, red coloring in the spaces between her freckles. "Besides, I'm not giving up my independence for some gold ring. Might as well put it in my nose and lead me around with it."

"Many women choose to be single." Katlynn swirled her milk. From the corner of her eye, she spied Cole's gaze on her.

Joy flicked off the oven and turned, wiping her hands on a green-and-white-patterned apron, a perfect color match for her silky blouse and earrings. "If you'd like to follow me, I can show you the family bible."

"Cole. A word," James said as they passed him on the way to the living room.

"If it's about your offer to buy us out, don't waste your breath."

Katlynn lagged behind, listening.

"Be reasonable. I don't want Ma getting married then foreclosed on. She'd be humiliated."

"You think we'd let that happen? Lovelands

look after our own. Like it or not, your ma's about to become one of us."

The protectiveness and pride in Cole's voice nearly broke Katlynn's heart. She hurried to join Joy. A moment later a red-faced Cole thumped down beside them on the couch.

"I marked the page." Joy heaved open an oversize book covered in faded black leather, a gold cross painted on its cover. Dry pages, yellow with age, rustled as she turned them. Katlynn sneezed at the musty smell.

"Bless you, dear."

She smiled at Joy's and Cole's concerned faces. "Thank you."

"Okay. Here it is." Joy stopped on an ink-filled page.

Katlynn and Cole leaned down to peer at it.

"Maggie Elizabeth Cade, born February 26, 1889, died May 31, 1907," Cole read out loud.

"She was only eighteen," Joy sighed. "Poor child."

Katlynn pictured the pretty young woman in the grip of her older, stern fiancé. Had she killed herself to escape a miserable marriage? Where did Everett Loveland's unexplained appearance, at the site of her death, fit in? A coincidence or something more…and what happened to Cora's Tear?

"Do you have any journals or letters belonging to Maggie?"

"There are a few places I can check. Lord knows the attic hasn't been cleaned in half a century. Let me get back to you."

"What's that mean?" Cole tapped an entry beneath Maggie's.

It read: Unnamed Cade (†*) May 31, 1907.

Joy took off her glasses and wiped them with her shirt hem. "It means," she said after a long moment, her voice slightly hoarse. "Maggie Cade was with child."

CHAPTER SEVEN

"Almost. Got. It," Cole grunted as he yanked on another box wedged between his aunt Susanna's attic rafters. Sweat streamed down his face and turned his wet T-shirt into a second skin. Two days spent organizing his aunt's house, working nonstop with his family and Katie-Lynn, tested his stamina.

His stubbornness, too.

When he started something, he finished it... and finished it right.

Except when it came to Katie-Lynn...

"Let me help." Katie-Lynn pulled back a rotted piece of wood holding the box in place.

Freed, the cardboard container crashed to the floor in a mushroom cloud of dust.

Katie-Lynn waved her hands in front of her face and then let out a huge sneeze.

Cole studied her, and his mouth twitched with humor. In baggy overalls over an army-green tank top, her hair tousled around her grime-streaked face, she looked ready for war, not a close-up. But she was pretty this way. Approachable. And the urge to kiss her naked lips, to hold her, had ridden him hard all day. "Did you take your allergy pills yet?"

"An hour ago." She stopped her search for a tissue when he held one up to her nose.

"Blow."

She honked loudly then laughed, rueful, as he tossed out the tissue. "Bet you do that for all the girls."

"Nope." Cole tore off the ancient box's tape, pinning his attention where it needed to be.

Needed, not wanted to be.

Because every minute he spent working with dogged, determined Katie-Lynn drew him more and more.

"*Some* of the girls?"

At her teasing tone, he glanced up into her warm blue eyes and was lost. She was the only girl—the only woman—for him.

"Hey." Katie-Lynn waved a hand in front of his face a moment later. "You in there?"

He ducked his head and tore open the box. "I'm here all right."

"You don't sound happy about it."

"I'm happy." Cole pulled out broken and mismatched sets of salt-and-pepper shakers.

Katie-Lynn examined a pair of ceramic corncobs. "No, you're not."

Cole peered at her briefly then returned to ripping old newspapers off figurines.

"You forget, I know you."

"Knew me," he clarified.

"So what's changed? You're still working at the ranch. You're not dating anyone. You only hang out with your family. Oh…and you're leading an Al-Anon group. That's different. In a good way. I'm proud of you for that, by the way."

He ignored the rising warmth following her praise. Why, after all this time and heartache, did her good opinion still affect him this way?

"What prompted you to do it?"

"The town held meetings about the rehab clinic, Fresh Start. Some wanted to shut it down. They said people with mental health or addiction issues didn't belong here. It got to me."

"Your mother wasn't happy in Carbondale."

Cole grunted.

"Are the meetings helping you?" Katlynn scooted to his side and grabbed another lump wrapped in brittle newspaper.

"Nothing left to be helped with." When he shrugged, his shoulder brushed hers, her bare skin silky soft against his. "She's gone."

"You're not."

"I'm not affected by it anymore."

"Liar."

He stopped sorting and peered at Katlynn.

They were so close, their eyelashes touched. "Why are you poking at me?"

She passed the back of her hand across her face. "I don't know. I just... Being around you again... I guess I still care."

"Why?"

"Why?"

"You've got everything you wanted—fame, fortune, rich men taking you out on yachts."

"So what if they have yachts? Money?" Exasperation filled her voice.

"They can give you things." His voice grew rough. "Things I'll never be able to."

His pulse raced as her gaze drifted from his eyes to his mouth. "You brought me flowers every day."

"Daisies were your favorite." His voice grew husky with memory, and his body tingled with sweet memories.

They looked into each other's eyes and Cole felt the earth shift. He wanted to tell her he'd missed her. That he was happy to have her back in his life again, but he was too afraid of ruining things to voice that thought. Heck, he was too afraid to even have that thought.

Katie-Lynn held herself still as if debating. Struggling. "No one else can give me this," she whispered.

Without warning, she wrapped her arms

around his neck, lifted her face and brushed her lips against his. The delicious taste of her, raspberry tart, made his eyes close and his hands fall to cup her waist. Coherent thought fled. With a groan, he kissed her back.

She was warm, her body needy. It had been a very, very long time since he held a woman—this woman—whom his body instinctively recognized. Longed for. Welcomed home. He took the kiss deeper, made it richer.

She was as bold and audacious as ever. She wasn't waiting for things to happen, and neither should he. Her hands were on his chest, then around his neck as he pressed her down to the attic floor. She was soft, in all the right places. He devoured her mouth, nips and bites that made her sigh. His hands slid up her sides then rose to tangle in her thick hair.

He angled her face the way he wanted, kissing her senseless, and her breath quickened, matching his, their gasps loud in the echoing space. When she dug her fingers into his back, urging him closer still, he let his weight fall on her fully. Their hearts thundered against each other. One leg rose, her knee pressing the side of his hip.

Cole knew he should pull away, but Katie-Lynn was intoxicating, grabbing his hair, kissing him like he was the very oxygen she needed to survive.

Narcotic. The woman was a narcotic. He ripped his mouth away, struggling for control where there was none. This was why you didn't get involved. Not even a little bit. Kissing Katie-Lynn for him was like an alcoholic having just one drink. No maybes. Just no. Her breathing was warm against his cheek, tightening even more of his muscles.

He rolled over and flopped on his back beside her, chest heaving. "I'm sorry."

Her fingers wound in his. "I started it."

"Are you sorry?"

Her grin was wide and unrepentant when he faced her. "Nope. I've been wanting to do that for a while."

"How long?"

"Twelve years. I've regretted leaving you a million times."

His heart stopped in his chest. Stunned. "But you never came back." When she'd left, it'd felt like she'd taken pieces of his heart with him. Pieces he needed to be whole.

Her expression turned inward. "There's nothing for me here."

Stung, he sat up and shoved to his feet.

Fool. She doesn't want you back.

A soft hand landed on his shoulder. "I didn't mean it like that."

"I know what you meant." He looked at his feet

and then slowly back up at her. "Been through it before. All my life."

"You're thinking of your mother."

His shoved his balled hands in his pockets. "She wanted to be a singer, but she got pregnant with me instead. Carbondale, my father, us… We weren't enough. It's the same for you."

She hung her head. "Do you blame yourself for what happened with your mother?"

When he didn't respond, Katie-Lynn's eyes rose to his. "Say anything, Cole."

His jaw clamped hard enough to break. At last, he bit out, "Every day."

"You were a baby."

"An unwanted one." He stared out the attic window at the distant, lonely mountain range.

"Your father wanted you."

"I made Ma's life miserable. It's why I…" He stopped and scooped figurines back into the box, resealing it with fresh tape.

"Why you what?"

The acrid smell of Magic Marker stung his nose as he wrote salt-and-pepper shakers on the carton's side.

"Cole. Please. Why you what?"

His eyes circled the boxes still stacked in the suffocating tight attic space, avoiding looking at her as the answer weighed down his tongue. It was a piece of his soul he'd buried, even from himself. "Why I never tried to stop you from leaving me."

Silence, heavy with unspoken words, unfurled in the space between them. Regret. Longing. Despair. Cole capped the marker and heaved the box. "Better get this downstairs. We're finished here."

"How come you never told me that?"

Cole turned at the door. Katie-Lynn's blue eyes glistened. "Would it have changed your mind?"

Her lips trembled. "Maybe. Probably."

"Then there's your answer. I don't want a woman sacrificing to be with me or who feels sorry for me." His wounded pride bled inside, steady and ice-cold. When she didn't speak, he trudged to the door.

"I'll look around a few minutes longer," he heard her mutter as he headed downstairs, grateful for the small reprieve. He needed to collect his thoughts and build his walls back up in case he revealed more.

"I'll take that," his father said, pointing to the box when Cole reached the bottom of the stairs. "Go grab a drink. We all just finished our break."

"Thanks, Pa."

A few minutes later Cole drained the last of his soda and surveyed the mostly organized living room. The dachshund snoozed in a dog bed, provided by Sierra, he'd wager, and the cats clawed a new scratching post.

"Cole!" Katie-Lynn shouted.

He stomped back up to the attic. "What is…" His voice trailed off and his mouth dropped open.

From Katie-Lynn's fingers dangled an old saddlebag with the initials ESL tooled in its leather.

"I took a last look around and spotted this, wedged up high in the back of the rafters." Her eyes were so electric, they practically sparked. "ESL. Do you think this belongs to—"

"Everett Samuel Loveland?" His heartbeat thundered. "Only one way to find out."

His breath stalled as Katie-Lynn pulled out each item: a midsize sheath knife, a tinderbox, a honing stone, a tobacco pouch and papers, a paper box of cartridges and a hair comb.

"Paper cartridge puts it in the right time period." Cole opened the small box and peered at the ammunition. "This was for a Colt revolver. Might be Everett's."

"I wish we could know for sure." Katie-Lynn scrounged around inside the bag then turned it upside down and shook it. A seam came loose, and a yellowed edge of paper poked out.

Cole cocked his head.

"Do you see that?"

Katie-Lynn's eyes lit. "Something's in there. Must be sewn inside the seams."

Cole unsheathed the knife and cut through the cloth lining of the saddlebag. Adrenaline surged when a piece of paper appeared. "Got something."

Katie-Lynn gripped his arm and peered over his shoulder. "Is that? Are those…?"

"Letters." He freed the envelopes and carefully deposited them on the floor. They were faded and worn, the ink barely legible.

"No return addresses." Katie-Lynn eased out folded sheets of paper with a shaking hand. She read aloud.

Carbondale, Colorado
May 2, 1907
Dearest,

I have but one thought, Everett, this afternoon of May, and it's of you; and I have one prayer, only; my heart, that is for you. That you and I might walk together again, might linger in our sacred spot, forget these many months and these mournful cares and become lovers again—I wish it were so, Everett, and when I look around and find myself alone, I sigh for you; a little sigh, a vain sigh, which will not bring you home.

I need you more and more, and the great world grows close, pressing me until I can barely breathe. I am comforted to hold a piece of you, dearest, inside me. To feel it grow, as does our love and our future, I pray. Each movement within drives away the shadows preying on my doubts, my fears that our blessed plans will be for naught. Surely, fate must give us a life together when we have already created one.

Everett, forgive me, darling, for every word I say—my heart is full of you, my thoughts, too. When I strive to share something beyond our world, the magical space we inhabit, words fail me. If you were here—and oh, that you were, my darling, we need not talk at all; our eyes would speak for us, and your hand tight in mine. Our love would be in darkness no more, but revealed, so bright, all will love us, too, and celebrate our happiness, our desire to be together. Always.

My daydreams bring you nearer, thoughts of you to chase the weeks away till they flee. My heart scampers so. I have much trouble to rein it back again, and school it to be patient. Four months is not forever, though it might feel so. I shall grow more and more impatient until that dear day comes.

All my love, and another's,
Maggie Elizabeth Cade

Katie-Lynn and Cole stared at each other, stunned.

Downstairs, the voices of Cole's family rose and quieted. A tree branch scraped against the attic's lone window. Somewhere a door slammed. An engine rumbled then quieted as a car drove away.

"This—this—" Katie-Lynn gasped, bright eyes wild. "This is everything."

"Sheds light on the situation."

She swatted him on the arm. "Tell me you're as excited about this as I am."

"On the inside." Which he was. His gut clenched, and his heart spun fast enough to make him motion-sick.

"Everett and Maggie were in love. A secret affair."

"And she was pregnant. She mentioned movement…"

"She signed it 'all my love, and another's.'"

"Baby Cade."

"Baby Loveland," Cole corrected, a sadness for Everett taking hold. Everett would have been a father, something Cole longed to become. But since the only woman he'd ever loved didn't share his feelings on the matter, his chances looked dim.

"It must be Everett's baby." Katie-Lynn pinched

the bridge of her nose and squeezed her eyes shut. "Can't imagine it otherwise."

"She seemed awfully keen to have Everett home." Cole stood and helped Katie-Lynn to her feet. "Plus, her expression in the engagement photo. She looked trapped."

"Unhappy for sure." Katie-Lynn returned the letters and items to the saddlebag. "Let's bring these back to the ranch. Wonder what other secrets we'll find?"

Cole shouldered the bag and ushered Katie-Lynn down the stairs. "Only one way to find out."

One thing was certain. Maggie Cade loved Everett Loveland, and it still hadn't been enough to ward off tragedy. Katie-Lynn kissed him and said she still cared…and it wasn't enough, either.

Whoever said love conquered all needed a swift kick followed by a heavy dose of reality.

"CARBONDALE, COLORADO, A sleepy town nestled in the foothills of the Rocky Mountains, is a peaceful, family-friendly place to live in America's heartland. Unless you're a member of the Loveland and Cade families, that is."

"Cut!"

Katlynn dropped her smile and struggled not to droop under the intense afternoon sun. Unseasonable temperatures hovered at seventy-five degrees. The sky looked as though it'd never even heard the word *cloud*, let alone seen one. How many more takes?

"That was fabulous, Katlynn. Truly. Genius." Gabe, her director, raked his hand through his unruly graying hair. "Phil!" he hollered to their lighting director. "Go to softbox to hide Katlynn's crow's feet."

Katlynn hid her wince as Phil emerged from an oak's shadow, a baseball hat shading his narrow face. "Not possible unless you want to move her under the tree or on the porch." He pointed to the Lovelands' ranch house.

"Crow's feet, my patootie," muttered Mary, blotting and powdering Katlynn's face. "You don't have a line on you."

"Maybe I should get Botox." Katlynn shuddered, imagining needles poking her skin. Many in the entertainment industry used it by their twenties. She was past due, really. In Hollywood, there was always someone younger, prettier and hungrier to take your place. Her pulse jumped like a rabbit at the possibility.

Mary clucked as she spritzed. "Who wants to look like frozen plastic? You have beautiful skin, Katlynn."

Katlynn smiled her thanks, her mind in overdrive. Hollywood gave her the spotlight, but it didn't give her love. Not the real kind. Not like…

her eyes lit on Cole. He was vaccinating calves in a distant pen, his cowboy hat and rolled-up sleeves accentuating his rugged good looks. Why had she kissed him yesterday? She blushed as she recalled the delicious weight of his body atop hers, the firm press of his lips taking control.

She'd like to blame it on impulse, but knew the reason was deeper—something she didn't dare name.

"And do something about those freckles, Mary!" thundered Gabe. "She looks like Pippi Longstocking."

Mary rolled her eyes and dabbed on concealer. "I keep forgetting to wear sunscreen."

Katlynn held still as Mary gripped her chin and peered at her intently. "I think they look cute. Plus, they give you extra color. No one's calling you a corpse at least."

Katlynn and Mary exchanged a wry smile. "There's that. Sorry about not fitting into the rose dress."

Last night, while reading through Maggie's letters, Cole grilled her a steak and a big, foil-wrapped potato she couldn't resist. Not when he'd heaped it with melted butter and lots of sour cream. Her mouth watered at the remembered taste of fluffy, buttery potato and juicy meat. Still. She should have resisted. Carbondale was sapping her willpower. Or was it Cole?

Mary waved an eyebrow pencil. "Jen sent backup wardrobe. Not to worry."

Katlynn smoothed down the body-hugging material of her yellow dress. Thank goodness for Spandex. Even if she could hardly catch her breath. No more steak, she vowed. Or equally tempting kisses with Cole.

"We're moving up to the porch," Gabe shouted to the crew. He turned and lowered his voice. "Katlynn, whenever you're ready, sweetheart."

"Sure thing."

She tromped over to the porch, angled her body, lowered her chin, sucked in her gut and opened her mouth for another take.

Three hours later Katlynn stood outside the county clerk's office, cell phone to her ear. "Hey, John. This is Katlynn. Leaving my fourth message. Will you please call me back or have Ma call? My number is…"

"How's your ma?" Cole asked when she ended the voice message.

"Her arthritis is bothering her, and she's caring for a household of my siblings and nieces and nephews."

"Not to mention overseeing a cannabis operation."

His laughing blue eyes set her heart aflutter. In his fitted green shirt and Wranglers, he'd never looked more handsome. Yet what she appreciated most was hearing him mutter "better" when she'd emerged from her room makeup-free, in an old T-shirt and borrowed jeans after her shoot.

For so long she'd believed the spotlight made her real. Visible. Now she questioned if the camera captured someone else—not her, after all. Cole was reminding her of who she used to be, of her authentic self…a person she might be wrong to cover up or be ashamed of. What was so bad about being regular like everyone else, anyway?

Her family situation was a case in point. Her mother had a tough time fitting Katlynn into her busy life…so what? It didn't mean Ma didn't love her. From now on she'd just drop by on her free time and arrange her schedule around her family's instead of the other way around like a normal person.

Not a star.

"Who'd have thought…my mother, a drug kingpin?"

"Leader of the Church Lady Posse," Cole deadpanned, cupping her elbow as they climbed stone stairs.

She laughed. "That actually sounds terrifying. No one messes with the church ladies."

"I know I don't."

They ducked inside the cool, quiet building and headed for the Historic Documents Library.

"How may I help you?" asked a short, fastidiously dressed man with a poof of blond hair.

Katlynn read the clerk's nameplate. "Hi, J.D. I'm Katlynn Brennon with *Scandalous History*." She shook the man's stiff hand. "My producer requested old surveys of the Cade and Loveland properties."

J.D. pressed his hand to his heart. "It's you."

Katlynn shot him one of her lower-wattage smiles since he looked ready to keel over. "Yes. It's a pleasure to be back in Carbondale. Would you have the documents ready for our review?"

J.D. strode around the desk and stopped in front of Katlynn, staring. "You're even prettier in person."

"Okay, buddy." Cole stepped in between them. "Let's leave the lady in peace."

J.D. emerged from his stupor to glare at Cole. "I'm not bothering anyone." He peeked around Cole's broad shoulders. "Am I?"

Katlynn shook her head. "Not at all." Though it was a bother, she admitted, then instantly took back the guilty thought. She wanted to be a star, and inconvenient attention came with the job. It rarely irritated her before. Cole's influence?

"I'm your biggest fan." J.D. tapped his shoulder. "I even have a tattoo of you."

"Really?"

Lord, don't let it be a naked one...

"Let me show you." He rolled up his sleeve to reveal an inked image of her sitting on a world axis. As cheesy as tattoos of her went, it wasn't half-bad.

"Very nice."

"Would you sign it?"

"We'd like to get on with our work." Cole widened his stance and hooked his thumbs in his belt loops.

Undeterred, J.D. raced to his desk, retrieved a Sharpie marker and passed it to Katlynn. "Please?"

"Of course." She scrawled her name on his biceps. "Now. If it's not too much trouble…"

"Right this way, Katlynn. *You're* welcome, at least." J.D. shot Cole a look so withering she nearly laughed. Cole shook his head and heaved out an exasperated sigh.

"Lifestyles of the rich and famous," he muttered under his breath.

"'Champagne wishes and caviar dreams,'" she whispered back, earning her one of Cole's traffic-stopping smiles.

"Here we go." J.D. gestured to a large oak table covered with oversize books open to property maps. "Last year we recovered files thought lost when the town office burned in 1922. Turned out they were stored in a councilman's basement and forgotten when he died. A recent homeowner discovered them."

"Lucky us!" Katlynn rubbed her hands together and sat in the chair Cole held out for her. "Thank you," she said to a hovering J.D. by way of dismissal.

The clerk remained, his feet seemingly glued to the floor.

"Scat." Cole rose to his feet, sending a squealing J.D. running for the front desk.

She shot Cole a narrow-eyed look.

"What? Too much?" he asked, all innocence as he took his seat again.

"It might be fine in a WWE wrestling ring."

"Then I guess I nailed it."

She playfully punched his shoulder and he laughed. And oh, man, she loved the sound of his laugh. Deep. Rich. "You're too much."

"Too much for you, maybe," he said with a wink that set her heart aflutter.

With an effort, she dragged her attention from one very tempting cowboy and focused on her work. They studied the oldest survey, dated 1887, for the next few minutes.

"Cole. Look!" She pointed to a shaded area running from Loveland property, straight through Cade land, to the Crystal River.

Cole picked up a magnifying glass and peered

at the tiny lettering beside the area. "Says easement."

Shock momentarily slackened Katlynn's mouth. She snapped it shut. "That means official access to the Crystal River was granted to the Lovelands when property lines were drawn. Cole. Your family has water rights' access."

Cole's nose flared and a muscle jumped in his jaw as he moved on to a survey map dated thirty years later. "It's gone here. What happened?"

"Strange." She cupped her hands and called, "J.D.!"

The clerk sprang from around the corner like a jack-in-the-box awaiting her bidding. "How can I help?" He held out a bag of red licorice. "Candy?"

"No, thanks. Can you explain why this easement disappeared?"

J.D.'s head whipped from one map to the other as he gnawed on a licorice stick. "Most unusual. Only a federal judge could have reversed a government-granted easement."

"A court case?" Cole's biceps tensed, hard as a rock, beneath her hand.

"Yes," J.D. answered, his eyes on Katlynn. "I can do some research, see if I can find any old lawsuits about it."

At Katlynn's smile, he flushed scarlet. "We'll

credit you and the Historical Documents office in the show."

Dots of perspiration slicked J.D.'s brow. "I won't let you down," he vowed, ripping off the end of another red stick.

"Thank you, J.D."

Back out in the hallway, Cole swept her in his arms and spun her in a circle. She was breathless and laughing when he set her back on her feet, his large hands spanning her waist.

"Do you know what you've found...what it means to me and my family? Getting back our water rights could save Loveland Hills."

"Cole," she warned, not wanting to burst his bubble, but needing to manage expectations. "It might not change anything."

He leaned down and pressed his forehead to hers, his breath warm and peppermint fresh on her cheeks. "Or...it could change everything."

CHAPTER EIGHT

"TWO OUTS. NOBODY ON," muttered Travis, pacing inside the softball dugout the following weekend. "Game's lost on the next pitch."

"Don't count out Katie-Lynn," Cole observed as he crunched sunflower seeds. "Pa was right to invite her to play."

Cute in denim shorts, a baseball hat pulled over her bright hair and a softball T-shirt with Loveland Hills emblazoned on the back, Katie-Lynn fit in with the locals competing in Fresh Start's fund-raising tournament. She took a couple of practice swings while standing at the plate, projecting confidence. To look at her, you'd never know it was the bottom of the seventh inning, fourteen to eleven, Cades.

"She's the last in our batting order and hasn't had a hit all day." Daryl pulled off his hat and dumped water on his flushed face. "She's doing her best, but let's face it. The Cades got us."

"We've beaten them plenty of times, too," Pa drawled, leaning on the dugout post.

"Whose side are you on?" Travis stopped pacing, his question an accusation, in full-on sheriff-interrogation mode. "You want us to lose so you don't upset your fiancée."

"It's only a game," Heath muttered, ever the family peacekeeper. "We'll get 'em next time."

"This is the last game of the tournament," Sierra reminded him. "Final inning."

"Who's got the last out?" hollered Justin Cade from shortstop. He crouched, ready for the easy ground ball he expected.

Cole spit out the salty seeds and stood. After a long, sweltering day competing to reach the finals, they faced their bitter rivals. The Cades had no call to shame Katie-Lynn…making her "out" a foregone conclusion.

After a player canceled, she'd stepped in and given it her all. No putting on airs or demanding special treatment. She competed without complaint, as eager to win as they were.

All proceeds went to charity, but something more personal was at stake than just winning the championship.

Bragging rights.

Pride.

Priceless to a family about to lose everything else.

"Come on, Katie-Lynn!" Cole hollered, clapping his hands. "Let's go."

Only her mouth-twitch showed she'd heard

him. After pointing her bat at James Cade, the pitcher, she rested it on her shoulder and bounced slightly on her feet.

"Go easy on her, James!" shouted Joy Cade from the stands. Her navy blouse matched her children's uniforms.

Cole held his breath when James strode forward. The ball arced against the blue sky. A half beat behind the pitch, Katie-Lynn hit an easy grounder to Justin.

"Son of a gun," swore Daryl, throwing his hat in the dirt and stomping on it.

"That's game," Sierra sighed into Cole's ear, turning to gather their gear.

Then something incredible happened. A miracle, really. Justin, for all his cocky trash talking, fumbled the catch. The ball bounced off his glove and shot into outfield.

Katie-Lynn's legs churned up dust as she hauled it to first base. Cole whooped with his teammates.

"Go, Katie-Lynn!" cheered her family from behind the backstop. Knowing how hard she'd been trying to connect with them, Cole had brought them to the game.

On the bag's edge, a red-faced Katie-Lynn bent at the waist, breathing hard, hands on her knees. When she peered up, she caught his eye and grinned at his thumbs-up.

"That's my girl!" he shouted, wishing it were true, then focused on their next hitter. Maverick. On break from his PBR bull-riding tour, he'd returned home to help with the fund-raiser.

Best of all, Maverick was top of their batting order.

Did they have a shot at coming back?

Maverick's arm muscles flexed as he swung a heavy bat.

"Hit it to short," hollered Daryl. "Maybe he'll boot another one."

Justin slammed his fist in his glove. "You're still down three runs, Lovelands. No more gifts."

"Shut it, Daryl," Boyd growled, when Daryl opened his mouth again. "They're about to be family."

"*Your* family." Travis rubbed the scruff on his face and peered at Pa uncomfortably. "Don't lump us into this marriage."

"Ball!" called the umpire when James's pitch went long.

Two more bad pitches followed. Three and oh. Cole eyed Maverick's confident stance in the batter's box, and his spirits lifted.

Come on, Mav, hit or walk... Keep us in the game.

"Just throw it in there!" screeched Jewel Cade from third base. "He doesn't want to hit."

"Come on, buddy!" Sierra urged, petting a

stray cat who'd wandered into their dugout. An animal magnet, Sierra was nicknamed R. Doolittle by Cole and his brothers long before she earned her veterinary credentials.

"Take the bat off your shoulder," Jared Cade catcalled from first.

James stared down Maverick for a long, stretched-out moment, the tension building to a knife's point.

At last, James flung the ball, a smooth, fast arc. Cole waited, hoped, prayed, for the welcome thud of the bat smacking the ball.

It dropped to the ground instead. Short.

"Ball four." The umpire pointed at first. "Take your base."

"Good eye, Mav!" hollered Cole.

Katie-Lynn jogged to second base and exchanged a quick glance with Lance Covington, a Cade cousin visiting from Denver. Lance smiled at Katie-Lynn and tipped his cap.

"Looks like they're going to choke!" Daryl rubbed his hands together.

Travis donned his batting glove, grabbed his bat and hustled to the batting box.

"Come on, Travis!" Cole shouted, clapping. Pumped. They had first and second. A homerun would tie it up.

"The only way they're going to win is if we

give it to them," hollered Justin Cade, adjusting and readjusting his hat. "These guys can't hit."

"They ain't seen nothin' yet," Pa muttered under his breath.

"That's the spirit, Pa." Daryl slung an arm around their father's shoulders. "Good to have you back."

Pa slid him a side-eyed glance and edged to the front of the dugout, peering intently at Travis.

Cole cupped his hands around his mouth. "Keep this rally going, Trav."

The first pitch dropped at the last minute onto the back of the plate, leaving Travis staring.

"Strike!"

"Come on. Come on. Come on," chanted Sierra, her face flushed, blond hair hanging down her back in a messy ponytail.

Another ball flew deep, pinging off a rear corner.

"He's a looker!" shouted Jewel Cade, triumphant, white teeth flashing in her freckled face.

"Put this one away," Jared yelled to James, pointing his glove at Travis. "Let's go home!"

James curled in all but his index and pinky fingers and waved them overhead. "Two down. One more to go."

"Don't pop the champagne yet!" Sierra jeered. The cat leaped from her arms and strutted to the stands.

Restless energy trembled through Cole's limbs. They needed this hit. All or nothing. "Crush it, Travis!"

Travis adjusted his grip on the bat and leaned in, ready to hit anything close. Meanwhile James stalled, rolling the ball in his hand, tossing it slightly as he squinted at the plate.

At last, James let loose. Strike.

"One more!" shrieked Jewel.

"You can do it, Daddy!" Javi, jumped up and down beside Joy and James's wife, Sofia. "You're Superman!"

On the next throw, Travis swung at the short pitch, ripping the ball far into center field. Katie-Lynn flew to third base, Maverick flat out running for second.

Every bit of air rushed straight out of Cole's lungs. Yes!

Cheering erupted from the dugout and their stands. "Wooo-hooo!" screamed Sierra, practically deafening Cole.

The fielder scooped up the ball and hurled it to James, keeping the runners from advancing farther as Travis took first.

Bases loaded!

Cole handed Daryl his bat and clapped him on the back. "You got this."

Daryl nodded, face set, and jogged to the batter's box.

For once, the smug Cades appeared sober and grim. They'd led all game and had seemed on the brink of handing the Lovelands a humiliating loss. Now momentum was against them.

James launched his first pitch and *bam*, Daryl, impulsive and impatient as ever, swung, hitting a rocket straight over the left fielder's head.

"Get gone!" Cole roared, heart in overdrive. A homerun would win the game.

The ball smacked the wall and bounced back infield. Katie-Lynn sprinted for home. Their third base coach, Uncle Emmitt, pinwheeled his right arm, waving Maverick on, then Travis. James held up his glove, catching the throw, cutting off Daryl at second base as Katie-Lynn, followed by Maverick then Travis raced across the plate, scoring the tying runs.

Cole caught Katie-Lynn in a bear hug, lifting her off her feet. He buried his face in the crook of her neck, breathing in her natural, earthy smell. His blood swam.

"I did it!" she gasped when he reluctantly set her down. Her blue eyes sparkled, filled with delight. All around them the fired-up Lovelands, and Katie-Lynn's family, whooped.

"Proud of you." He tipped down her cap brim to stop himself from kissing her hard and fast.

"Hey," she protested, laughing, as she stumbled slightly, temporarily blind.

When her hand landed on his abdomen, he froze as did she. His eyes squeezed shut and his heart felt like it'd fly out of his chest. No matter where she touched him, even if it was just his hand in an innocent way, he felt it everywhere. The euphoria of her spread from his head to his toes, electrifying every inch between, making him want to grab on to her and never let go.

"Sorry." She eased back, her hat now twisted back on her head so the brim pointed down her neck.

He grinned at the picture she made. Sweaty. Red-faced. Ready to kick butt. He loved this side of Katie-Lynn.

No denying, he was falling for her again, and he was powerless to stop it. He could feel it, like a train with no brakes, coming faster and faster, straight for him. Soon, it was going to crash, and it wasn't going to be pretty.

His head called him an idiot and a glutton for punishment. Not because of his feelings for Katie-Lynn, but for letting down his guard when a future together wasn't possible. Yet his heart insisted she was his girl, his other half—the one he'd been waiting for all the time she'd been away.

"We can do this!" Maverick pumped a fist in the air as Cole grabbed his favorite bat.

The crowd howled when Katie-Lynn stopped

him with a hand on his arm and kissed his cheek. "For good luck."

His pulse tripped all over itself. "No luck needed." He chucked her under the chin before jogging to the plate.

I only need you.

"We're all even!" Sierra bellowed, sounding as wild as the animals she treated.

"Hold him. We'll get 'em in extras." Jared Cade reached behind and pulled one foot up to his back, stretching his hamstring.

"Looks like the choke is about to be complete," Travis hooted. "Boomer's on deck."

"Play deep!" James waved back the infield and outfield, knowing Cole's reputation as a power hitter.

Jewel stopped chewing her gum, blew an enormous bubble then sucked it back in. "Your luck's run out!"

Cole grasped each end of his heavy bat and lifted it skyward. He twisted at the waist, stretching his back, stalling to settle his nerves. To focus. The Cades' laughing, cocky expressions suddenly disappeared. Now they looked dead serious. Intent on getting him out.

Cole swung the bat a couple of times, his thundering heartbeat the only sound he heard as he brought it up to his shoulder. He needed at least a double to bring Daryl home.

James hurled the first pitch.

"Strike!"

"All right!" cheered the Cade fans.

"Nice pitch."

Nerves twisted in his gut as he dug the tip of his cleat into the dirt, grounding himself. If James threw a close pitch or a good pitch, Cole would swing. He didn't want to be down two strikes.

A flat pitch winged Cole's way. Short, he judged, leaning forward to watch the ball drop in front of the plate.

"Ball!" announced the umpire.

Air rushed from Cole's lungs.

"Good eye, son," Boyd called.

Buoyed by his father's praise, every muscle in Cole's body tensed, ready to deliver a smash hit. James chucked the ball again. With barely a second to process, Cole judged it too deep and didn't swing. When it ticked the back of the mat, he winced.

"Strike!"

He swore under his breath and backed up in the batter's box, expecting another deep pitch. Using his wristband, he wiped the sweat streaming into his eyes.

The ballfield was now deathly silent, everyone's attention focused on the next make-or-break pitch. It all came down to this moment.

Swinging the bat, Cole pointed the tip at a waiting James, staring him down. "Gonna get you," he silently communicated. An unruffled James Cade glared back, their family's one hundred and twenty years of animosity on full display.

Cole snapped his bat to his shoulder. His mouth was filled with a hundred cotton balls, his heart jackknifing in his chest. James chucked the next pitch.

Deep...

Cole strode forward, twisted slightly and swung with all his might. The slightest vibration, the ball coming off the end of the bat, signaled he'd lined a clean, solid hit.

Jared leaped, but the drive flew over his head, straight down the right field line.

Yes!

Cole tore down the first base line and tagged up. Panting, he watched Daryl race to third base. A quick check over Cole's shoulder revealed the right fielder rocketing the ball home as Uncle Emmitt waved Daryl on for the winning run.

"Go! Go! Go!" screamed his family.

"Get him!" roared the Cades.

The fans leaped to their feet. Pandemonium.

The Cades' catcher planted himself in front of the plate just as Daryl and the throw arrived. The ball whacked the catcher's mitt. Before he could tag the runner, Daryl raised his arms, knocking the catcher's head and plowing him over. The ball bounced out of his glove. On the plate, Daryl jumped up and down as the umpire waved his arms. Safe.

Score!

Win!

Justin Cade raced to the plate, his face dark as thunder, hands clenched into fists. Without breaking stride, he punched an unsuspecting Daryl. The hit to his jaw spun him around.

Oh—heck, no!

In an instant the Cades and Lovelands rushed the brawling players. Fists flew, legs kicked, elbows rammed. A sock to the eye, followed by a stomach jab, knocked the breath out of Cole. He grabbed Justin in a headlock and hauled the flailing hothead out of the melee. Katie-Lynn held back a raging Sierra while Jewel threw down as hard as the boys. Even though her punches seemed to bounce off Maverick's steel gut, she didn't let up. Heath shoved Maverick, knocking him to his knees, then grabbed Jewel's elbow, dragging her from the violent fray.

The umpire blew his whistle,

Boyd yelled, "Quit it, boys!"

"Stop now," Joy ordered, her soft voice authoritative. "You're acting like children."

"Animals," Boyd corrected. "Y'all are better than that."

Everyone froze.

Justin stopped struggling and Cole released him. Jewel yanked free of Heath. Katie-Lynn let go of Sierra, who reached down and pulled the catcher to his feet. The rest lowered their raised fists and hung their heads.

"You're making a spectacle of yourselves," Boyd barked, his face beet-red.

Concern spiked for his father, who took daily medication for his blood pressure.

"Now this'll be on TV." Joy pointed to the *Scandalous History* camera crew who'd been filming their game.

"I'll make sure it's not in the cut," Katie-Lynn said, her eyes on Cole. He gave her a brief nod of gratitude.

The crowds dispersed, leaving the two families facing off on the otherwise empty field.

"Are you proud of yourselves?" Boyd demanded.

"Their catcher was blocking the plate," Daryl protested.

"You hit him," Jared accused. "A dirty play."

"Just like all you Lovelands," muttered Justin.

"What'd you say?" Impetuous Daryl advanced, and Boyd shoved him back.

"Stand down. All y'all. We're about to be family or are you forgetting that?"

"We'd like to," Maverick growled.

A sobbing Joy hurried off the field.

"Now look what you've done. I'm ashamed of you. All of you," Boyd thundered, then raced after Joy.

The Cades and Lovelands drifted off to their respective dugouts and gathered up their belongings.

"Can't stand those jerks." Daryl yanked off his shirt and mopped up his sweat-streaked face.

"You're going to have to for Pa's sake." Heath packed up the bat bag and slung it over his shoulder. "For the wedding."

"If we even make it that far," muttered Travis. He chugged the rest of his sports drink, hurled it in the trash and stalked off the field.

Katie-Lynn waved to her family and turned to Cole. "Thanks for inviting them. Must have taken some strong-arming to get them here."

Cole shrugged. "Not one bit. Though I might have mentioned the market potential for Keith's cannabis operation."

Katie-Lynn's mouth curled. "Why limit themselves to church ladies?"

He grinned back. "Exactly."

She trailed her hand down his arm. "But seriously, thank you. My ma's never seen my show since she doesn't get cable. Who'd have thought I'd get her attention playing softball?"

Seeing her this pleased filled Cole with pride. He could make her happy…if she'd let him. "Feels good, doesn't it?"

"Yes. I'd better say hi before they catch a ride home with my uncle…or Keith gets arrested."

Cole stopped Katie-Lynn and waited for the rest of his siblings to clear out. "I appreciate you not airing this on your show."

"Can't imagine you'd think I would."

"The Cade-Loveland feud on full display. As hot as ever. A wedding in jeopardy. It'd make good TV. Ratings. Isn't that what you need to keep your show? Your job?"

"Some things are more important," she said obliquely, staring at him for a long minute before scooting outside the dugout, leaving him to wonder.

Had Katie-Lynn's priorities begun to change?

Was that something she'd mentioned—him?

CHAPTER NINE

"PA, ARE YOU sure I can't get you an inversion table for your back?" Katlynn asked later that evening.

Her family had surprised her by inviting both her and Cole over to celebrate the tournament win. After a meal of pot roast followed by strawberry shortcake, the group now crowded on the back porch, lounging on molded plastic chairs. A sense of familiarity settled in her bones. Participating in her family's after-dinner ritual was like donning a pair of old, forgotten jeans and discovering how much you'd loved them. Missed them.

"I'm not hanging upside down like some bat." Pa removed his index finger from a teething Frankie's mouth. "Though this kid's turning into a vampire. Michelle, come get 'im before I wind up needing a rabies shot."

Cole's low chuckle vibrated in the short space separating them on the porch swing. He'd washed up after the game, but still wore his softball pants, revealing long, muscular calves. They were crossed at the ankles, beside her own, as they rocked companionably on the front porch swing.

She released a contented sigh. All the world, including herself, seemed at peace. This was what true mindfulness meant. Beyond her family's cleared backyard, the setting sun clung to the horizon, coloring the clouds in orange-red streaks. In the dense bushes, lightning bugs flashed while crickets chorused, a nice change from the bright lights and traffic that'd become her constant companion in LA.

"I'll take him, Michelle." Katlynn strode to her father. "And congratulations on your promotion. Head of the bakery. That's amazing."

Michelle dropped back into her chair and shot her a grateful smile. "Thanks, sis. Been rolling out so many pie crusts I think I got tendinitis."

"Baker's elbow?" teased their older brother John.

"Just don't get arthritis like me." Ma fanned herself with an old issue of *Reader's Digest*.

"Here, baby," Katlynn crooned, scooping up a wide-eyed Frankie. His head swiveled from her to his mother, and his face puckered. "It's okay. I'm your aunt Katlynn. Not a stranger."

The baby opened his mouth, preparing to scream if the blotchy red blooming on his chubby cheeks was an indicator.

"Ohhhhhh! Better put him down, Katie-Lynn,"

her brother Martin warned. "Looks like he's in a horn-tossin' mood."

Katlynn dropped onto the swing and dug her free hand into her purse. "Look what I've got for you." Katlynn cooed as she slid a new flip-flop into Frankie's mouth, mid-wail, cutting him off. When Cole extended his finger, Frankie wrapped his tiny fingers around it.

"Well. I'll be." Katlynn's mother let out a short laugh. "Guess you two had his measure."

"Where'd you get the flip-flop?" Michelle shook her long bangs from her eyes.

"Walmart." Katlynn almost laughed at the sight of her family's astonishment. Even her brother Keith's drooping lids rose. "What? You think I'm too good to shop at Walmart?"

"No." Pa was the first to recover. "Glad to see our Katie-Lynn's still herself is all."

"Better yet, they were on clearance," she added, smiling when she caught her mother's approving nod. In a large family with plenty of mouths to feed, the ability to save a dollar was prized.

Cole draped his muscular arm across the swing top and the delicious weight of it, touching her back, raised goose bumps.

"Katie-Lynn's always had a way of coming out on top," observed John. Their old sibling rivalry echoed faintly in his voice. Growing up, they'd been competitive since they were closest in age. And coat size.

"If it wasn't for Katie-Lynn leading the softball rally, we wouldn't have beat the Cades," Cole pointed out.

Her heart turned to mush at the warm admiration glowing in his blue eyes.

"She's always made us proud," Pa declared, surprising her. "Even when she read those books and spoke in that funny accent for a spell. Remember that, honey?"

Ma nodded, smiling.

"I remember!" Michelle exclaimed. "Her teacher had them reading Shakespeare, and Katie-Lynn started talking like them..."

"Wouldest thou passeth the salt," Martin intoned, mock-serious. Michelle giggled, and Ma smiled behind her raised hand.

"Hey," Katlynn protested, her lips twitching at the undeniable comedy of her pathetic attempt to speak in rhyming couplets. "I was just trying to be different."

"You were different, all right," John mumbled around a toothpick. "Like that time when you tried dyeing your hair black with shoe polish, and it come out green."

"What'd they call her at school?" Michelle swatted at a nagging mosquito.

"Alien girl," Katlynn laughingly admitted,

humor and time lancing the sting from the humiliating memory.

Cole and the rest of the group joined her, their gales of laughter growing louder and louder in the still night until some bent at the waist while others wiped away tears.

"Ma gave me that uneven bowl cut to hide it," Katlynn gasped out, her eyes streaming. "But I think it made it worse."

"Definitely worse," Keith added, now sitting up, his smile wide and loopy. "One ear was showing. The other covered up."

"And that was my eighth grade graduation picture!" Katlynn lapsed into giggles again.

"I can dig it up somewhere. I don't think Cole's ever had the pleasure of seeing it." Pa began to heave himself from his chair then dropped down again at the loud chorus of *no*s!

"I'd like a peek at it, sir." Cole's words ended on an *oomph* as Katlynn elbowed him in the side and mouthed, "Never."

"That picture gave me nightmares," Keith murmured, leaning back in his seat again, eyelids lowering.

When Katlynn chucked the other flip-flop at him, he neatly caught it in the air then winged it at an unsuspecting John's head. It bounced off his forehead.

"Hey!" John threw it back, but hit Martin instead, who then hurled it back at Keith.

"Me! Me! Throw it at me!" Timmy leaped in the air, trying to catch the sandal as his uncles began an impromptu game of keep-away.

"Never claimed to be a hairdresser," Ma protested, chuckling. "Besides, I gave all you kids bowl cuts. None of you complained."

"To your face." The Brennon siblings grinned, nodding at Michelle's revelation.

"We did the best we could." Ma sighed.

Pa patted her hand. "Yes, you did, sweetheart."

"My favorite Katie-Lynn memory was when she ran off for three days, and we all pretended not to notice." John tossed the flip-flop to Timmy, ending the game.

Katlynn stiffened. "You noticed I was gone?"

"Noticed?" Martin rolled his eyes. "Ma, Pa and us older kids took turns watching over you while you camped at the creek."

"What?" Shocked, Katlynn's numb fingers let go of Frankie's flip-flop. "No one said anything when I got back."

Cole grabbed the sandal before it hit the ground and returned it to Frankie's mouth.

"That's because Pa told us not to." Michelle arched her eyebrows at their ruddy-faced parent.

"Why?" Katlynn asked, mystified.

"Figured you had your reasons for wanting to

be alone," Pa said. "I supposed you'd work out whatever was in your head and then come back home, to those who loved you."

Katlynn turned, her gaze landing on Cole. He'd taken Frankie from her and talked softly to him as he wiggled the flip-flop in his mouth.

Cole caught her stare and nodded as if his thoughts were aligned with hers. *Home...with those who loved her.*

"Sitting up all night against those rocks probably started my back problems," her father said, pulling her from her thoughts, from the truth resounding in her soul.

"Pa!"

Pa waved a hand at her. "Just teasing you, darlin'. Wasn't any trouble to make sure you were safe."

"Why didn't you just haul me home?"

"In a big family like ours, everyone needs a little privacy now and then."

Nods circled the porch, leaving Katlynn speechless and blinking the sting from her eyes. All this time she'd felt lost in a crowd. But being part of a tight-knit, loving group had its benefits, too...

Her eyes strayed to Cole's handsome face as he patiently held the flip-flop for a gnawing Frankie. It struck her how little she'd understood, or fully appreciated, her past.

"I like you, Aunt Katie-Lynn." Timmy stopped playing with the cat and looked up at her. "Will you come back for Christmas?"

"Well—uh—I—don't know about that, honey." Michelle stalled, casting a nervous glance Katlynn's way. "Your aunt might be busy. She's very important. Lots of other people to see."

Katlynn pictured her annual holiday trip to St. Barts and juxtaposed it with the warmth of her family. No comparison. How had she ever imagined there was? "I'll come back…if I'm welcome."

Ma clapped her hands and beamed. "We'll have a real family Christmas, then. Imagine it. All of us together for a holiday at last."

Cole stood and held out a hand. "We'd better head back."

Katlynn passed a now sleeping Frankie to her sister and hugged her mother then her father.

"Love you, darlin'," her pa whispered in her ear before releasing her. It was only the third time she recalled him saying it.

"Bye, now!" She dashed away tears before making her unsentimental father uncomfortable, then ducked into Cole's truck.

Minutes later Katlynn quit belting along with a Faith Hill tune when her cell phone vibrated, a familiar number flashing on the screen. Cole cranked down his truck's stereo system as she hit the speaker button.

"Hylda?"

"Oh, thank *God*." Her agent's nasal voice, a sound resembling an autotuned cat in heat, scratched through the speaker. "I've been trying to reach you for days. Why haven't you returned my texts?"

Cole covered one ear and mouthed "Ouch" before returning his hand to the wheel.

Katlynn rolled her eyes and decreased her phone's volume. "Reception's spotty out here and—"

"Never mind," Hylda cut her off, brusque. Ruthless and all business, she was one of Hollywood's top agents with little time to waste. Rumor had it she'd negotiated a six-million-dollar commercial deal and had a mani-pedi while giving birth to her first child last year. "I've got an offer from *Celebrity Survivor*. Are you interested?"

The truck slowed as they approached a road work site illuminated by large outdoor lights. She glimpsed Cole's quick glance from the corner of her eye.

"The show where they starve and physically and emotionally torture you for months?"

"Sounds fun, right?"

"Hylda…"

"Imagine how thin you'll get."

"I don't care about that." As soon as she said the words, Katlynn knew them to be true. Eating real food, wearing regular clothes, relaxing her workout routines this past week had been a vacation from her regular life...or maybe this *was* regular life and what she'd been living for the past twelve years was just a facade. Glittering on the outside, empty and bare on the inside.

Hylda laugh-snorted. "Good one, Katlynn. Anyway. What should I tell them? It'd be great exposure, and given what's going on with *Scandalous History*, we need to be thinking of ways to keep you relevant."

Fear tolled in Katlynn's chest. "Have you heard anything more about the show?"

Hylda hummed under her breath, a tick of hers usually heralding bad news. "Ultima's moved forward on *Millennial Millionaires* and ordered a pilot."

Katlynn gasped, and Cole squeezed her hand, a warm, fast, reassuring grip, before releasing it.

"Nothing's been decided in terms of replacing *Scandalous History*. Lots of pilots are made and forgotten." Papers rustled in the background, a sign her agent multitasked as usual. "Tape the episode of your career, come back strong and we'll see where we stand. If all else fails, call Seth Rutherford. You went yachting with him in

St. Barts, and his father owns Ultima. He looked pretty smitten in the tabloid pictures."

The truck leaped forward as they cleared the orange cones. A glance at the lit dash revealed the needle pushing seventy-five and Cole's white-knuckle grip on the steering wheel.

"I went with a friend and barely spoke to him."

"The article said you two were canoodling."

"They always say that." She fought the urge to squeeze Cole's arm, to reassure him.

Reassure him of what?

He had no competition?

True enough, but she'd led him on already when she'd kissed him in Aunt Susanna's attic. She wouldn't mess with his heart when she had no intention of staying in Carbondale perma-nently…no matter how much she enjoyed being home with him.

"Wouldn't hurt you to reach out to Seth," Hylda insisted. "Let him buy you dinner. See how things go…"

"I'm not getting involved with him for my ca-reer!"

"Come on, Katlynn. You know how things work out here. This is Hollywood, not Cartoon-ville, Colorado."

A dark scoffing noise erupted from Cole.

"It's Carbondale," Katlynn gritted out. Of course she knew how things worked in Hollywood. She'd accepted those unwritten rules long ago. Only they didn't sit well with her anymore, not after spending time with a man of integrity, honesty and determination. Cole wouldn't compromise his values, or himself, to get ahead; he wouldn't change who he was. He was confident in his own skin and adamant in what he believed.

And what did she believe?

She wasn't sure anymore except for one thing.

She was falling for Cole Loveland again. Hard.

Lord help her.

Hylda yawned. "Shall I Fed-Ex the contract?"

"Fine." Katlynn rattled off the Loveland Hills's address.

"And I'll message Seth's assistant about a dinner date when you're back."

"Are you going out with Seth Rutherford?" Cole asked tightly when she ended the call, his voice a low, deep rasp.

"No."

Only Cole's long exhale and the powerful throb of his V8 engine filled the silence.

"You don't have to do that crap," he said.

Her mouth dropped open. "*Celebrity Survivor*?"

Cole nodded.

"You heard Hylda. I need to keep myself relevant, especially if my show's canceled."

"You'll find something else."

"Not right away, and the public might forget about me."

"And that's bad because…?"

She rubbed her damp palms on her jeans, grappling with her answer.

"Come on, sweetheart," Cole coaxed, his gruff voice tender. How she loved the soft side to this tough guy, a part of him he always reserved just for her. "Tell me what's really going on. Pretend we're at our Say Anything tree and don't hold back. Not from me." The feel of Cole's calloused fingers, threading through hers, steadying her, halted her tumbling thoughts.

Truth time.

"Remember how I used to complain about growing up in a big family? How no one noticed me much?"

Cole nodded.

"All I ever wanted was to feel like I counted. The only way I feel like I even exist is when others see me," she admitted.

"I see you," Cole said quietly. Then, in a hushed voice she had to strain to hear, he murmured, "I've always seen you."

Her heart swooned. First her family, now this… "Cole. I—" Her buzzing phone stopped her from revealing the truth she'd been about to spill.

Saved by the bell.

She spotted the Cades' home number on her screen and tapped the answer button.

"Hello?"

"I found something, something belonging to Maggie Cade." Joy's excited voice practically bubbled through the speaker.

Cole turned his head sharply in Katlynn's direction. Her pulse picked up steam. "What is it?"

"After the game, things here were…ah…a little tense."

A short bark of laughter escaped Cole.

"Is that Cole?"

"Hi, Joy."

"I know Justin is sorry for giving you the shiner."

"I'm sure he is," Cole said drily.

"Suffice it to say," Joy said, "I'm not proud of my children's conduct."

"No one was innocent," Cole reassured her. "I'm sorry, too."

"Kind of you, Cole. Thanks." Joy's sigh floated softly through the phone's speaker. "I hope… I hope we can find a way to come together."

When Cole agreed, Joy cleared her throat. "Anyway, I decided to peek around the ranch's old carriage house. I had a hunch if any of Maggie's things remained, they'd be in there. No one's gone through that junk in decades. A hope chest with Maggie's initials was under a pile in a far corner. At first, I didn't find much of anything. I was about to close it when I realized it was narrower inside than the outside suggested."

"A false panel?" Katlynn's voice rose, urgent.

"Yes. And inside it was a journal. Maggie Cade's personal diary."

They exchanged a swift look, Cole's eyes beaming at her in the dim. As he cranked the wheel, turning, Katlynn breathed, "We'll be right there."

Thirty minutes later they sat beside each other in the Lovelands' lantern-lit gazebo, far from everyone's prying eyes as they read through Maggie's entries.

"'December 24, Tuesday,'" Katlynn read aloud. "'Our Christmas tree went up this night. It was beautiful beyond imagining. I swooned, fancying the Lord watching over us, delighted at our tribute to His mighty grace.'

"'I had twenty presents among which was Cora's Tear, which Gran most graciously gifted to me! She would not countenance any objections as to my relative youth, declaring my age now—eighteen—old enough to pass down to the oldest Cade girl for her dowry as is our tradition. I dream of finding my one true love, a heart to know mine. I pinned Cora's Tear to my shawl and shall fall asleep with it, hoping it sends me dreams of a future as bright and shining and beautiful.'"

Cole cleared his throat and turned the page, his rough fingers lingering over Katlynn's for a breathtaking minute.

"'December 25, 1906,'" he read. "'This seems very like Sunday as we went to church this morning—we were again tortured by a most frightful new hymn which I must confess, I didn't know a bit, so sang La La to it! At which Everett Cade, the youngest of our neighbors, caught me. He gave me a most improper wink. When I lifted my nose and glared, he grinned without the least concern to propriety. That was when I noticed how handsome he was. Oh, diary. He's not the kind of man a proper young lady of means should notice. Yet his dimples, one in each cheek, lend him such a rakish air. I fear I became utterly taken with him.'"

Katlynn laughed. "I sense chemistry…"

"Everybody loves a bad boy." Cole flipped the page.

"Yes, we do…" She slid him a sideways glance. Beyond the gazebo, June bugs banged against the screens as moths whirred and fluttered, seeking light.

"Am I a bad boy?"

"Let's see." Katlynn tapped her chin, breathing in the cool mountain air, fresh balsam and columbine. "You're stubborn. Fiercely independent. Thickheaded. A loner. Extremely protective of those you love." She paused and touched the black-and-blue ring around his eye. "Does that hurt?"

"Only when you touch it."

His wry tone conjured a smile from her. "And you're sarcastic."

"Verdict is…"

"Trouble."

"What's that mean?"

Goose bumps rose on her arms at his expression, an intense mixture of hope and longing that pierced her straight through. "Trouble for me. Cole, I don't want to care about you."

"Don't *want to*," he said slowly, rubbing his jaw. "Which means…you do care?" His eyes lit up.

"I can't do anything about it, but yes."

His grin was sudden and enormous and did funny things to her heart…like turning it into a somersaulting gymnast. "Same."

She biffed his shoulder. "Now that's romantic."

"Hey." Cole rubbed his shoulder, mock-offended. "You're the one who called me trouble. Is that how you speak to people you care about?"

"How should I speak to you?" Her breath caught when his grin faded, and his gaze swerved to her lips.

"I prefer actions to words…" He leaned down and brushed her mouth with a heady, pulse-jumping kiss.

Katlynn pressed a hand to his chest, halting him, pulling back. "Let's figure out Maggie and Everett's romance first."

"And then?" Vulnerability shaded his deep blue eyes and tightened the corners of his mouth.

"We'll see where we stand."

"Kind of like *Survivor*."

"Shut up and give me the journal." Katlynn forced her attention back on the entries. "'At our church dinner, Everett took three servings of the pudding I served! He was quite dashing and most persistent, coaxing me to dance the jig with him. I quite lost myself, laughing and making a spectacle in a most unladylike way. At my mother's glare, I begged off, telling Everett that proper ladies don't dance the jig with strange men. And he said, "You're not proper. That's what I like about you. That and your pretty strawberry blond hair."'"

"'Oh, diary. I must admit how very vain I've become of my hair after his compliment, and how often I've sat at the glass, brushing it, picturing his dark, twinkling eyes, hearing him say he liked me.'"

Cole whistled. "Maggie sounds smitten."

"He's taken with her, too."

They read through several more passages chronicling the growing, illicit romance between Maggie and Everett. All around them, bullfrogs serenaded the rising half-moon while a cool breeze drifted through the screen.

"'A kiss cannot be stolen when given freely,'" Katlynn read aloud from a passage dated February, 1906. "'And I bestow it most fervently on Everett when we meet upon the ridge each dawn, with only the rousting mourning doves and rustling Scotch pines to bear witness.'"

Then, in March. "'On a bed of the softest moss, to the burble of a spring-fed brook, I have quite lost myself in Everett and he in me,'" Maggie wrote. "'We became one; a holy communion of heart, soul and body. Now we are joined, we shall never be put asunder. Everett wishes to speak to Pa, but without means to provide for me, as though I need more than his love, we must wait.'"

Katlynn traced Maggie's scrawled words, absorbing the young woman's joy and dreams. She'd been Maggie once. In love and naively certain of her own unending happiness. Unlike Maggie, however, she'd had a choice, one she now second-guessed. "They were meeting secretly."

When she shivered, Cole slipped his arm around her shoulders and pulled her against his solid warmth. "Remember the letter where she asked Everett to return home and meet her?"

Katlynn stiffened. "She said she buried a priceless secret there."

"Cora's Tear," Cole said quickly. "Why?"

"Let's keep reading."

Katlynn and Cole skimmed several more pages then stopped. "'Oh, black day, why did you dawn?'" she read from an April entry. "'Pa has announced I must marry a man thrice my age. A horrid, joyless person who promises to give me everything I want when all I desire is Everett. When I rode out to meet Everett, Mr. Farthington's servant followed me and nearly glimpsed Everett, who hid himself in the mulberry bushes. I will not marry him! Pa and Mr. Farthington have set a wedding date and Cora's Tear is to be part of my dowry. I will not let him have it or me!'"

Another few weeks of passages, then, "'I am with child. A miracle beyond imagining that brings my beloved and me joy and sorrow. To our surprise, Everett's been offered a position to build the new Crystal River railroad line. However, he must leave me, a separation we must bear for the greater good. He promises to be back before my wedding to Mr. Farthington, with enough cash on hand to win my father's blessing. He will not have it any other way, though I beg him to take me with him. He's too proud to gain another man's fortune by marrying into it and determined to find a way to provide for me himself. Stubborn man, how I do love him.'"

"Sounds like a Loveland," Cole said, his voice thick.

"Loyal, honorable and stubborn all right." Katlynn eyed Cole. "This proves he didn't want Cora's Tear."

"We need to prove it to the Cades and end the feud before the wedding." Cole swatted away a hovering mosquito. "There's bound to be more fights otherwise."

"An episode this scandalous might be enough to save our show." Her heartbeat quickened. "But we need more evidence."

Their fingers twined, locking around each other. "We'll get it," Cole vowed.

"The ink's smeared." Katlynn peered closer at the next entry. "She was crying."

She pressed the tip of her finger to the blurred script then read, "'Oh, evil, despicable man. In desperation, I have confided to Mr. Farthington that I am with child and begged him to release me, but he will not. He says I've proven fertile, and he's in need of an heir. If I confess to my parents, he will claim the child as his own and deny Everett.'"

Katlynn's eyes flew to Cole, whose slack jaw and wide-eyes reflected her own shock. "'Yes. He knows about Everett and me,'" Katlynn continued in a shaking voice. "'His servant man spied my beloved the night he followed me and has watched me ever since. Worse, he arranged for Everett's job to rid himself of his rival. I cannot let him succeed… How does one outwit a monster?'"

"Poor Maggie. She was trapped and alone," Katlynn murmured. "Everett shouldn't have left her."

"He wanted to do right by her. Provide for their future," Cole said gruffly, then turned the next page. "'Fear lays heavy in my heart. There are whispers in town, rumors Mr. Farthington may have killed his wives for their money. Today, government agents visited his home while we had tea. I overheard mention of missing funds, and an audit of his financial records. Now he intends to move up our wedding date. Does he plan to marry me for my dowry then take my life, too? I must write and urge Everett home, or I shall be lost to him forever.'"

At last, they reached the final entry in the journal.

"'Tomorrow is my wedding, a blasphemous day that must not be. Will Everett meet me tonight at our special place? I've heard no word. I buried our future there and if I cannot reach him, then let him have this piece of me and the future denied us.'" Katlynn's throat constricted, rendering her speechless.

Cole guided her head down to his shoulder and read on, his voice hoarse. "'But I shall not despair. My beloved will come for me and our child.'" Cole stroked the top of Katlynn's head, gently, reverently, his fingers sliding lower to thread in her hair. "'A love like ours cannot have been created in vain. Life, please let us live. Love, please let us love. I am a fanciful girl who wanders in fairy tales. I pray for my happily-ever-after.'"

Katlynn stared up at Cole, his face blurry through the wash of her tears. "She didn't get her wish."

"Neither did Everett." Cole's arm tightened around her.

"And she buried Cora's Tear. It wasn't on her when they found her body because she'd hidden it. Where?"

Cole rubbed his jaw. "Their secret place. We need to reread the journal for geographic clues and triangulate a location."

"She mentioned moss. Columbine. Scotch pines. A spring-fed brook. A mulberry bush."

"We'll talk to Pa and look at the property maps again."

Katlynn nodded. "And what about Clyde and

his financial issues? Was he after Maggie for her money?"

"Might have been."

"Enough to kill for it?" She crossed her arms over her chest, a bone-deep chill settling inside.

"He had her followed once, at least. But how do we prove he had motive?"

"We need Crystal River Railroad's financial and government grant records."

Cole's brow creased. "What'll that give us?"

"A start. The one Maggie and Everett never got."

CHAPTER TEN

"Ms. Brennon?"

Cole and Katie-Lynn stopped in the county clerk office's main hall, turned and spied J.D., the Historical Documents clerk. Every muscle in Cole's body clenched. Did J.D. have information on the missing water rights' easement?

His hand settled on the small of Katie-Lynn's back protectively—as her rabid superfan neared. J.D.'s hands shook, and his eyes bulged. Katie-Lynn had confessed how much she needed to be seen and J.D. saw her, all right. She'd always belong to the world, to her fans and herself, and him not one bit. She'd confessed she still cared for him, though. Enough to change her life so they could be together? Or should he be asking himself the same question? He was beginning to suspect he should. But he needed his privacy. Loving her would make his life public. He'd live under a microscope, in a phony world full of fake people.

When it came to him and Katie-Lynn, there were no easy answers.

"Hey, J.D." At Katie-Lynn's megawatt smile, the clerk stumbled to a halt. "We stopped by Historical Records like we'd arranged, but it was empty."

J.D. held up a crumpled paper bag with a large grease stain engulfing the bottom half.

"Were you having lunch?" Katie-Lynn prompted gently. "We finished up at the financial office earlier than planned."

Based on Maggie's journal, they'd requested Crystal River Railroad's grant documents as well as government audits.

J.D. nodded, opened his mouth, closed it, then blurted, "Olive loaf."

"Well, now, that's my favorite luncheon meat."

"Liar," Cole muttered under his breath, biting back a grin.

Katie-Lynn shot him a quick, withering look, closed the distance between herself and J.D. and looped an arm in his. "Were you able to find out anything about the easement?"

The question broke J.D. from his trance. "Yes," he gasped. "Follow me."

Cole reached the door first. He wrenched it open, heart in mouth, and ushered them inside. "What'd you find?"

"A court case." J.D. heaved a ledger from behind his desk and dropped it to the table with a thud.

Cole fumbled to open the book at its marked spot.

"Let me." Katlynn's calm voice eased his rampaging pulse. Sliding a fingernail behind the tab, she flipped open the tome.

Cole bent down and scanned the faded page. "Cade, plaintiff versus Loveland, defendant, June 1, 1908." His gaze snapped to Katie-Lynn. "The Cades sued my family."

"Almost a year to the day after Maggie's death."

"And Everett's."

"'Complaint,'" Katlynn read. "'Plaintiff, Josiah Cade, by his undersigned attorneys, Weston and Weston, brings this extinguishment of easement suit asking the court to terminate the granted property easement in accordance with Article 631 of the Civil Code. The easement granting Archibald Loveland livestock access to the Crystal River through Josiah Cade's property unduly burdens the servient owner through egregious misuse of aforementioned easement.'"

"We had an easement." Cole heard his words from a distance, as though someone else spoke them, his tongue, his mouth, his body, numb. Seeing it on a map was one thing, but reading it in print struck him physically. Viscerally. If the original easement was still in place, his family's financial troubles wouldn't exist. "What's a servient?"

"The person whose property has the easement." J.D. shook a couple of mints in his hand, popped them into his mouth and extended the container to Katlynn.

She scanned the front page of the document and accepted the mints, murmuring her thanks. "This is the summary of 'misuses.'"

Cole frowned down at the numbered list. "'Diluting of cattle blood lines and adversely impacting auction sales revenue.'"

"Are they claiming your Brahmans bred with the Cades' Longhorns when crossing their property?" Katie-Lynn asked.

"Yes." Cole's back teeth ground. "Which'd never happen. Experienced ranch hands and cattle dogs keep herds apart. No one benefits from interbreeding."

"Second complaint is destruction of property including fences, grounds and outbuildings."

"Herds running roughshod over a neighbor's property? First, it's not neighborly. Second, that'd injure our cattle, too. We'd never allow that." Cole scowled. "The Cade lawyers must have been as greasy as fried lard to come up with this list of lies."

Katie-Lynn nodded. "Third complaint is an increase in traffic using the easement to the detriment of servient herds' water access." She paused and tapped her fingernail against the page. "Wasn't there an increase in your ranch's livestock and finances immediately following Maggie's death?"

J.D. leaned close. "My grandma always said it was proof the Lovelands sold Cora's Tear."

Cole shot him a hard look.

"C-c-course my grandma was slipping a tad. One time she wore her brassiere over her dress to Sunday services..."

Cole turned back to Katie-Lynn. "What's that have to do with this case?"

"My guess is the increased number of Loveland livestock tramping through Cade property reminded them of what they'd lost—a precious family heirloom and a beloved daughter."

Cole rubbed the back of his hand across his eyes. "They filed this lawsuit to punish my family."

"Seems so."

"They'd already killed Everett. What more did they want?"

"Maybe to force the Lovelands to come clean about the jewel? They'd drop the lawsuit in exchange for its whereabouts?"

Cole stared at clouds chasing each other across the deep blue sky. Where was Cora's Tear? Out there somewhere... The key to solving this mystery, clearing his family's name and mending the feud once and for all. "Only we had no knowledge of it."

"But the Cades thought you did. Maggie kept her plans to hide it and run away a secret."

Cole watched as a lone red truck barreled down the distant highway heading out of Carbondale. "She confided in Clyde Farthington."

"Who had a motive to keep them apart." Katie-Lynn's voice rose. "If he'd been skimming funds from the grant, and faced an audit, he'd need a quick influx of cash to return the monies."

Cole tore his gaze from the truck and exchanged a long look with Katie-Lynn. Would the requested grant and audit paperwork reveal incriminating evidence?

"The ruling's here." J.D. flipped to another page.

The quiet hum of a copier and the pungent smell of forgotten brewed coffee filled the air.

Katie-Lynn cleared her throat. "The court rules the servient estate is unduly burdened by an unreasonable use of the easement by the dominant owner."

"The dominant owner is…"

"The users of the easement, the Lovelands," Katie-Lynn clarified for Cole. "As such, it extinguishes the easement. Any attempt by the former dominant owner to use the easement henceforth shall be viewed as trespassing."

"That's a travesty," Cole bit out. "Excuses to take away my family's rights."

"I quite agree." They turned to see a stooped, gray-haired man wearing a seersucker suit and a pair of black-and-white wingtips. His cane thumped on the floor as he slowly advanced to join them.

"Hey, Uncle Peter." J.D. held out a chair for his relative, who lowered himself carefully, smoothed his suit and crossed his hands atop his cane. "These are the folks I told you about. Katlynn Brennon's from *Scandalous History*. Remember?"

Katlynn extended a hand. "How do you do?"

"Peter Stockton, Esquire. And may I say, my dear, that you are even lovelier in person. It's an honor to meet you."

Katie-Lynn smoothed strands of hair back to her messy ponytail, her lightly freckled cheeks glowing pink. Mr. Stockton was right. She was a hundred times prettier now that she'd begun looking like herself again.

"It's a pleasure to meet you, as well." Katie-Lynn's rosy lips lifted in a winsome smile. "Are you from around here? I detect an east coast accent."

"Astute of you, my dear. I'm a retired property attorney from New York. Moved to be with family after my wife passed."

"I'm sorry to hear that." Katie-Lynn pulled up a chair, her expression a perfect blend of sympathy and kindness. Knowing exactly what to say, how to behave, wasn't an act. Beneath the polished facade beat the heart of a real woman.

A woman he was falling in love with. Again.

"My condolences," Cole muttered, doing his best to be part of the conversation. He'd socialized more alongside Katie-Lynn this week than he had in the years they'd been apart. For a guy who didn't like talking, he'd done a lot these days, and not minding it…much. His hermit life no longer held its appeal, and it'd be harder to let her go this time. Now he knew what life—if you'd call what he'd been doing living—was like without Katie-Lynn in it.

"My nephew mentioned your investigation." Strands of white hair lifted from Mr. Stockton's mostly bald head when he doffed his straw hat and laid it on the table. "It intrigued me enough to consider the matter myself. Last night I read these briefs and came here to offer my services. Free of charge."

Cole's head jerked back. "Services?"

Mr. Stockton smiled slightly at Cole, his thin lips disappearing to reveal a row of pale yellow teeth. "We'll appeal the termination ruling in a higher court."

"To reinstate the easement?" Katie-Lynn's eyes shone with the same hope rip-roaring through Cole. He wanted to shoot out the lights and shout hallelujah to the county. He dropped a hand to her soft shoulder to anchor himself lest he float clear to the ceiling.

Mr. Stockton donned a pair of glasses, peered at the ruling and pointed to the judge's signature. "Jedediah Cade. A relative."

Cole's mouth dropped open. This lawsuit wasn't justice. It was fixed.

"We have access to the Cade family bible." Katie-Lynn pulled out her cell phone. "It may confirm the relationship."

Mr. Stockton waved a wrinkled hand. "J.D. already established the connection through historical records. He was Josiah's brother. He'd followed his sibling west and practiced law before the county appointed him justice."

"Why'd he hear the case?" Cole sat in the chair Mr. Stockton indicated. "It's a conflict of interest."

"He should have recused himself." Mr. Stockton pulled butterscotch candies from his suit's breast pocket and passed them around. Seemed a sweet tooth ran in J.D.'s family. "However, judges were few and far between back in those days. The Lovelands could have appealed the decision to a higher court. The evidence was flimsy at best, the arguments flawed."

"Why didn't they?" Buttery flavor filled Cole's mouth.

Mr. Stockton pointed to the case's cover page. "The Lovelands represented themselves whereas the Cades hired a legal team. The Cades could afford a lengthy court battle, and the Lovelands, presumably, could not. Perhaps they'd over-extended themselves by increasing their live-stock, cattle they no longer could keep watered."

"So, we gave up?"

"Like my nephew, I'm a bit of a history buff and have followed your family's feud." Mr. Stockton's deep-set eyes gleamed behind his lenses. "As I recall, the Lovelands dammed up the Crystal River farther upstream to flood your property and stop its flow to the Cades?"

Cole nodded, recalling the family lore.

"And your family was also charged with tres-passing when caught driving cattle across the former easement."

"Doesn't sound like they gave up." Katie-Lynn's eyebrows met above her nose. "They fought back the only way they could."

"And over time, the easement was forgotten." Cole rubbed the back of his tight neck, marvel-ing. "What do we do now? I won't accept char-ity, though your offer's appreciated."

Mr. Stockton carefully removed his glasses, polished them with a pocket square, then stowed them away. "I suspected as much given your fam-ily's reputation as being—"

"Stubborn?" Katie-Lynn grinned, lightly kicking Cole's boot under the table.

"Proud," Mr. Stockton supplied, giving Cole a warm, assessing glance. "In lieu of a retainer, I'll accept a percentage of the settlement."

"Settlement?" Cole echoed, pinching the bridge of his nose where a headache formed.

"Once the easement is reinstated, we'll sue the Cades for damages, the financial hardship caused by the denial of your usage of the easement. I'll take an agreed-upon percentage. If we lose, we both get nothing."

Cole's mind raced as he considered the ramifications of such an action. The timing was terrible. His father loved Joy and was about to marry her. If they took legal action, Joy might side with her children and Pa could lose his chance at love. The thought of causing his father pain sliced his heart. Yet they stood to lose the ranch, his family's legacy, a condition caused by the Cades. Deep down he knew he had to do the right thing.

Cole's jaw clenched. Justice was long overdue, though he'd wait until after the wedding to bring the suit, something he and his siblings had the legal right to do since they were shareholders in the ranch. In the meantime, what Pa didn't know wouldn't hurt him. Joy surely couldn't blame him. With any luck, she might persuade her hotheaded children to settle out of court.

He grasped Mr. Stockton's hand and pumped it. "Sir. You have a deal."

KATLYNN PEERED DOWN at the Loveland Hills's survey map spread out on the kitchen table the following morning. "These dots with squiggle tails are natural springs?"

"Yes." Cole flipped bacon sizzling on the stove. "There're a couple near the ravines we'll ride out to and check today."

"If they have Scotch pines and mulberry bushes around them, we may discover Everett and Maggie's secret meeting spot."

Cole cracked a couple of eggs over another frying pan. "And Cora's Tear."

Excitement bubbled inside Katlynn. This story was juicier than she'd imagined. When she'd briefed the show's team last night, they'd cheered for a certain season renewal and congratulated her on a sure-to-come Emmy. Her eyes drifted to Cole's broad back as he added slices of cheese over the frying eggs. In her chest, her heart swelled with an almost pleasurable ache. She'd always loved her eggs that way, and he remembered.

The Emmy glimmered in her mind's eye, the symbol confirming she mattered. Yet the statue seemed diminished somehow. Less important... Since coming home, spending time with Cole and her family, her perspective had shifted along with her feelings. His quiet confidence, devotion to his family and protective nature were as magnetic as ever. She was falling for him again. Yet loving him meant retreating from the world to live privately, where no one would see her.

Cole said he saw her.

Her family cared.

Was it enough? She wanted it to be. She was successful now. Shouldn't her need to be noticed be filled?

The toaster oven dinged, and Katlynn hurried to grab the warm slices. After dividing them onto a couple of plates, she buttered them then returned them to the toaster.

"You remembered," Cole said in her ear as he reached around her to grab the salt and pepper.

She shivered at the warm brush of his lips against her sensitive flesh. "Extra butter, extra melted."

His deep blue eyes searched hers. "My favorite."

"Mine, too."

The air between them heated, their faces drew closer, they were lost in each other's gazes…

"Not to interrupt you two lovebirds, but can a fella squeeze in here for a cup of joe?"

At Boyd's amused voice, Katlynn grabbed the

toast from the toaster again, tossed them on the plates and fled back to the table, her cheeks red.

From behind her raised coffee mug, she murmured, "Morning, Boyd."

"Appears to be *quite* a good morning," Boyd said, his eyes on his son as he poured himself a cup of coffee. "What are you two doing up this early?"

Cole slid the eggs onto the toast, forked bacon slices beside them, then sauntered back to the table. "We've pinpointed a few places where we think Cora's Tear might be."

Katlynn stared down at her megacalorie plate, imagined Mary's disappointment when she couldn't zip the rose dress for the next taping, and cut through the soft, cheese-covered egg, anyway. Her eyes closed in appreciation at the rich, buttery flavor exploding on her tongue.

"How'd you figure that?" she heard Boyd ask.

"Just some documents we've been going through," Cole said evasively. They'd decided to withhold the information about Cora's Tear and Maggie and Everett's fates until they had all the facts. Ever a man of his word, Cole kept mum except for filling in his siblings about the lawsuit. All agreed to serve the Cades after the wedding.

She nudged the toe of his boot in approval and he winked at her, smiling slightly, as he munched a slice of bacon. A warmth started in her torso and spread to the tips of her fingers and toes. Carbonated sunshine. He was more delicious than the food.

"Is that the area you're looking at?" Boyd pointed the end of his spoon at the black circle on the map.

When Cole nodded, Boyd rubbed his jaw. "Huh."

"Hey, Pa." Sierra swooped into the kitchen, kissed her pa's cheek and filched a slice of bacon from Cole's plate. A short-haired tabby trotted at her heels. "Are you still coming into the clinic with me to look at the bald eagle? We're releasing him today, so this is your last chance."

Boyd continued staring down at the map.

"Pa?" Sierra waved a hand in front of his face. "You okay? I mean, we should have apologized about the fight before now, but we're all sorry about the softball game, and we won't shame you at the wedding. Promise."

Boyd lifted his head and offered up a slight smile. "Appreciate that, darlin'."

"Can I get anyone some juice?" Sierra called as she headed to the fridge.

"I'll have some." Cole studied his father, who'd returned his undivided attention to the map. "What is it, Pa?"

Boyd's forehead furrowed. "It's just… I've had

an offer to buy this exact section of land. Several times."

Surprised, Katlynn swallowed her coffee wrong and choked. Cole raced around the table, eyeing her closely until she stopped coughing. A napkin materialized before her streaming eyes, dabbing at her tears.

"You okay?" he asked beneath his breath, passing her his glass of water before sitting in the chair beside her.

"Fine, thanks."

Beneath the table, Cole's large hand cupped hers, holding it gently as if it were a priceless object he didn't want to drop. The tenderness of his touch tripped up her heart.

Sierra dropped into a chair on Katlynn's opposite side. "Thought I was going to have to perform the Heimlich. I've never done it on a human before."

Katlynn glanced at the map's circled areas. Who'd offered to buy the track? Was it a coincidence or something else? And how to think straight when Cole was driving her crazy with this secret hand-holding?

"Pa? You okay?" Sierra prompted.

Boyd passed a hand over his face. "Just got some things to think on."

"You're not planning on selling that land, are you?" Cole was back at the stove now, peeling more bacon from the package and dropping it into the pan. At the tabby's meow, he slipped it a piece.

"Would help us out," Boyd mused.

"We don't break up Loveland Hills," Cole insisted, his broad shoulders tense.

"It's a high offer." Boyd lifted his coffee mug and drained it. To Katlynn's eye, his hand shook slightly.

His financial troubles must surely be weighing on him. If they could find Cora's Tear, broker a deal to return the easement rights, the pressure of living on the brink of bankruptcy would end for this deserving family.

"How much?" Cole tapped an egg on the side of the fry pan and turned.

"Funny thing is, when word got out that Katlynn was here to do the story, the buyer upped his offer again." When Boyd named an exorbitant amount, Cole's egg splatted to the floor.

"That'd sure make things easier around here." Sierra finished her juice, grabbed her bag and pulled on her boots. "You coming, Pa?"

Boyd nodded and rose.

"Why'd anyone pay such a crazy amount?" Katlynn mopped up the broken egg then chucked the sodden paper towel in the trash. "I don't know the going rate for land around here anymore, but..."

"Hasn't changed much. The natural springs are a plus, I reckon." Cole folded his arms across his chest, his finger tapping the pronounced curve of his biceps. "Who's the buyer?"

Warm spring air curled through the room when Sierra eased open the door. "Must be an out-of-towner. Maybe one of those fracking outfits?" She ushered the cat outside then followed.

Boyd fiddled with the brim of his hat before settling it on his head. "That's the strange thing. The man's local and his family's been after this property for generations."

A strange premonition lifted the tiny hairs on Katlynn's arms. "Who?"

"Clyde William Farthington, the fourth."

CHAPTER ELEVEN

COLE LOOSENED HIS death grip on Cash's reins and turned him down a lane of flowering apple trees. Since Pa's revelation, a sense of bewilderment seized him. His mind whirled, his thoughts jumbled puzzle pieces. Once he fit them together, they'd reveal the big picture. His gut told him Pa's disclosure brought them closer to solving the mystery of what'd happened to Everett, Maggie and Cora's Tear. But how?

"Clyde William Farthington," Katlynn mused aloud as they ducked beneath low-hanging tree branches. "Why would he want this section of land? It can't be a coincidence."

"No." Cole jerked sideways when a honeybee whizzed by his ear, racing for the pink blossoms permeating the air with a thick, heady scent.

"So, what's the connection?" When they walked down a slope and encountered a brook, Katie-Lynn's white gelding, Spirit, sidestepped, balking. She controlled her skittish mount and guided him over the water, easy as pie. Being away hadn't done her horsemanship any harm. "Clyde's ancestor was engaged to Maggie Cade."

"And he knew about her and Everett." Cole waved Katie-Lynn ahead when the trail narrowed, and patted Cash's steaming neck while they waited. It was hotter than blue blazes, the unseasonable warm weather continuing for its fourth day. They'd been riding under full sun for an hour now to reach one of the natural springs on the survey map.

"Clyde didn't care about Maggie's pregnancy." Katie-Lynn peered over her shoulder at him, her pretty, freshly scrubbed face framed by her white cowboy hat. "How strange to claim a child that wasn't his."

"He needed an heir. Maggie wrote his previous two wives were infertile."

"And they died in bizarre accidents. Suspicious, don't you think?"

Cole watched Katie-Lynn's trim back and narrow waist as she swayed gracefully in the saddle ahead of him. She looked all sorts of pretty in her frayed jeans and yellow T-shirt, her hair pulled back into a loose braid with a daisy clip. And those little black leather boots…for some reason they drove him crazy. His fingers curled around the reins again, itching to touch her. Hold her. Kiss her. Tell her…

Tell her what?

"Cole?" Katie-Lynn prompted without turning.

He cleared his throat—and his head. "One wife drowned. The other fell down a flight of stairs and broke her neck. Sounds suspicious."

"They were rich heiresses, and he had a lot to gain from their deaths. He took their money, killed them when they didn't give him a child, then moved on to someone who could."

"That's a statement right out of an episode of *Scandalous History*. Has anyone ever told you that you look like its host?"

"All the time."

Their laughter carried in the wind, and Cole got lost in the sound of Katie-Lynn's joy. It wove around him like a spell, gripping his heart, making him long for things he knew he could never have...

"Maybe I should open the show with that line," she teased.

"It's a keeper," he drawled.

Cash's hooves skidded on a mossy rock. Cursing himself for not paying better attention, Cole directed Cash from the path's edge. The patch of Scotch pines they passed beneath blocked the sun and created a temporary dim, cool spot. "Cora's Tear was Maggie's dowry."

"It would have solved Clyde's audit problem if his company was under scrutiny."

Cash pulled up alongside Katie-Lynn when

they emerged onto the side of a dense, purple-covered hill of flagrant columbine. "We'll know tomorrow when we get the records."

Katie-Lynn closed her eyes and tipped her head back. Her white-gold braid fell past her shoulders, and the smooth expanse of her neck drew his eye. Never in his life had he found anyone or anything as beautiful as Katie-Lynn.

"This is heaven." When she opened her blue eyes, they met his then slid away. "I forgot what this feels like."

He nudged Cash closer, so his leg brushed hers. "How what feels like?"

"To be lost in something grand, to wonder at the incredible instead of trying to be that wonder."

His eyebrows rose at her revealing statement. It gave him hope, and an opening. "You're not happy in LA."

Her head snapped around. "That's ridiculous."

"Is it? Then tell me…what makes you happy there?"

"The people."

"You have a lot of friends? People you can trust?"

Katie-Lynn fiddled with the scalloped neckline of her shirt. "Nobody trusts anybody in Hollywood."

"Why's that?"

"Everyone wants something… It's hard to tell if someone's being nice because they like you or need a favor."

"And these are your friends?" he chided.

Spirit shook his head, as if in agreement, freeing himself from a tormenting fly.

Katie-Lynn shrugged. "There's so much more to do there. Parties, restaurants, events…"

"You don't eat. Or at least you didn't when you first came home." He tore his eyes from her troubled face and watched butterflies dance above the columbines' white/yellow centers.

"There are certain expectations—of who you need to be."

"Being yourself isn't good enough?"

"No."

"So not being yourself, starving and having no real friends makes you happy? Sounds lonely."

Katie-Lynn leaned forward, threw her arms around Spirit's neck and rested her head against him. "I'm successful there."

"And that's enough?"

She buried her face in Spirit's silver mane.

"Katie-Lynn." He slid his hand down the length of her slim arm and twined his fingers in hers. "Is it enough?"

She straightened and stared down at their joined hands. Loaded silence. Then she whispered, "No." Her eyes flitted up to his. A few strands of her golden hair had come out of her braid and were blowing lightly across her cheek. She stole his breath. Each and every time he looked at her, she stole his breath.

His heart, too.

"Nothing's ever been enough except—except when I'm with you."

Her admission was like an earthquake running through him. His mind, his heart, cracked in two. He hadn't known how much he'd needed to hear those words until this moment. They erased the long, lonely twelve years he'd spent without her as if waking him from a bad dream. "Katie-Lynn." He lifted their hands and pressed his lips against her knuckles, holding her hand there. "Nothing's enough without you, either."

Having her so close, with her fresh scent enveloping him, the warmth of her skin pressed against his mouth, made his blood rush through his veins like liquid fire. With a groan, he leaned over to cup the back of her head, angling it up to his. Her lashes fluttered to her cheeks, and she lifted her mouth.

A rattle sounded from the bushes nearby. Cole tensed at the familiar, deadly sound. Cash reared slightly. Spirit scrambled backward. They fought to control their mounts when an enormous diamondback coiled in front of them, within striking distance.

Cash snorted, and Spirit whinnied, both horses dancing nervously on the trail. "Easy, boy. Easy." Cole drew his pistol slowly, staring intently at the poisonous snake. Its venom killed in minutes. The snake's head rose, its tail shaking, not backing down. With lightning speed, it lashed out at Spirit.

Cole squeezed the trigger.

The snake, shot through the head, collapsed to the ground. A spooked Spirit lit out, galloping pell-mell through the field. Katie-Lynn's scream pierced his heart like a stake. The horse had taken control and was in no mood to give it back.

"Hi-yah!" Cole kicked Cash and leaned low over his head, racing flat out after the runaway gelding. His pulse roared in his ears, his heart exploding in his chest. Just over the hill was a drop-off high enough to kill Katie-Lynn and her horse if she couldn't redirect Spirit in time.

Katie-Lynn pulled on the reins to little effect. Her hat blew off her head, and her braid streamed behind her. "Whoa! Whoa!" she shouted. Spirit's hooves ate up the ground, kicking up dirt as he flew from one danger straight into another.

"Come on, boy!" Cole urged Cash on, harder still, asking him for everything he had left in him. They were gaining on Spirit, but not fast enough. The drop-off loomed.

"Oh, my God!" Katie-Lynn cried when she spotted the ledge.

"I've got you!" Cole hollered, grabbing for Spirit's reins. Thirty or so more strides and she'd go right over. His hands swatted air. The leather straps danced just out of reach.

Cole's muscles tensed as he rose in the saddle, preparing to grab Spirt's reins. No room for error. He had to time this exactly or he'd lose Katie-Lynn just as Everett had lost Maggie. Leaning forward, he snatched up the reins and forced his mind to relax despite the approaching edge. A runaway horse had to be guided, not stopped. Trying to halt it was futile since it was too frightened to cooperate. Even if he could pull hard enough on one rein to double back, he'd handicap Spirit, making the gelding lose his balance and topple them over the edge regardless. If he yanked on both reins, the extreme pressure would become something else Spirit thought he needed to escape.

No.

Cole had to allow Spirit to see where he was going and keep his legs under him, or he'd panic further.

"Don't clamp your thighs," Cole shouted at Katie-Lynn as Spirit's hooves thundered on the hard ground. Any move Spirit made could bounce a braced rider loose. Cole eyed the nearing ledge, the wind whistling in his ear. They could easily sail right over.

Don't think. *Do.*

Cole blacked out the looming cliff and pictured himself riding through a field, confidently guiding Spirit, controlling his emotions. Next, he focused on the rhythm of his breathing, then on the rhythm of Spirit's surges.

"No," Katie-Lynn sobbed as the heart-stopping drop-off yawned before them, a vast valley nearly at their feet.

Only ten strides away...

"Don't cry, Katie-Lynn," he urged. "I won't let anything happen to you."

He began tugging on the reins a little each time Spirit surged, then relaxed his grip to allow the stride, putting himself in time with the horse's gait and focusing Spirit's attention back on him so he heeded his master.

Seven strides...

Gradually, Cole gained control and began shaping Spirit's strides instead of just riding alongside them.

Three strides...

Katie-Lynn clutched the saddle horn, her mouth a silent "O" of terror as the edge flashed up at Spirit's hooves. Cole cried, "Whoa!" and pulled harder on the reins at the last possible minute.

Miraculously, Spirit stopped, sides heaving, his head hanging over the precipice before he backed up a few paces. Cole leaped off Cash then hauled Katie-Lynn into his arms. Her body quaked against his, and he smoothed his hands down her back. "Shhhhhh…darlin'," he murmured in her ear. "You're safe. I've got you."

But you could have lost her.

This time, forever…

"We almost died." She buried her head in the space where his neck met his shoulder.

He placed a finger beneath her chin and tipped her damp face up to meet his. Their eyes met for one earth-quaking moment. "But we didn't."

"Or we did and this—this is heaven." She gazed up at him through spiked lashes. "Thank you for saving my life."

"Could say I've become rather attached to it."

She laughed, and the sound was sweeter than music. It was the thing he'd missed most about Katie-Lynn, her free-spirited laughter. She reached up to stroke his cheek. "Guess that makes me a lucky girl."

His pulse pounded in his temples; his head spun. The rational part of his brain sort of shorted out the moment her hand touched his face. Common sense? Out the window. Prudence? What was that? Logic? Who could be logical when her delicious mouth was a breath away from his?

When her soft body brushed against his? When her scent turned his muscles to granite? The last of his self-control crumbled, replaced with a mix of pent-up adrenaline and passion he couldn't extinguish.

He tugged her hand away and backed her against a tree, crushing his lips to hers, his hands gripping her waist. Her gasp against his lips might have been shock, maybe dismay, but one glance at her darkening eyes told him neither one of those was what she was feeling. Not even close.

"Is this heaven, Katie-Lynn?" he whispered against her lips, drowning in the raspberry tartness of her mouth.

"Yes," she breathed. "It always is when you hold me."

His heart headed into cardiac arrest from the aftershock of her words. It pounded hard enough to hear.

He covered her mouth with his, kissing her hot and reckless. As his hands slid down her back, his chest heaved against hers. She was fire in his arms, her mouth soft and eager beneath the claim of his lips. In an instant, he saw his mistake in kissing the only woman he'd ever loved… would only love. This intimacy brought her dangerously close, fitting into the empty spaces she'd left behind.

It'd crush him all over when she tore loose again. He shouldn't expect anything more. It was just as stupid to expect anything more from her now as it had been twelve years ago.

Katie-Lynn was who she was. Sociable, outgoing, citified. And he was who he was—rooted, traditional, an introvert.

"We need to stop," he rasped out.

"Not yet." She kissed him back harder, holding on to him as if she still teetered on the ledge and he was her only lifeline.

"Make me stop, Katie-Lynn. Please…" he begged, knowing he'd never let her go if she didn't stop this. She had him too far gone emotionally to turn back.

"No," she said simply, wrapping her arms around him, kissing him just as hungrily as he was kissing her.

Being near Katie-Lynn was like being in the center of a tornado. All his senses tumbling, spiraling, flying out of control, while at the core, at his center, was the relentless pull to draw even closer.

Magnetism.

He couldn't separate himself from her. Maybe he never could. She was a brand on his skin. "Push me away."

"Never," she whispered, pulling him even closer.

"Don't say things you don't mean," he said gruffly, his lips trailing along her neck. The natural, earthy smell of her soap, fresh laundry, horses, sweat, made his lungs expand, the more to draw her in.

"Working together," she murmured, tilting her head back, letting him kiss the hummingbird pulse at the base of her throat. "Seeing you every day... I don't want to stop being together."

"Then we're not stopping." He moved his lips back up to hers and stared down at her. Her eyes lit up, and she gave him the full force of her smile. Oh, but she was pretty. Pretty as a pie supper. "Once we start this, we can't go back, Katie-Lynn."

She gulped, a hint of nervousness finally showing, and when she nodded, he was a falling-down barn one good blow from collapsing. For so long he'd convinced himself he only wanted the ranch, but his time with Katie-Lynn showed him there was more to life.

"This is what I want." Her hands skimmed up his chest, over his shoulders and clasped behind his neck as she stared up at him.

Instantly he was hung in the past, remembering the first time they'd kissed, the night of his mother's funeral. She'd held him as he'd cried, and he'd felt as though she was the only thing holding him together. He cared about her now just as much as he'd cared then.

Even more.

He could scarcely believe she was here with him, that he was getting a second chance with her. A second chance at love.

Whoa, slow down. No one said anything about love.

Twelve years ago, she'd made it clear she didn't want to be tied down to Carbondale, or him. Why would things be different now? He sucked in a long, deep breath. "You want me? Us?"

"I'm falling for you again, Cole. I can't deny it, but…"

His heart squeezed with an ache only she could soothe. "But…" He nibbled his way along her jaw, molding her body to his. Their quick breaths synchronized when he reached the soft lobe of her ear and drew it into his mouth. "Say anything, darlin'."

"But I can't make any promises," she gasped. "There are a lot of people depending on me for the show…and…I'm not sure I'm ready to give it up to move home."

Her words hit him like the first slap of a blizzard. Cold and stinging. He stared at her mute, then twisted away. Talk about mixed messages. Was she as confused as he or just jerking his chain? When she caught him by the hand, he stopped.

"Cole," she pleaded. "Please, understand…"

"No. *You* understand," he said without turning, regret bitter on his tongue. "I'm not some leading man in a Hollywood script. These aren't just words. This isn't pretend. It's real. For me, anyway."

And with that, he stomped off and corralled the horses, vowing to keep his distance. Emotionally, anyway. Katie-Lynn had nearly destroyed him once. This time, he suspected, she might finish the job.

AT HER PRODUCER's pointed look, Katlynn returned the half-and-half containers to the diner's bowl and dumped an extra packet of artificial sweetener into her coffee instead. She sipped the scalding fluid, the temperature barely registering. If she burned her tongue so be it. She deserved to suffer for her reckless behavior with Cole earlier. Why had she kissed him?

Again.

She peered out of Pete's Kitchen's window and watched the quarter moon crest Mount Sopris. It shed no light on her situation. Adrenaline was a convenient excuse for giving in to temptation. Gratitude for saving her life was another.

But it went deeper and was much more complicated.

Stars glimmered in the wide, dark sky, brilliant without smog or lights of the city to conceal them. What was she hiding behind the smile she aimed at her producer as he droned on about the episode's early buzz and teaser previews?

She'd fallen for Cole again. Period.

When he'd rescued her, it'd seemed like he saved her life in other ways, too. She hadn't even known she needed to be rescued from herself... from her empty life. But the truth stared her dead in the eye when she'd nearly fallen from that bluff.

She was unhappy in LA. All her accomplishments seemed smaller, less consequential, when viewed from Carbondale. Something about the majestic Rockies put life into perspective. She had a lot to figure out and shouldn't be giving a straight shooter like Cole mixed signals. His words, actions, affection were real, he'd asserted...as were hers. Yet she couldn't act on them until she'd figured out a path forward for them.

Was a long-distance relationship possible? He'd been against it once, but maybe time had softened him on the idea? Or should *she* compromise? She'd attained some fame and still she felt unfulfilled. Time to rethink her life goals, the most basic and important of which being happiness.

Only now Cole was avoiding her.

He'd spoken just a handful of words while they'd inspected the first of the two springs they'd targeted, noting the lack of mulberry bushes or Scotch pines, before heading home in silence. After untacking the horses, he'd disappeared to his cabin on the ranch and hadn't emerged for supper. A long talk with her mother earlier, when she'd stopped by to visit, hadn't clarified the situation much. Ma advised her not to play with fire unless she wanted to get burned…and to remember she wasn't the only one she'd hurt in the process.

Her shoulders slumped.

"Hey. Don't look so defeated, Katlynn." Her producer, Tom, snapped his fingers at a passing waitress. She shot him a quick glare without stopping. "I just got a call from *Celebrity* magazine wanting an inside scoop on the Cade-Loveland mystery. You're going to be a bigger star than ever."

She yanked her smile back on. "Great." More attention from people who didn't know, care about or need her…unlike Cole, or the Lovelands or even her own family, she was discovering. While chatting with her mother, Michelle had arrived while Katlynn was chatting with her mother to pick up her kids, heard Katlynn's troubles and joined the conversation despite having just worked a twelve-hour shift. In LA, she paid big bucks for someone to listen. Here, people did it because they cared.

Her coffee mug left a damp ring on their booth's wooden table when she set it down. "If it's all right with you, I'd like to call it a night. I've got some notes to write up and after a day in the saddle..."

"With your ex-fiancé?" Tom's eyes gleamed as he sniffed a forkful of lettuce before taking a delicate bite. "I still think we need to use that in the story."

"What? No!"

"*Celebrity* magazine would like to."

"How do they even know about—" She broke off and stared at her smug producer as he chewed. Suspicion coiled tight in her gut. "You didn't."

Tom spread his hands and a red onion slice dropped from his fork. "It might have slipped out. Gives the segment a more human angle. Anything to sell a story...free publicity for us."

"It's not just about publicity. This is my *life*."

"Oh, honey." Tom squeezed a lemon wedge over his salad. "You surrendered that long ago when you became a celebrity. Didn't you read the fine print in your contract?"

"This isn't funny, Tom. And Cole didn't sign

up to have his love life exposed to a bunch of strangers."

Tom shrugged. "You have the right to keep things off the record for the interview. I'm just advising you to—" Another passing waitress, carrying steaming platters of meat loaf and potatoes, snared his attention. He leaned out of the booth, snapping his fingers. "Server! Hey. Waitress."

"Why don't you just whistle?" Katlynn slid down in the booth, embarrassed by his high-handed behavior. In LA, people catered to Tom's powerbroker behavior. Here, it came across as entitled and obnoxious.

Tom puckered his lips and blew an anemic wheeze of air. "I would, but I don't know how."

"You can't treat people like that."

"Who? Them?" He jerked his head at the hustling, red-faced waitstaff. The humid air fogged the lower half of the windows circling the crowded, rustic room. "They're just waitresses. They don't count."

Her blood fired at his dismissive words. "Who does, then? Me?"

Tom patted her hand. "Of course. You're our star."

Her gut clenched at the once cherished label. "I count because I get to dress up and talk on TV? That makes me better than Sally over there?"

Katlynn gestured to a pregnant woman bussing a table with one hand pressed to the small of her back. "Who, I believe, is raising three kids alone while her husband fights a forest fire? Or what about Jenny? She—"

At her name, Katlynn's old classmate stopped by their table. She flicked limp brown locks off her round face and smiled. "Hey, Katie-Lynn. Heard you were in town. Wasn't sure if you'd mind if I said hi, you being—ah—you and all."

"It's good to see you." Katlynn shot her a warm, welcoming smile and firmly ignored Tom's rude pleas for pepper. "If you're on break, can you sit with us? Let me buy you a cup of coffee."

"Oh. No. We're not allowed to do that." Jenny's smile fell as she cast a quick glance back at the kitchen. A florid man wearing a Manager badge shoved open the swinging door and stalked into the restaurant. "I'll be in trouble for talking too long since this isn't my station, but I wanted to say I'm a big fan. You sure done us proud. And sir, I'll pass your request on to your server."

With that, Jenny scurried away.

Tom crossed his arms over his chest and shot Katlynn a smug look. "See. Even they know you're better than them."

"Are you insane?" Katlynn raised her voice over the thunderous crash of dropped plates at the end of the bar. A good-natured cheer rose from the diners seated at it while the sound system blared a George Strait tune. "Did you see the yellow ribbon over her name badge?"

Tom flicked his eyes to the ceiling and heaved an aggrieved sigh. "Ribbons were over in 2010."

She pulled apart her paper napkin, shredding it. "It's not a fashion accessory here. It means she lost someone in the war. Sacrificed a loved one. What have I ever sacrificed except for unrestricted breathing because of my shapewear?"

"Speaking of which..." Tom's assessing gaze fell on her, and she struggled not to squirm. "When we were filming yesterday, Gabe noticed you might have put on a few pounds."

She gasped, her emotions veering between shame and anger. "What if I have? Does skinnier make me better?" Tufts of white paper drifted from her fingers to the table. "Does being richer make me better? Younger? Those are impossible standards. Unrealistic."

"It's our business."

"Well, maybe I don't want to be in *your* business anymore."

Tom chuckled slowly, knowingly. "Oooh... now I see."

"See what?"

He tapped his chin. "What are you looking for? A ten percent increase in next year's contract?

Fifteen? Have Hylda call me. You know how we handle these matters."

"It's not about the money," she said through gritted teeth.

Tom stared at her uncomprehendingly. "What, then? You want a bigger dressing room? A producer credit?"

"I'm thinking of quitting," she blurted, honest with herself at last.

Tom gripped the table's edge and leaned forward, his voice low and urgent. "Be reasonable. Lots of people are depending on you. If you quit, that's even more ammunition for Ultima to replace us with *Millennial Millionaires*. Not to mention we have you contracted for twelve more months."

She sighed and slumped back in the booth.

"Excuse me, miss? Ma'am?" Tom called when their server passed by a third time. "See. I was nice, and it still didn't work. This would never happen to me in Hollywood," he grumped.

"You're a big shot there. Here...you're just another pain-in-the-butt customer on a busy night."

Tom speared his salad and waved his fork at her. "You're enjoying this, aren't you?"

"Immensely. Now tell me what you really wanted to talk about that couldn't wait until morning."

"Have you heard of Senator Reardon?"

"Yes," she admitted cautiously. She recalled Cole's grandfather from his picture in papers and on TV as he'd accused the Lovelands of covering up his daughter's murder as a suicide.

"He heard about our episode and wants to be included."

Shock rolled through Katlynn, flattening her. "Not a chance in hell." No way would she allow Cole and his family to suffer through the man's hurtful accusations again.

"Since you know the family, shall we say, intimately, I suppose you know what he wants to say."

"A pack of lies."

"Allegations," Tom countered.

"None of them proven."

Tom waved his American Express card at another server then lowered it when she whizzed by. "He says the ex-sheriff, Boyd's brother, refused to investigate. Sounds like a cover-up."

"It wasn't," Katlynn denied flatly. "The Lovelands are decent people who suffered a tragedy."

Tom tapped the edge of his black card on the table, a speculative gleam in his eye. "Or Boyd Loveland saw an easy way to cash in on his wealthy wife's inheritance to save his struggling ranch."

"Take that back," she growled, fierce.

"I'm just saying, there are always two sides to every story. It's our job to present them."

"I'm sure there's an alternate explanation for a secret military base operating in the desert than building new weapons...like aliens...but I'm not reporting on it. I'll leave that to TMZ."

"Don't be hyperbolic." Tom smothered a yawn. "You've always been practical. Think of what this angle does for our story. The feud begins when a Loveland's accused of murdering a Cade for her priceless jewel. Now, another Loveland, who may have killed his wife for her money, is about to marry a wealthy Cade widow... Will she meet the same fate?" Tom's eyes glowed, a scandal-monger on the scent. "Think about it, Katlynn."

"I am, and the answer is no." She glared at him. "I promised the Lovelands not to stir up controversies that'd jeopardize the peace of their upcoming wedding."

"It's not like you signed anything." He peered at her closely. "You didn't sign anything, did you?" He pulled out his cell. "I can get a hold of legal and—"

She held up a hand, forestalling him. "I gave my word."

Tom's shoulders, covered by his expensive suit, lowered. "Good. So there's no reason we can't—"

"I won't go back on my word," she insisted.

Like Cole said, words here mattered. They were real and not spoken lightly.

"If you won't do it, I'll have Ashton interview the senator for the segment."

"Ashton?" she gasped. Ashton Reince was a slick, smooth-talking Hollywood up-and-comer who'd take her job in a heartbeat. He filmed supplementary segments for their episodes and lived to sniff out scandal, stoking it to the highest degree. "You can't let him near the senator. He'll have the county demanding the case be reopened when he's through with the interview."

At last, their server stopped at their table and passed over a pepper shaker.

"I asked for cracked pepper." Tom scowled. "Not ground."

"Is he pulling my leg?" she appealed to Katlynn.

"Sadly, no."

When the server scampered away, Tom shook the pepper over his salad with short flicks of his wrist. "We've already booked the senator. It's either you or Ashton. Who's it going to be?"

She bit her lip, ignoring the sting. Only she could manage such a difficult interview and keep it from becoming something tawdry or worse. She had to control the message. Caught between a rock and a hard place, she blurted, "Me, but on one condition."

"Which is?" Tom's cell buzzed.

"Let me also tape a segment interviewing Boyd Loveland and Joy Cade ahead of their wedding. They were each other's first loves, an angle that'd spice up the story without turning to innuendo and unproven accusations."

"They didn't fail in some suicide pact, did they?" Tom asked without looking up from his phone, his thumbs whizzing over the digital keys.

"No."

Tom finished his text, stowed his phone and sighed. "Pity. Okay. Get both interviews, and we'll see which one works better. Deal?"

Katlynn sagged back in the booth. "Deal."

She'd do the interview of her life to portray Senator Reardon as a grieving, but very misguided parent, and Joy and Boyd as star-crossed lovers finally getting their second chance at love. When she finished, there'd be no question which segment the superior angle was, the production team's choice clear.

Hopefully...

Yet they might still choose Senator Reardon...

Cole would see it as a betrayal.

Should she tell him or wait until her production company picked the segment?

If he knew now, he'd be even angrier with her... In the window's reflection she caught her frown. No. Better to wait.

When he saw the finished project, she hoped he'd understand she'd only had his best interests at heart…

CHAPTER TWELVE

"JOY. BOYD. WELCOME to *Scandalous History* and congratulations on your engagement." Katlynn aimed a serene smile into the camera just behind Boyd's left ear. Farther back in Loveland Hills's front parlor, directly in her line of vision, stood a protective Cole. His stance was braced and wide-legged, arms folded across his broad chest.

Sticky dampness pooled beneath the arm-holes of her floral-patterned dress. Aluminum reflector shields, set up around Boyd's front parlor, bounced light straight into stinging eyes she willed to keep wide and open. Despite the conditions, she stayed mindful, as her life coach would advise her. If she messed up this interview, the production might go with the fractious segment she'd taped yesterday with Senator Reardon. She could not let Cole down, even if he still barely spoke to her, despite their fruitless rides out in search of Maggie and Everett's secret meeting spots.

At least her family welcomed her. Just last night she'd babysat John's and Michelle's kids on their bowling league night and now knew every word to every song in *Frozen*. The irony of the lyric "Let It Go" did not escape her.

"Cut!" Gabe pointed at the tabby cat stalking haughtily across the room's colorful braided rag rug. It leaped onto a chintz chair matching the one on which Katlynn sat, lifted a leg and began giving itself a bath. "This is a closed set!"

"Ginger! Sorry about that…curious cats…what can you do?" Sierra slipped past the sound crew, scooped up the protesting cat and hurried from the room.

"Pa!" Heath called from the hallway. "Have you got the keys to the backhoe?"

"Probably left 'em in my overalls' pocket," Boyd hollered back. "Check the wash."

Gabe shoved his hands in his hair. With his mouth hanging open, eyes dark and wild, he so closely resembled the painting "The Scream," Katlynn nearly laughed. "Are you expecting any more visitors? Pigs wandering in for breakfast?"

Cole shrugged. "We usually eat 'em for breakfast, but I can ask my brother Daryl to round some up for you."

Gabe sputtered. By the look of him, her director teetered on the brink of one of his infamous tantrums, a mood that might ruin this crucial segment.

The recalcitrant senator had proved more challenging than expected, answering her pointed questions with persuasive answers. They would have raised doubt in her mind if she hadn't already known the truth. She had to nail Joy and Boyd's piece so the senator's footage became cutting room floor fodder.

When she caught Cole's speculative stare, she willed back the flush rising in her cheeks. She hadn't explained her absence when she'd left to meet the senator. Keeping a secret this big from Cole felt wrong, even if it was for the right reasons.

"Gabe," Katlynn said. "We're ready when you are."

He muttered to himself as he reset the shot. The key grip curled his fingers down, "Three, two..." Then a silent point.

"Joy. Boyd. Welcome to *Scandalous History* and congratulations on your engagement," Katlynn began again, her voice modulated and warm. "From all accounts, your upcoming wedding has been a long time coming."

Joy smoothed a nonexistent wrinkle in her navy skirt until Boyd caught her hand in his. "It sure has," he said. "I'd planned on asking for her hand over forty-two years ago."

Katlynn angled her head and leaned forward. "Tell me about how you two first met."

"Met? I couldn't get away from her." Boyd

chuckled, earning him a playful tap on his arm from Joy, who relaxed slightly.

Good.

Act like your natural, charming self, Joy. As for Katlynn, it was tough to focus with Cole watching her like a hawk.

"Is that true, Joy?"

Pink suffused her cheeks as she tucked a silver strand of her bob behind her ear. "He might be exaggerating a tad."

"She was a petite little thing. On the scrawny side," Boyd began, the lines of his face easing as he looked down at Joy with a smile. "And a couple years younger than me. I remember thinking she had big eyes and an anxious smile. A pretty gal, but skittish."

"And what was your impression of Boyd Loveland, Joy?"

Joy studied their clasped hands before lifting her head and gazing straight at Katlynn. Given the camera practically resting on her shoulder, it was a good angle. "I thought he was the handsomest cowboy I'd ever seen. He was helping at the county fair's 4H livestock exhibit, throwing hay bales like they were made of cotton candy. When one of the guys whistled at me, Boyd scolded him, told him to respect a lady."

"I don't remember that," Boyd exclaimed.

"A lady has to have some secrets."

Their affectionate, teasing exchange was enough to melt the cameras for goodness' sakes. Katlynn's muscles loosened. Joy and Boyd were naturals. Two regular folks finding happiness at long last. How could the show not prefer this angle? Was Cole pleased? She didn't dare check in case his expression threw her off; she was in the zone.

"And were you smitten right away, Boyd?"

Boyd shook his head. "My friends called Joy my shadow because she followed me everywhere, especially after she kissed me when we played seven minutes in heaven."

Katlynn sensed the crew's rapt attention and Cole's intent gaze. The normally silent set seemed to have entered a sound vacuum. Not even a breath could be heard. "Seven minutes in heaven? Sounds scandalous."

"She was terribly persistent." Boyd let out a long, suffering sigh, a hint of amusement running through it. The mixture of exasperated affection reminded her of Cole so much, she ached. How to get him to start talking to her again?

Joy rolled her eyes. "Every gal was after you. I had to get your attention somehow. When he spoke up to that boy at the fair, I knew he was the one for me. I wasn't going to quit until I got my man, but Boyd played hard to get."

"Really?" Katlynn angled slightly in Boyd's

direction. Just behind him, she glimpsed a slight smile curving up Cole's lips. Did he think she was doing a good job? The possibility filled her with a helium-tank's worth of bright, bubbly air. "Why, Boyd? You said you thought she was pretty…"

"I knew, straight off, to keep my distance." Boyd absently toyed with the blunt ends of Joy's hair. "She wasn't a casual dating kind of gal, and I was too young to get tied down. Some people called me wild back in the day."

"What changed your mind?"

"Homecoming dance my senior year. I'd been crowned homecoming king and scored the winning touchdown. I felt invincible. Untouchable. Then Joy asked me to dance."

"And you turned me down." Joy folded her arms across her chest and shot Boyd a mock-glare.

"First time." Boyd hung his head and rolled his eyes up to the camera, his expression hangdog. "Second and third time, too."

Katlynn shook her head ever so slightly in sympathy. On TV, the slightest movement was magnified several times over. Less was always more. "How'd that make you feel, Joy?"

Joy closed her eyes briefly. "Like a fool."

Boyd pressed a light kiss to her temple. "When

I saw some gals laughing at her, I got angry, so I asked her to dance."

"Out of pity?"

"It was more complicated than that." A smile curled Boyd's mouth, and his eyes took on a far-away look. "She looked real pretty that night. I still remember her dress. Yellow with beaded straps. It floated around her like a cloud. She'd fixed her hair different, too, pulling it up on the sides and curling it. For the first time I noticed her long neck and pretty ears." Boyd chuckled. "Funny the things you remember."

Cole cleared his throat, twice, and Mary, the show's hair and makeup guru, gasped "Awwwwww" from the sidelines. Was Cole remembering their first date, the dreamlike moment they'd shared at his birthday party before tragedy struck?

"Cut!" hollered Gabe. Joy and Boyd straightened, looking slightly confused. "What part of *quiet on the set* isn't being communicated here?" He subsided when Cole cocked an eyebrow at him, oozing quiet menace.

Mary clucked as she dabbed powder on Katlynn's forehead. "Those two are a dream. What's that thing my son's always saying? Relationship goals? Boyd and Joy are mine."

Since Mary moved on to freshening Katlynn's lipstick, she simply nodded, her eyes seeking out

Cole again. Joy and Boyd had found a second chance at love; could she and Cole do the same? Like Joy, Katlynn fell in love with Cole at first sight. Sometimes the heart knows…and can't forget.

A moment later the cameras rolled again.

"When we hit the floor, the band swung into a slow tune," Boyd continued his story slowly, bringing the avid listeners back in time. "She put her arms around my neck and smiled up at me, her eyes big and dreamy, and I warned her, 'I'm not falling in love with you.' She just kept smiling."

Boyd scrubbed a hand over his eyes, and a short laugh escaped him. "But I did. I did. As soon as I held her, I knew she was the one."

"You knew that quickly?" Katlynn asked.

"It was more a feeling than a knowing."

Out of the corner of her eye, she glimpsed Mary throw a hand over her mouth to stifle another "Awwww…" The same feeling coursed through Katlynn. A kaleidoscope of emotions flitted across Cole's face, shifting and fusing, one into the next. Was he identifying with Joy and Boyd as much as she did?

"What forced you two apart?"

Joy peeked up at Boyd through her frameless glasses, her hazel eyes wide and slightly dark with regret. "My husband, God rest his soul."

"A love triangle," Katlynn mused, putting the "salacious" spin on the words Gabe loved. The intrigue just kept coming.

Joy placed her hands over her knee; her mouth turned down in the corners. "He'd always been sweet on me, but I never saw him as more than a friend. Besides, Boyd and I were serious, and I wasn't the two-timing type."

"Most loyal gal that ever was," Boyd interjected.

Joy reached over and squeezed Boyd's hand. "Then me and Boyd went jumping from this huge Scotch pine atop cliffs into a spring-fed ravine. My parents had warned me never to go up there because of the underwater rocks, but I never listened well back then. They were always lecturing me about something or another, especially about Boyd. They didn't approve of me dating an older boy. Said he was too reckless. Wild."

The mischievous smile playing on Joy's lips had Katlynn guessing Boyd had been the tamer one in the relationship.

"So, you went diving, your parents found out and they forbade you from seeing Boyd again?"

Disappointment deepened the faint lines around Joy's mouth. "Worse. I landed wrong and broke my leg and pelvis. I was laid up in the hospital for weeks and Boyd never visited, not once. It crushed me worse than the fall."

"Why didn't you visit, Boyd? Guilt?"

Boyd opened his mouth then snapped it shut when Joy continued. "I thought so, at least at first. I even wrote him letters, but he never wrote back. My only visitors were my parents, a couple of girlfriends and Jason Cade."

"Your future husband."

"Right. Except I was still too hung up on Boyd to have any feelings for Jason. The day I got released, I phoned Boyd, but his mother told me he'd joined the marines and shipped out the day before."

Katlynn's eyes swung to Boyd. "Without leaving word?"

Boyd and Joy shook their heads in tandem. "It hurt me bad. Over time, I picked myself up, told myself to stop pining for someone who didn't care about me and to learn to love the young man who did. When Jason proposed, I accepted."

"Then what happened?" Katlynn leaned forward, all ears. She loved finding the heart of a story, and every one of her instincts told her she'd struck gold.

"Boyd came home on leave the following Christmas and asked if he could see me. I didn't tell anyone, just snuck out and met him. When I showed him my ring, he got really quiet. I asked if he planned on congratulating me, but he refused. He claimed I broke his heart."

Katlynn's on-air, sympathetic expression felt completely natural for the first time in a long time. "Did she, Boyd?"

"Cut!" Gabe shouted. "Katlynn, sweetheart. You look stunning as always. But the face you're making is creating a line between your eyebrows."

"So?" she challenged, empowerment coursing through her. Fine. She was showing a few more lines and extra pounds. So what? Spending time amongst regular folks again, with Cole, her family and the Lovelands, had made her comfortable in her own skin...with who she really was.

Gabe's mouth dropped open and Mary giggled from the sidelines. Their pregnant lighting tech gave Katlynn a thumbs-up. Two female sound engineers exchanged swift, nodding smiles.

Yes. This is what Hollywood needed. A host who wasn't afraid to show her age or her predilection for cheesy eggs.

Speaking of which...her stomach growled. She'd only had time to inhale a yogurt before this taping.

"How about just mildly empathetic?" Gabe wheedled, softening his normally abrasive tone even further for her. "Project with those beautiful eyes. Facial muscles are passé."

And part of our basic biology...at least for those not shot up with Botox.

When the camera light flickered on, Katlynn puckered her eyebrows again, taking advantage of her star status. Gabe wouldn't dare challenge her a second time in front of the crew. "Did she break your heart, Boyd?"

Boyd blinked up at the whirling ceiling fan. "Clean in half. When she told me I had it wrong, that I'd crushed her by not visiting, by not answering her letters, I knew something bad had happened. I went to the hospital every day, leaving word with the nurses, but they never allowed me to see her and returned the gifts I'd left. I thought she was mad and wouldn't forgive me for daring her to jump at the ravine."

A short silence descended, broken by the living room's chiming grandfather clock. After a moment Joy blew out a long breath. "We just stared at each other for the longest time. Not comprehending. My parents had always been protective. They must have wanted to keep away the man they held responsible for nearly killing their daughter."

Joy stared down at her white heels; a perfect match for the belt spanning her waist. When her eyes rose, her lashes blinked fast, swatting back tears.

"What happened next?" Katlynn coaxed.

"I cried."

"I cried, too." Boyd guided Joy's head down

to his shoulder. "I swore it wasn't too late for us. We could make this right. Then she threw up."

"As in…"

"Vomited all over his shoes. I had morning sickness." Joy peered up at Boyd. "And that was that. When I confessed my suspicions about a baby, Boyd got so still I thought I'd stopped his heart and killed him outright."

Boyd rested his cheek atop Joy's head; the loving picture they made nearly broke Katlynn's heart. "I thought she'd done me all over again. Could hardly breathe. It took everything I had to wish her and Jason well and leave. Never spoke to Joy again until a couple years ago, at a bereavement support group."

The small smile playing on Joy's lips triggered Katlynn's memory. "Did I hear you got kicked out for talking too much?"

"We had a lot to catch up on."

"I can imagine. How did your children take the news of you two getting reacquainted?" Katlynn didn't have to see Cole's frown to sense it. He didn't want her asking tough questions, but this was her job. One she loved. Yet she'd have to quit it to be with Cole unless some other compromise existed…

Boyd shifted against the floral-patterned couch cushion. "Might say it took them some time to warm up to the match."

"And are they supportive?"

"We're counting on it," Joy said, her eyes just a trifle sad. Cole shifted his body weight to his other leg. Hopefully, this interview would help ease the tension that'd flared anew at the softball game. "Tonight's our rehearsal dinner so fingers crossed everyone gets along."

"And no one gets killed," Boyd added with a wink, although the strain around his mouth belied his lighthearted gesture.

"If you could go back, change things, would you?"

Boyd and Joy stared at each other for a long, potent moment before facing Katlynn again. "No," Boyd said as Joy shook her head. "We've each raised children we'd never wish away. And the time apart has only made me appreciate what a lucky man I am to have this second chance. She's the wind behind me, pushing me forward. The light in the window calling me home."

This time, when a sigh rose from the crew, Gabe just kept filming. Katlynn supposed they'd have to address the sound issue in editing, but the moment was too pure to spoil with a cut.

"I love you, Boyd Loveland," Joy murmured, her hand on his cheek.

"I love you, Joy Cade. Can't wait to tell the world so next week and make you mine at last."

"Congratulations, Joy and Boyd, and thank

you again for sharing your powerful story with us today."

"Cut." Gabe strode from behind the camera, his movements quick and electric. Like Katlynn, he smelled a good story…maybe even an Emmy-worthy one. "Let's shoot a few more reaction shots and outtakes and then we're done. Excellent job as always, Katlynn."

"Gabe? May I take five?"

His eyes narrowed on her face, assessing. "Do we have a skin anesthetist on call? Maybe some Botox during your break?"

"He can take that Botox shot and shove it where the sun don't shine," Mary growled beneath her breath when Katlynn joined her in the walk-in pantry they'd converted into a dressing room. "You look gorgeous just the way you are."

"Thanks, Mary. Would you help me with something?"

"Sure, honey. Anything."

"Could you get me out of this shapewear and then burn it?"

Mary grinned. "My pleasure."

When she emerged, Cole cupped her elbow and led her aside. "You did a good job in there," he said gruffly. "Thank you for—for showing the truth."

Her senses sang at the approval in his voice.

"I always do, even when it's confusing and messy. Cole...the other day when I kissed you—"

Cole shook his head, cutting her off. "I've had time to cool off. You don't know your mind yet. Neither of us has figured out how to make things work."

"But we want to," she whispered when a couple of crew members ducked past them, rubbernecking.

"Yes..." Cole glanced back into the living room at Joy and Boyd. "Hearing my pa talk about Joy, how he remembered so much of their first dance, reminded me of us. I've never forgotten how pretty you looked when I picked you up for my birthday party." One side of his mouth tipped up, and he shook his head. "I still couldn't believe you'd said yes. And when you opened the front door in your yellow sundress, white daisies in your curly hair, a little pearl necklace around your throat, I thought I was the luckiest guy in the world."

Her knees dipped at his confession. "I felt that way, too. You were the first person who'd ever noticed me. And in your blue dress shirt and tie, I'd never seen anyone handsomer. I'll never forget that night—how you looked, but mostly how you made me feel. Special."

"I grew up stuffing down everything in my life, whether it was family secrets or my feelings.

I wanted to hide who I was. Then all the negative attention after Ma killed herself… I wanted to just disappear…" He paused and cupped her face. "But you wouldn't let me—you always wanted everyone to know who you were—and I was just the guy who discovered you first."

"The only man that's ever counted."

He blinked at her. "You mean that?"

"I—I do. There's been no one else."

Cole's hands dropped to her waist and squeezed, his smile wide. Pure, unadulterated happiness. "I want a second chance with you."

Her heart exploded at his confession. When she opened her mouth to answer, he shook his head and continued. "I'm a one-woman man, Katie-Lynn. When I gave my heart twelve years ago, I gave it for keeps. All those things we talked about in our Say Anything tree… I've never told them to anyone else. A part of me belongs only to you, maybe more than it even belongs to myself. I'm still yours if you want me."

"I do, Cole," she gasped, her breath coming too quick to catch. "It's just…how could it work?"

"Would you consider coming home for good? I've seen you with your family, the community. You're happy here. And you're miserable in LA. I can fulfill you, Katie-Lynn, shower you with more attention than you'll ever want. So much, you'll probably be begging for privacy…if you'd give me the chance."

Her brief laugh trailed off as the sobering reality of what he'd proposed sank in. "So, you still won't compromise? I'd have to give up everything to be with you?"

"Think of what'd you be gaining."

"I—I—" She hesitated.

This interview reminded her of how much she loved her job. Yet she loved Cole, too. Why did she have to give up one for the other? A niggling sense of foreboding took hold; he won't give up anything but expected her to?

She swallowed back her concern as she drank in his tender, vulnerable expression. Surely, he wouldn't be that selfish. They'd work out the particulars later.

Cole framed her face with both hands, and his eyes delved into hers. "You don't have to give me an answer now, but will you think about it?"

"Yes," she whispered before his lips captured hers in a kiss as soft as a dandelion's wish.

"For now," Cole said, pulling back, "let's focus on a mystery we *can* solve."

At her relieved nod, he continued. "The swimming spot Joy mentioned…" His eyes were a deep, intense blue as he peered down at her, willing her to see the significance.

Her thoughts raced backward, rewinding the

interview then stopped. Understanding snatched every bit of air from her body.

"It had a spring-fed brook," she gasped.

Cole gripped her hands, excitement coursing from his fingertips. "And a tall Scotch pine to jump from. It could be Maggie and Everett's meeting spot."

"We need to talk to Joy and Boyd to pinpoint the spot."

Cole peered out the window beside them. "I'll ride out. Should be able to make it back in time for the rehearsal dinner."

"You'll wait for me?"

Cole released her hands to cup her face, his calloused palms so gentle, she ached. "I always have."

CHAPTER THIRTEEN

COLE GUIDED CASH up the rocky incline, closely eyeing the rugged terrain leading him and Katie-Lynn to his father's swimming hole. Nervous anticipation left him restless and shifting in the saddle. Would they find the jewel? Solve the mystery? Hearing Joy's hope for a reconciliation spurred his mission to clear his family's name and resolve the feud.

But solving the mystery meant ending his time with Katie-Lynn if she chose LA over him again. He snuck a glance at her as she squinted over her mount's head, concentrating on the treacherous ground. In a pink shirt tucked into faded jeans, the tips of her black boots peeking out from the hem, she looked herself, which was to say, as pretty as a summer dawn. Yet she'd looked professional and polished earlier when she'd interviewed his parents, her skill impressing him deeply. She was good at her job. What's more, she enjoyed it.

Seeing her in action made him question if she really was miserable in LA. The lifestyle might be lacking, but the work—the spotlight—set her aglow. If she gave it up, could he make her as happy as she'd looked in front of the camera? Or would she feel as miserable and penned-in as his mother?

His jaw clamped. Katie-Lynn wasn't his ma. She was a strong woman who knew her mind. She wouldn't abandon her dreams for him. That wasn't what he was asking...or was it?

She said she wanted a second chance, too. Like all Lovelands, he prided himself on his patience. When it came to Katie-Lynn, though, his fortitude failed him. He wanted to know, now, if they had a shot at happiness. If she left again, she'd take his heart with her. Without her, he'd have no need of it, anyway.

He could follow her to LA...

Cash stumbled slightly as they crested the bluff and emerged atop a tree line. "Whoa, boy," Cole muttered, steadying his paint horse. Katie-Lynn rocked in the saddle as Spirit clamored up and over the edge next.

Compromise. He'd never considered it before, but now he wondered. He'd given her an all-or-nothing ultimatum when they'd been engaged. Had he played a part in driving her away by trying to hold her back? If he hadn't been so adamant about her leaving, maybe things would have worked out between them.

Was he repeating the same mistake this time around?

If you keep doing what you've always done, don't expect a different result...

"That was steeper than it looked," she gasped, once they moved onto the flat-top, needle-covered ground.

He dragged in a gulp of crystalline air: pine, fresh water and the wildflowers coloring the path. "It's no wonder Joy's parents thought Pa reckless for coming here."

A twig snapped behind them. Cole twisted in the saddle, peered at the shadowed brush, then faced front again.

"Did you get a chance to read over the documents J.D. sent over?" The exertion colored Katlynn's face and drops of moisture dotted her brow.

He doffed his hat and waved it in front of his hot face. "Daryl needed my help with the backhoe. Anything interesting about the Crystal River Railroad's grant?"

"It confirmed Maggie's journal account. Shortly before she died, the land grant office issued a letter of intent to audit Clyde's company for 'misappropriation of funds.'"

He sucked in a quick breath. "He'd been skimming money from the grant?"

"Yes. The completed audit proved a large

amount of the grant was not accounted for, the books falsely inflated."

"What'd he do with the money?"

"J.D. wondered that, too. Knowing Clyde was from Chicago, he did some digging and found old tender notes between Clyde and a gambling outfit there."

Cole resettled his hat on his head and pulled the brim low over the strong sun slanting through the pine canopy. "Tenders, as in monies owed?"

"Right. And he was in debt up to his ears. He needed to marry Maggie Cade fast to get her jewel and settle his accounts."

Silence reigned as he digested the information. Clyde had ample reason to force a pregnant Maggie to marry him.

Another crack splintered the quiet. Cole whirled in the saddle but caught only the slightest movement, a flash of brown. Was an animal stalking them? The hairs on the back of his neck rose. A grizzly? He unsnapped the fastener securing his pistol to his saddle.

"An animal?" Katie-Lynn glanced over her shoulder briefly, her hand clenched around the reins.

"Sounds like."

"Grizzlies are hungry in the spring." Katie-Lynn's voice dropped to a whisper. Her face paled.

"Let's pick up the pace." He squeezed Cash's sides, easing him into as fast a trot as he dared with the bluff falling away on either side of them.

"It makes sense now why Clyde moved up the date of the wedding." Katie rode straight-backed beside him. Her eyes darted over her shoulder.

Cash snorted, a trumpeting sound he usually made when he sensed danger. "Easy boy." Cole patted Cash's soft neck.

Spirit nickered in answer. Did he fear a predator? Cole drew his pistol and rested it on his tense thighs.

"The government would have pulled his grant if he failed to return the missing funds. He married a Jane Eleanor Prescott, a whale oil heiress from Maine, shortly after Maggie's death and settled up his account."

"How long did she last?"

"Long enough to give him a son…or someone's, anyway. She actually outlived him." Katie-Lynn eyed Cole's gun. "You think we should stop?"

Cole twisted round in the saddle, spied nothing unusual, then shrugged. "Whatever was following us must have stopped. Besides. We're here."

They dismounted, tied their horses to an oak tree and began scouring the area. No mulberry bushes, Cole noted with disappointment. Or Scotch pines. Maybe Joy's memory had been off?

"For you." Cole picked a flower and tucked

the purple bloom behind Katie-Lynn's ear. Her wide, delighted smile rose to her sparkling eyes.

When he leaned forward, she pressed a hand to his chest, stopping him. "We agreed to focus on this mystery for now."

He slid his hand down the length of her slim arm to tangle with her fingers. "Never said we couldn't have fun while doing it."

Her mock-frown lasted all of two seconds before she broke off laughing. "You're incorrigible."

"Persistent."

She looped her arms around his neck. "An attractive quality in a man."

He slid his arms around her and flattened his palms against her slim back. "Oh, yeah?"

"Yeah." The teasing smile playing on her lips fired him up from head to toe.

A thump to their left sent them stumbling apart. Cole grabbed his gun from the back of his waistband, pushed Katie-Lynn protectively behind him, and peered at the thick, swaying brush. Their short, quick breaths mingled with the soft slap of water twirling against the rocks below.

"Grizzly?" she whispered in his ear, shivering.

"No," he said grimly, nodding at the pair of rabbits chasing each other through ferns. "They'd smell it."

"Mountain lion?"

"I think it's a bigger predator."

"What do you mean?"

"Follow my lead and act normal," he whispered in her ear. "I think someone's following us."

"Well. Don't see any mulberry bushes," he said loudly, wandering closer to the source of the sound.

"And these trees aren't Scotch pines," Katie-Lynn pointed out, nonchalant. If she was nervous or scared, she hid it well.

Not much frightened Katie-Lynn, he thought, pressing his lips together to hold back a grin as she prodded a large stone with her boot, her movement exaggerated. "Though these would make a perfect hiding spot for Cora's Tear."

At a muffled gasp from the bushes, Cole pounced, grabbed a crouching man by the scruff of his neck and hauled him out. "Who are you, and why are you following us?"

Katie-Lynn froze in place, gaping at the man twisting in Cole's grasp.

"I-I'm just out taking a walk." The stranger ducked his head and pulled his hood tighter around his face. "Same as you."

Circling him slowly, Katie-Lynn eyed their captive. She stopped and slipped off his hood. "I know you… You're part of my crew. Jerry Stubbs. A gaffer. But why…?"

Cole's grip loosened in surprise, and the man tore loose.

Stubbs was aptly named. The middle-aged man was no taller than Katie-Lynn, but roughly twice as wide, with a broad, cherubic face, wide blue eyes and a petulant droop to his small mouth.

"Please, Ms. Brennon," Jerry pleaded. "I don't want any trouble."

"Won't be any trouble if you start explaining yourself," Cole growled.

"What's going on, Jerry?" Katie-Lynn prodded gently. "We've known each other a long time. Just last month I was at your daughter's christening. Frances Jean. Such a pretty little girl. Now, tell me why you're following us?"

Jerry's shoulders slumped. "I'm sorry, Ms. Brennon."

"I appreciate that, Jerry, but what I really need is an explanation."

"My wife, she's on unpaid leave and with Frances Jean coming along, money's tight."

Cole opened his mouth to demand Jerry get to the point, spotted Katie-Lynn's sympathetic nod and shut his trap. No one knew how to draw a story from a person better than her.

"I understand," she murmured, her voice soothing. "A man needs to provide for his family. You're in a tight spot."

Jerry's mouth curved into a grateful smile. He

looked ready to throw himself at Katie-Lynn's feet. "When that man offered me money to follow you, I—I said no at first. Then he upped it to triple the amount…and diapers…they're expensive, you know?"

"Very expensive," Katie-Lynn agreed. "And this man…he sounds extremely persuasive. Who did you say it was again?"

"Clyde William something or another. The fourth." Jerry clapped a hand over his mouth and spoke through his fingers. "Wasn't supposed to say his name to anyone."

Shock locked up every joint in Cole's body. Why would Clyde have them followed unless… a dark suspicion took hold.

"You didn't tell just anyone. You told me." Katie-Lynn's friendly smile disguised the surprise she had to be feeling. "What'd he want you to do?"

"First off, I wasn't going through with all of it, push come to shove, so to speak."

Enough.

Cole leaned down, stopping just an inch from Jerry's face. "What were you supposed to do?" he barked—ready to bite.

Jerry shook in his boots. "I-I'm supposed to follow you and report everywhere you go."

Katie-Lynn made a sympathetic noise. "Doesn't sound so bad."

"It gets worse, Ms. Brennon," Jerry sighed.

"Then it's a good thing you're confessing everything now." Katie-Lynn nudged Cole aside to step in between him and Jerry. "Otherwise you'd have lost your job when I reported you. That's the last thing you want given your financial struggles."

Jerry's face turned ashen, and Cole marveled at the genius of Katie-Lynn. She had a way of sneaking up on a person, disarming them, making them believe she was harmless and then, just when your guard was down, *wham*, she blindsided you.

"Since you've decided to do the right thing, though, we'll keep this between us, okay? And the sheriff." Her white-gold hair flowed over her left shoulder as she cocked her head, her expression serene. No sign of the clever mind working fast behind her guileless baby blues…

Jerry jerked his head up and down. "I want to do the right thing."

"Tell us what gets worse, then," Cole demanded, bad cop to Katie-Lynn's good.

"He said you were searching for some old brooch, and if you found it, I was to take it from you and bring it to him." Jerry pulled a handgun from his pocket and passed it over to a wide-eyed Katie-Lynn. "By any means possible."

Cole's gut burned. Clyde William Farthington,

the man who'd been trying to purchase this land from his father, whose ancestors before him had attempted the same, was hunting Cora's Tear... and was prepared to kill Katie-Lynn for it.

"You'll go to the sheriff with this story?" Katie-Lynn asked.

Jerry nodded. "I'm sorry, Ms. Brennon. I wouldn't have gone through with it."

"I believe you."

An hour later they dropped Jerry off at Travis's office, hopped in Cole's truck and headed down the highway to Clyde William Farthington's mansion.

"How does Clyde know Maggie hid Cora's Tear in this area?" Katie-Lynn rested her heels on her seat, circled her arms around her raised knees and dropped her cheek to them.

Cole pressed harder on the accelerator. "Not sure, but we're about to find out."

"I'M AFRAID MR. FARTHINGTON is indisposed," intoned Renata, Clyde's maid, as Katlynn stood beside Cole on the mansion's front steps. "Please check back tomorrow, or, preferably, call first."

When she began to shut the door, Katlynn gripped its jamb, requiring Renata to either crush her fingers or keep the entrance open. "May I beg a favor?"

Think.

How to get in there?

Renata glanced at Katlynn's hand, her upper lip pulled tight in disapproval. Clearly Renata did not like a scene. That could work.

"I'm afraid I'm feeling a bit unwell myself. A long day riding," Katlynn babbled, ignoring Cole's side eye. "Could I trouble you for a glass of water before we go?"

Renata studied Katlynn as she drooped against the doorway, wedging her shoulder in the gap. When push came to shove, no one knew how to gain entry like an investigative reporter.

"I can't imagine what my production company would think, let alone the tabloids, if word got out I fainted here." Katlynn infused her voice with a slight gasping hoarseness. "You know how the paparazzi loves to speculate on pregnancies. They'd drag Mr. Farthington into a crass story for refusing me a glass of water."

Behind her, Cole camouflaged his chuckle with a cough.

Renata sighed and opened the door wider. "Come in." She pointed to the front parlor. "Please wait here."

Her short heels clattered on the black-and-white tiles as she marched away.

"Where is he?" Katlynn turned slowly in a circle. "I'm not leaving without answers."

"That's two of us. Hey. Look." Cole pointed

to a pair of gardening gloves beside a pair of open doors off the parlor leading to an indoor terrarium. The faint strains of opera music floated from the space. "Could be in there."

"Let's check it out."

Humid, moist air smothered them the moment they stepped into the glassed-in space. Katlynn glanced out one of the clear panels; the weather had been sunny for several days but was about to break. Thunder growled in the distance and she could feel the coming rain in the air flowing through an open door that led to an outdoor rose garden.

"Mr. Farthington!" she called, stepping deeper into the room. Potted orchids crowded shelves on either side of the space. They filled the room with a cloying, floral scent.

Cole stopped her with a hand on her arm and a point out into the garden. On a bench amidst bright roses framed by trimmed boxwood hedges, sat Mr. Farthington. White drifted from his mouth as he puffed on a cigar. A wide-brimmed straw hat shaded his face. He appeared to be napping.

Katlynn's chin lifted. No one smoked while they napped. She'd bet her last dollar he was faking. "Mr. Farthington!" She advanced down the white gravel path. Beneath her boots, the hard stones ground against each other. "A moment of your time?"

"I've been expecting you," he said without lifting his lids.

Katlynn's eyes met Cole's and he shrugged, as surprised as she.

With a sigh, Clyde opened his eyes and straightened on the bench. "Won't you have a seat?" he asked, his cigar dangling from his mouth.

The surreal moment seemed to steal sensation from her legs. It felt as though she floated to the bench.

"How did you know we were coming?" Cole demanded, dispensing with the niceties. Her heart swelled at the tough, rugged man, the delicate roses surrounding him only accentuating his masculinity. He wasn't smooth or sophisticated like the men she'd met in LA, but he was a good man, a man of principles, integrity and strength. He didn't waver or equivocate, especially when it came to her, as she'd discovered today. He'd never stopped caring for her and wanted her back...

Clyde removed his cigar from his lips long enough to say, "I received a call from your brother, Sheriff Loveland. Claimed some wild story about me having you followed. Quite ridiculous."

"Is it?" Cole paced forward and loomed over

the gamine man who, in his tan linen suit and expensive loafers, looked as though he'd stepped off a yacht in St. Tropez. Cole's chin jutted. "Whose gun did Jerry have?"

"Who?" Clyde asked, shooing away a curious bee.

Katlynn called on her interviewer skills to study his body language. Despite his off-handed speech, he seemed nervous. His hands were steady as he replaced his cigar in his mouth, but there were lines of strain around his eyes, and his jaw was set in a way at odds with his casual talk. The humid day was warm, but it was not so warm as to justify the slick of sweat at Clyde's temples.

"The man you hired to steal a jewel from us, using any means possible." Katlynn smiled blithely. "I believe that comes with charges of conspiracy to commit grand theft."

"And murder," Cole added, his teeth clenched.

Clyde's face darkened, and his hands fisted at his sides. "You have no proof. A jury wouldn't believe such a crazy story. I'm well-known in this town. My family has a long history here. A reputation."

"So does mine." Cole pointed a finger in Clyde's face.

With Clyde distracted, Katlynn slipped her cell from her pocket, scrolled to Gabe's number, selected text and hit the microphone button to transcribe and record the conversation. She muted the volume to keep them from hearing Gabe.

"Lovelands," Clyde spat, "are white trash. Broke-down cowboys."

Emotions shifted like sea currents beneath Clyde's blotched skin as Katlynn glanced from one man to the other.

"I'd rather be a poor, honest man than a rich thief. *If* you're any kind of a man, tell us why you're having us followed."

Clyde's slit eyes rested on Cole, hard and bright as diamonds. "No one will believe you, anyway."

"Seems my brother's leaning in that direction."

"The infamous Loveland lawmen…a tradition in Carbondale for generations. You think that'll scare me?"

"If it doesn't, you're an idiot."

Katlynn leaned forward and straightened Clyde's tie. "Mr. Farthington, if your family has some connection to Cora's Tear, think of the historical implications. You'd mentioned you were a history buff. This is your chance to make a name for yourself. Surely, your family's part in this Cade-Loveland feud is an important one, an untold story. Let me share it. Imagine the celebrity, the notoriety, you'll gain." She stared directly into his eyes. "The miscommunication with Jerry can be a nonfactor, and Sheriff Loveland will drop the investigation into the attempted murder and grand theft charges."

Clyde paled slightly. "An investigation for attempted murder?"

"Wouldn't you rather the focus be on the past than the present?" she cajoled. "If you're the key to resolving the Cade-Loveland feud, you'll be a hero...not a petty criminal."

In the distance, lightning forked against a gray-purple sky, the charged air electric.

"Which is it, Farthington?" Cole demanded, his arms folded across his chest.

"Mr. Farthington," Renata huffed, appearing in the doorway. "I tried to turn them away, but—"

With a graceful wave of his hand, Clyde dismissed her. "Leave us be, Renata."

"Why has your family been trying to purchase the parcel of land by the bluffs from the Lovelands?"

"We were ordered to."

"By?" Cole demanded.

Clyde sighed. "By Clyde the first. From his deathbed."

"A deathbed confession." Intrigue crackled along Katlynn's spine. She sat ramrod straight, schooling her face to conceal her excitement. At last...the truth. She could smell it.

Clyde nodded. "My ancestor had gotten into a bit of financial trouble and—"

"Siphoning government funds to pay off his gambling debts," Cole interrupted. "We know all about it...and why he moved up the date of his wedding to Maggie. He needed the jewel."

Clyde's hand rose to his chest. "How did you—"

"We're investigators. It's our job," Katlynn replied, firm. When she met Cole's eye, the proud expression he wore squeezed her heart.

"One you appear to be quite good at," Clyde mused, recovered from his shock. "I see I have no choice but to tell you everything."

"Beginning with?" Katlynn prompted. Open-ended queries loosened up reluctant subjects. As if to punctuate her question, lightning forked, quicksilver, in the distance. The air swarmed around her, pressing.

"Before he died, Clyde begged his oldest son, in confidence, to continue his lifelong search for Cora's Tear." Clyde dropped his cigar to the ground and squashed its glowing tip with his shoe. "It was promised to him as part of Maggie Cade's dowry and, by rights, belonged to him."

"Not her family?" Katlynn prodded gently.

Clyde pulled a monogrammed handkerchief from his breast pocket and dabbed at his glistening forehead. "It was part of the betrothal agreement."

"But she died before they were married," Cole insisted.

"Yes. Unfortunate." Clyde waved the white cloth, dismissing Cole's claim, before pocketing it again.

"Indeed." Katlynn signaled Cole with her eyes to let her take the lead. He put Clyde on the defensive. Even the worst villains didn't see themselves as the bad guy. The trick was to make them believe you understood their point of view and would portray it on the show sympathetically. "I imagine your ancestor must have been quite desperate when he was informed of the railroad's audit."

Clyde heaved an aggrieved sigh. "He would have resolved the matter had his fiancée not been a simpleton."

"How do you mean?"

"Taking up with another man," Clyde sniffed. "A penniless younger son."

"Maggie?" Katlynn rounded her mouth, aping surprise.

Clyde leaned forward and patted her knee. "Oh, yes. She was sleeping with a Loveland." Clyde's glance flitted dismissively over Cole, who now stood as still as a statue. "Everett Loveland."

"But how would he have known that?" Katlynn asked with just the right amount of breathless anticipation. "Seems like Maggie would have been too clever to flaunt such a tawdry romance..."

"Indeed." Clyde nodded at her approvingly. "My ancestor knew better than to trust an uneducated, ungrateful minx. He had her followed, discovered their trysts and arranged to send Everett away with a job offer."

"He worked for the Crystal River Railroad," Cole said.

"With him out of the way, he could persuade the young woman to see the error of her ways." Clyde uncrossed his legs and leaned forward, his elbows on his knees.

"Only she didn't come to her senses, correct?" Katlynn angled her body sideways to maintain eye contact, her connection with Clyde. "She continued to care only for Everett."

Clyde nodded. "Correct. A silly, useless girl."

"She could have had it all," Katlynn mused aloud. "Money. A position in society, a name people recognized. She wasn't sufficiently grateful for Mr. Farthington's attention."

"She deserved what she got," Clyde muttered, low.

"Say that again," Cole growled.

Clyde's shoulders hunched. Thunder rumbled, low and deep. Closer now. "Her death was her own fault."

"Not Everett's?" Katlynn prompted. The unspoken truth swelled in the space between them as surely as the water ballooning the dark clouds overhead.

Clyde studied his hands as they twisted in his lap. "No."

"But many believed Everett killed her...unless you know something no one else does."

Clyde glanced at her sharply, and she held her breath, watching as he calculated his next response.

"A secret so explosive you'll become a household name for sharing it?" she prompted, dangling the bait.

Clyde's lids lowered. "You're a clever one, I'll give you that."

"Excuse me?" Disappointment curled tight inside Katlynn. She'd nearly had him on the hook. Now he was pulling away.

"You're trying to trick me into a confession."

"If you don't confess to me, then Ultima Productions will demand one," she pronounced, switching tactics, reading her subject. "When they take you to court for threatening the life of one of its stars."

A trio of sparrows swooped low over the hedges to land on a birdfeeder, twittering in the sudden, tense silence.

"Are you threatening me, Ms. Brennon?" Clyde asked coldly.

"Merely reminding you of the facts." She lifted her chin, meeting his haughty stare. Matching it. In this moment she wasn't speaking to him as a star. She was Katie-Lynn Brennon, a simple girl from Carbondale, Colorado, who deserved and demanded answers about her small town's worst unsolved crime.

"Clyde visited her the night before the wedding and spied her sneaking away," Clyde intoned, speaking as slowly as a funeral dirge. "He confronted her on the bluffs. When she admitted to running away to marry Everett, he insisted on knowing the whereabouts of the jewel or he wouldn't free her."

"Insisted?" Menace now darkened Cole's voice.

"Wouldn't he have known the location since he'd had her followed?" Katlynn asked.

"Alas, his hired man suffered a fatal heart attack before showing Clyde the spot, though he'd described the general area."

"The land your family's been trying to purchase to conduct your own searches." Katlynn pulled her shirt collar from her damp neck. Beneath her clothes, her body felt slick. Clammy.

"Yes," Clyde said, impatient. "We've gone over this before."

"Let's get back to Maggie, then." Cole rested

the tip of his boot on the bench leg and leaned closer to Clyde.

"She proved to be quite a fighter." Clyde sank back in the bench, putting as much distance between himself and an encroaching Cole as possible. "She struck Clyde. When he grabbed her, merely to restrain her since she was becoming quite hysterical, she stumbled out of reach and fell off the bluff."

Cole's eyes, dark with horror and shock, clicked with hers for an electric moment. Astonishment and dismay vied for a place in Katlynn's chest with a certain feeling of satisfaction. The truth—at last.

"Clyde killed Maggie Cade."

Clyde, the fourth, shook his head. "It was an accident, of course."

"All of Clyde's women died in accidents," Cole insisted. "That's no coincidence."

"Well... I..." Clyde sputtered.

"So why didn't he tell the authorities?" Katlynn asked, sounding as offhand as possible to get Clyde to relax again.

"He heard hooves approaching and hid when he spied the man who'd tried to steal his intended."

"Everett," Cole breathed. His nostrils flared.

Clyde nodded. "The Cades arrived a moment later searching for Maggie. When they spotted

Everett with her, they assumed he killed her and strung him up."

"And Clyde didn't try to stop it?" Katlynn jumped in to ask, beating a red-faced Cole.

"And implicate himself?" Clyde gave a short, dismissive laugh. "Why would he do that?"

"Because it's the right thing to do." Cole paced before the bench now, his hands tightly clasped behind his back. "The honest thing."

Lightning cracked, near enough to make Katlynn jump. She'd suggest they head inside, but it'd break the spell. The Cade-Loveland feud, solved at last. Exaltation mingled with anticipation. Joy and Boyd would be delighted by the news and have the wedding they deserved... and she'd have unraveled one of America's longest unsolved mysteries, elevating her and her show. If she was planning to leave LA for Cole, it shouldn't matter, but it did. It did. This was a possible Emmy-winning scoop, the culmination of her life's work. It'd be hard to turn her back on it.

"The right thing?" Clyde scoffed. "Such bourgeois sentiments. Maggie was dead regardless, and Everett...his hanging saved him from a meaningless existence."

"Your ancestor did them a favor, as you see it?" Katlynn pressed, covering up her distaste.

"Maggie's death was regrettable, I imagine, but Everett's...well..."

"Didn't matter," Cole bit out.

Clyde shrugged. "Cora's Tear belonged to my ancestor until Everett tried stealing a woman and dowry that didn't belong to him."

"But her heart was Everett's. That's more valuable than a thousand Cora's Tears," Katlynn said, her eyes on Cole.

"Sentimental mishmash." Clyde retrieved another cigar from the box beside him and patted his pockets in search of a lighter. "Would have thought that beneath you, Ms. Brennon. In any case, my family has sought the jewel ever since."

"The jewel doesn't belong to your family," Cole insisted through clenched teeth.

"It was rightfully ours."

Katlynn raised her eyebrows. "And you killed to get it."

"Now...see here, Ms. Brennon."

Katlynn held up her recording cell phone and unmuted the volume. "Did you get all that, Gabe?"

"Every word," her director gasped. "Tell Mr. Farthington we'll be sending our representatives tomorrow with a contract."

Clyde's scowl smoothed, and a pleased light entered his eye. "A contract? Will I be in the episode?"

"You'll be its star," Gabe assured the odious man. "Next to Katlynn, of course."

"No. I'm happy to let Mr. Farthington shine," she demurred, her eyes on Cole. "Stardom has lost its appeal lately."

A stunned smile transformed his rugged face to breathtaking handsomeness. They had much to celebrate after finding a way to bring peace to the families at last.

If only she wasn't still at war with herself...

CHAPTER FOURTEEN

COLE CHEWED SLOWLY on a tender spare rib, half listening as Heath's guitar twanged inside Shorty's outdoor dining tent. Contentment filled him as he watched Joy and Pa swap bites from each other's plates. The sweet-smoky scent of hickory barbecue drifted in on the cool evening air and mingled with the children's shouts. Cade grandkids chased his brother Daryl's son and daughter around cloth-covered tables formed into a horseshoe perimeter for tonight's rehearsal dinner.

So far everyone behaved themselves. Even Justin had shot him a half smile when Cole and Katie-Lynn arrived at the church to practice for tomorrow's wedding. With little time for big announcements about Clyde's revelations, he'd simply taken his place in the wedding party, amazed the rehearsal and now the dinner went off without a hitch.

Cole spied Katie-Lynn at the end of a table, speaking animatedly with Brielle Thompson. Katie-Lynn exclaimed over the sparkling engagement ring Justin gave Brielle recently, and Cole pictured the small, heart-shaped ring still in his nightstand drawer. Was it too small for Katie-Lynn now? Was the life he offered her?

Justin ambled up behind Brielle and pressed a kiss to her shoulder. Hard to believe a man with a death wish like him had turned his life around for a woman.

Love did strange things to a man.

Changed him.

Was Cole changing? He'd stopped being a complete hermit while investigating with Kat-lynn…but was it enough to win her back? He still preferred obscurity and she wanted the spotlight.

At Amberley's shoulder tap, Katie-Lynn turned and embraced the legally blind barrel-racer. The right person motivated you the way Jared Cade inspired his wife, Amberley. He'd refused to let her give up her dreams of touring with a professional rodeo group. In fact, he'd stopped playing pro football to manage her career.

Love meant making a sacrifice.

Katie-Lynn's pretty face glowed beneath lantern lights swinging from the tent poles. Jared joined the women and slung an arm around Amberley. Was Jared happy after giving up the Broncos? Did he regret the sacrifice? Resent his wife?

Love shouldn't be conditional.

True.

Katie-Lynn said she no longer cared about being a star. Had she decided to come home to him? Tonight, he'd take her to their Say Anything tree. They'd vowed to speak only the truth there. He'd listen, hoping they'd reach some sort of compromise.

Heath transitioned into a slow song, prompting Jared to sweep Amberley into his arms and waltz her in the space between the tables. James, Sofia and Javi joined them, swaying together, too, James's daughter, Jesse, dozing on her father's shoulder. Cole smiled at the domestic scene, imagining himself as a dad, Katie-Lynn by his side. A glimpse of Daryl's sullen wife, refusing his younger brother when he entreated her to dance, sobered Cole. Daryl ducked his head as he stalked away, but not so fast Cole missed the defeat on his face. His poor brother. It killed Cole to see Daryl miserable.

"When should we tell them?" Katie-Lynn whispered in his ear, making him jump. She pulled out the empty chair next to him and sat. Her eyes danced, her grin infectious.

"After dessert?"

Katie-Lynn followed his gaze to the tower of slightly tilted, mismatched cupcakes Sofia baked for the event. "They're going to be thrilled. I still can't believe we solved the feud. I suppose it hardly matters if we find Cora's Tear now."

Cole rubbed his lightly bristled jaw. "We've been hating each other for no reason."

"What a waste."

"Misunderstandings shouldn't keep people apart." Cole reached for Katie-Lynn's hand and cradled it.

She pressed her palm to his, laced their fingers together and squeezed. "I agree."

"Since we've solved this mystery…" He probed her eyes, gauging her mood.

Her gaze fled his, and she withdrew her hand. "Right. We need to talk about us."

"Is that a bad thing?" His heart throbbed painfully in his chest. Was she going to reject him? He steeled himself.

"No." Her cheeks blew out with the force of her exhale. "It's just a lot to figure out all at once."

His stalled lungs burned. "Pa said love was more a feeling than a knowing."

"I—"

Katie-Lynn cut off at the arrival of a stooped man in a familiar tweed suit. He leaned heavily on his cane, flanked by J.D. What was Peter Stockton doing here? When Cole and his siblings last spoke with him, Mr. Stockton agreed to prepare the filing to appeal the easement decision and sue for restitution.

"Uh-oh," Katie-Lynn gasped. "You don't think—"

"No." Cole watched as Mr. Stockton leaned down to ask a question of Javi, James's son, who, in turn, pointed out his father. "He's not supposed to serve papers until after the wedding."

A familiar camera crew appeared. Dread formed like a cannonball in Cole's stomach and then exploded.

He must have made a noise because Katie-Lynn now gripped his arm. "Cole. I swear. I have no idea why they're here."

He slanted her a quick, assessing look. "Who invited them?"

"Not me."

To Cole's horror, J.D. handed James a thick envelope with an official-looking mark on the front. Pa rose from his seat, took Joy by the hand, and joined the group. Cole and Katie-Lynn hurried over, as well, along with the rest of the family. Heath quit playing and a heavy silence descended.

"James Cade?" asked J.D., looking straight into the camera. He'd teased his blond poof to gravity-defying heights and wore a sleeveless muscle shirt highlighting Katie-Lynn's tattoo.

"What's this about?" Pa demanded.

"I'm James Cade." A muscle flickered in

James's jaw. "You'd better have a good reason for interrupting a family get-together."

"Gabe, why are you filming?" Katie-Lynn demanded. Her director waved off her comment.

"Stop. This is a mistake," Cole thundered, fully gleaning the men's purpose. Cold, hard dread coiled in his gut.

"Is this a bad time? Oh, dear," Mr. Stockton said. "Forgive me. When J.D. suggested we serve the court summons here, I thought it odd, but he assured me…"

"What did you do?" Katie-Lynn gestured between J.D. and her crew. "Did you contact my show about Cole's plans?"

J.D. hung his head. "When a production assistant stopped in for some research, I mentioned the lawsuit. Then Gabe contacted me and…well…he said I'd be on *Scandalous History*!"

"That's no excuse to ambush people and hurt their lives," Katlynn fired back. Anger blew off her in waves of heat. She had nothing to do with this media stunt, clearly. "Cameras off, Gabe, or I'll quit, and you'll miss the biggest scoop of your career."

Gabe signaled the cameraman to stop and backed up a step. "You've got something better?"

"Yes. Why didn't you run this by me first?"

Gabe shrugged. "I make the calls."

"We're supposed to be a team."

"What are the summonses about?" James demanded, chin jutting. "Are you suing us?"

"Not at the moment," Cole admitted.

James tore open the envelope and the group collectively held its breath as he scanned the documents. A moment later he lowered them, his face a thundercloud.

"Lowlife Lovelands," James stormed. "Suing us for damages caused by some easement denial none of us has ever heard of?"

"I assure you it's quite real," proclaimed Mr. Stockton. He filled them in on the easement's litigation history.

A babble of angry voices rose when he finished.

"Quiet!" thundered Cole's father. The group hushed. "Cole. Did you do this?"

He hung his head slightly. "Yes."

"And you hired an ambulance chaser to sue the Cades without telling me?" Pa turned to Mr. Stockton. "No offense meant."

Pete Stockton lifted his chin. "None taken."

"The timing wasn't right to include you." Cole pressed his lips together as regret swelled, threatening to suffocate him.

"Who else knew?" Pa stared at his sheepish offspring. "You've all been keeping this from me?"

"We didn't want to cause a problem before the wedding, Pa," Sierra entreated.

"Too late," growled Justin, ripping the papers out of his brother's hand. "Says here you're suing us for access to our land and five million dollars in damages."

An angry howl erupted from the Cade clan.

"Now, now," Joy soothed. "Boyd won't allow such a thing. We're going to be one family now. Right, Boyd?"

Pa stared at his children then back at Joy, the lines around his mouth deepening. "All this time, we should have had access to the Crystal River?"

"The termination of the easement ruling was a travesty of justice," Mr. Stockton proclaimed.

"Boyd," Joy pleaded. "Please assure me of your intentions."

Pa's features scrunched in fierce concentration. "Understand, Joy. We're about to lose Loveland Hills. I want no part of restitution payouts, but if the easement was returned, we'd have a viable future."

Joy gasped as if she'd been struck. "Boyd Franklin Loveland. Are you allowing this case to proceed?"

"I won't lose my land. It's my family's legacy."

"But you're willing to lose me?" Joy's pained expression pierced Cole, straight through the heart.

"It doesn't have to be that way," Pa entreated.

"You said I was worth a thousand ranches," Joy said, brokenly.

Pa reached out his hand. "Joy…"

"You're not trespassing on our land," James interjected. Firm. Hard.

"Trespassers will be shot," Justin growled.

Jared folded his arms across his chest. "There are valid reasons we'll block you."

"Cattle interbreeding?" Cole challenged, recalling the issues raised in the old lawsuit. "That'd weaken our herd, too. Experienced ranch hands know how to keep the herds apart, unless you're saying *you're* not up to the job."

Jared grabbed Justin's cocked fist in midair.

"Your operation's going under," drawled James with aggravating self-control. "Not ours."

Daryl shoved to the front, teeth bared. "Because we've been denied water access."

"What about your cattle trampling our fences, huh?" Jewel thrust her freckled face between her brothers'. Her expression momentarily softened when she met Heath's stare. The color between her freckles filled in—pink. "Just last year your cattle took down one of our lines, and we lost twenty head."

"We've been investigating a cattle-rustling case in the area," Travis interjected.

"A convenient cover," James grumbled.

"Are you calling us cattle thieves now?" Cole's fists clenched.

"My family deserves an apology," Pa said, low and intent.

"I'd ask for the same if I thought you'd give it," Joy replied, her color high. "Why'd we think this would ever work?"

Pa grabbed the back of a chair. "What are you saying?"

"Our families will always be on opposite sides. And I'm glad Mr. Stockton served us sooner rather than after—" Her voice caught. When Pa reached for her hand, she jerked it away. "After we made the biggest mistake of our lives."

With that, Joy fled the tent, her family hot on her heels.

"Go to her, Pa." Sierra tugged at their father's arm. "Hurry."

Pa dragged in a deep, ragged breath. "No. She's right. We were stupid to think we'd bridge our divide. I won't let my ancestors' ranch go under if I have a chance to turn things around. It's my duty. And a man has his pride. Joy deserves better than a bankrupt, homeless ex-rancher."

"But what about love?"

At Sierra's question, Pa blinked up at the tented ceiling. "Was an old fool for thinking I'd find it this late in life. Love's not in the cards for everyone, no matter how much we wish otherwise."

Cole's throat constricted. He'd gone and done the one thing he'd vowed to prevent: hurt his father and ruined his wedding. "Sorry, Pa."

Pa's glistening eyes met Cole's. "It's okay, son. We've always been alike. You did what I would have done—looked out for your family. For your heritage. Can't fault you for that."

After Sierra escorted their slump-shouldered father to the parking lot, Cole flicked his gaze to Katie-Lynn, who was now deep in conversation with her director.

Was he like his pa?

Was love not in the cards for him, either?

He and his father were both stubborn. By not compromising, he'd driven Katie-Lynn away just as his pa lost Joy. Watching Katie-Lynn doggedly solve an old mystery proved she was good at her job. He'd been wrong to hold her back in the past…but what about now? Could they find a way to compromise?

His father's and Joy's breakup reinforced the need to find a way to compromise or he'd lose Katie-Lynn again.

This time forever.

He didn't want to be alone any longer, even if it meant being part of Katie-Lynn's world, but how?

"WHERE ARE WE GOING?" Katlynn pleaded when Cole's horse, carrying them both, plunged down a slope early the next morning. The inside of her bitten cheek stung. "And can I remove the blindfold?"

"Nope." Cole's deep voice, spoken directly into her ear, sent shivers of awareness dancing down her spine.

She leaned back against the hard planes of his chest. Arms of steel bracketed her body as he guided them to an unknown spot. Why the secrecy about their destination? He'd woken her before dawn, giving her only a minute to dress and meet him outside. She'd forgotten this spontaneous, romantic side of him. Was he taking her somewhere special to discuss their second chance...one he wanted on his terms?

Could she agree to them?

A knot twisted the sensitive muscles of her stomach. The tantalizing scent of Cole, leather and a dash of spice on clean male skin, did little to settle her. She'd promised to talk about next steps once they solved the Cade-Loveland mystery. If she and Cole had shared the news last night, would the wedding still be on today? Everything fell apart so suddenly, she hadn't even informed her film crew yet, hoping Boyd and Joy might still reconcile. With the wedding set to start at 2:00 p.m., though, the chances of their happily-ever-after were dwindling fast.

Katlynn exhaled a quivering breath as she pictured Boyd's stricken face and Joy's tears. Boyd claimed they'd been foolish to try again, insisting some differences couldn't be breached.

Did the sentiment apply to her and Cole, too?

She swayed with Cole as Cash scrambled up another incline, relishing the feel of Cole's arms wrapped around her. No one made her feel this way. Protected. Cherished. Like she belonged.

Was it enough?

She wanted things to be different for them this time around…

"How much longer?" she asked.

"I'll tell you when we get there," he drawled, sounding more amused than annoyed.

"You're an aggravating man, Cole Loveland."

"Happy to return the compliment, Katie-Lynn Brennon."

He answered her giggle with a deep chuckle that rumbled through her. All around rose the twitter of waking birds accompanied by rustling branches overhead. They must be in a wooded grove based on the thick balsam scent she breathed. Cool air, fresh scrubbed from yesterday's rainfall, fanned her flushed cheeks. "I'm sorry about what happened."

Cole's muscles tensed. "It's not your fault. I should have told Pa about the case."

"You were trying to save the ranch."

Cole's long exhale blew past her cheek. "But I broke his heart doing it."

"He let Joy go. *He* chose the ranch."

She strained to hear his response but only the *clip-clop* of Cash's hooves reached her ears. "Cole?"

"Yeah."

"What are you thinking about?"

"How lonely Pa's going to be again." The sad note in Cole's voice tolled inside her, a hollow sound. Was he thinking of himself, too? Of them? "I've seen Pa happy before, but with Joy…he was someone else."

"How was he different?"

"He was…complete." Cole pressed a feather-light kiss to the crown of her head then rested his chin atop it. "You make me feel that way, too. Whole."

"Cole," she gasped, touched to the marrow of her bones.

"I reckon everyone's born with a part of them missing," he mused, his voice a deep rasp. "The person you love is the piece you spend your life looking for. Some'll never find it. Others won't recognize it. Worst is when you don't hold on to that person when you're lucky enough to find them."

She turned slightly in the saddle and slipped

an arm around his lean waist, holding tight. "I'm glad we found each other again."

With the reins in one hand, he linked his fingers with hers. "I'm not letting you go without a fight." He brought Cash to a halt. "You're my missing piece."

He slid off the horse and large hands gripped her waist. As he lowered her to her feet, she clung to his strong forearms. He dropped a kiss against her cheek, then her eyelids through the bandanna, while she tried to control her pounding heart. "Can I take this off?" She touched her bandanna's knot.

"Not yet." He curved a hand around the nape of her neck.

She started to speak, but his lips found hers. Her mouth parted on a gasp as he kissed her tenderly as if she was the most treasured thing on earth. Her blood sang. Her soul soared. Euphoria.

His arms tightened around her, crushing her against his chest. With each breath they took, the other seemed to inhale. Their chests rose; their hearts pounded. Little shivers shot through her when he deepened the kiss, stealing her air.

His fingers dug into her neck in a firm hold. Blindfolded, she wasn't prepared for the intensity of his kiss, but she quickly caught up, her other senses heightened without her vision. Her lips parted under his onslaught, and a strangled, needful sound rose up to break the silence.

As the force of his kiss tilted her backward over his arm, her body sparked to life and her heart swelled and thundered. The rush of sensations crawling across her body was maddening and beautiful and scary-intense. She skimmed her fingertips over the soft, clipped hair at the back of his neck. His skin was warm and smooth under her clenching fingers.

Cole's lips left hers, and he breathed fast and harsh as though he'd run right up Mount Sopris. When he spoke, his voice was hoarse as he pressed his forehead against hers. "You undo me. You have no idea how you undo me."

He gripped her hips, bringing them closer. When he kissed her again, it was that deep, scorching kind that pushed her to the edge of the cliff. She was ready to jump off headfirst, to finally feel everything for Cole she'd denied herself since she'd returned home.

Her fingers skimmed over his broad shoulders then lower to dig into the taut skin of his biceps as his free hand slid down her back. Time slowed to a crawl and his mouth never left hers, his lips soaking up her responses like he was starved for water. She felt glorious. Alive. Better than under a million spotlights, before a million viewers… swimming in raw sensation.

The kiss felt incredible—amazing—and it made her think of what she'd lose if she returned to LA, how lonely she'd be without Cole, her missing piece.

His lips pulled away and his body shook against hers.

She wondered what he was thinking, but he tugged off the bandanna before she could ask. Their eyes met, and something seemed to fracture in his gaze. In that moment she knew exactly what romance was. Romance was the look in Cole's eyes, the connection they'd been fighting tooth and nail.

She mentally raised a white flag. Waved it hard.

"Do you recognize where we are?"

Huh? She couldn't focus on anything but Cole… Still, she forced her eyes off his handsome face and peered around them. Mulberry bushes circled the small clearing. A pair of Scotch pines sprang from the edge of a bluff. Closer still loomed a familiar gnarled oak.

"Our Say Anything tree!"

Cole leaned in and stole another kiss. When their lips parted, her eyes remained closed. "Figured it'd be a good place to talk."

Excitement shoved away her nerves. "Think we can still climb it?"

"Only one way to find out."

Cole tied up Cash, boosted her up onto a lower limb and began ascending behind her.

"I forgot how beautiful it is up here!" she called down to him, pausing to watch the sun's golden orb break across the pink horizon.

Fingers of light probed the valley at their feet. Rays gilded the majestic peaks in the distance and illuminated the sea of trees waving below. There was a magical quality to a Colorado Rockies' sky that stirred something in her. The sky was bluer than blue, the air fresher. Cleaner. She'd forgotten how heights like this exhilarated her. At this elevation, the weight of her life, her troubles, her worries, dropped away, sandbags cut from a rising balloon.

"I haven't." Cole lowered himself onto the thick branch, his back against the trunk. Gripping her hand, he guided her down in front of him so their legs dangled in the air, swinging. His strong arms wrapped around her. They made her feel feminine and safe against his powerful breadth.

She angled her face and caught his stare. "You're not even looking at the view."

"I'm looking at you. There's nothing else I'd rather pay attention to."

She planted a kiss on his lightly stubbled chin. "It feels so good to be back home." The wind flowed more briskly up here, swaying the smaller branches overhead. "And didn't we used to climb higher than this?" she asked.

Cole peered up. "Yep."

"Guess we were more agile then."

"Or had less sense."

She laughed. "True. But I like this spot. Let's carve our initials in it. Leave our mark."

He swept her hair from her shoulder and dropped his chin to it, snuggling her close. The warmth of his body seeped through the thin cotton of her shirt. "You're so beautiful. I haven't been able to think of anything but you since you came home."

Her cheeks flushed as he lowered his lips to her neck and trailed kisses to the sensitive skin just beneath her ear.

She ran a hand through her hair. "I'm sure I look a mess. I didn't have a chance to brush my hair, put on makeup—"

"You look like heaven to me, Katlynn."

The sound of his deep, raspy voice sent her heart careening in her chest. She closed her eyes and gripped his knees. "You called me Katlynn."

His mouth was working magic on the curve of her neck, sending goose bumps down her arms.

"Watching you at work, seeing your professional side," he murmured against the hollow at the base of her throat. Her pulse throbbed. "It's impressive. You're good at your job. Guess I'm getting used to Katlynn."

"Can you care for her?" She twisted around to better see his face.

"I love her," he said simply. He looked down at her with a smile so genuine and full of emotion that it stole her breath.

"I—I love you, too."

Joy exploded on his face. "You make me so happy." He took her in a needful kiss, leaving her weak-kneed and giddy. Her mind spun a dozen ridiculous what-if fantasies.

What if they got married like she'd wanted? A big wedding, full of friends and family, one where they'd broadcast their love, not keep it only to themselves like he'd wanted... And then what if they had kids? Two. No. Three. And a dog... Cole would ranch and she—she'd do what? Her happy thoughts wobbled. Raise children? Keep house? Those were important responsibilities, and extremely rewarding, but somewhere, deep down, a sense of claustrophobia squeezed the thought. Would such an insular world be enough?

"God, I missed you," Cole murmured against her temple when their lips drew apart. "Every day you were gone was a drop down a dark well."

Years of longing and regret brewed in her belly. "I missed you, too."

"We're soul mates." He rested the side of his

head atop hers when she faced forward again. "Destined to be together. The only question is how?"

She opened her mouth to say she'd quit, move home, but only silence, soft as bats' wings, flew out.

"You can say anything here," Cole prompted, the vulnerable note entering his voice squeezing her heart. "Remember?"

She nodded. "No judging."

"No arguing," Cole added, listing another rule for their special spot.

"No repeating what we say to anyone else."

Another wind gust ruffled their hair and Cole pulled her closer still, shielding her. "And always telling the truth. Even the hard ones. So, say anything…Katlynn."

She stared out into the glowing valley. "The problem is I don't know what to say. I don't know what the answers are."

"Could you be happy here?" Cole cleared his throat. "You said you didn't care about being a star anymore."

"I don't—but I still love my work."

"And you're good at it."

"Maybe I'll be better at loving you."

"But would you be truly happy?"

She hesitated, and his leg muscles clenched beneath her hand.

"Katie-Lynn," he prodded. "Say anything."

"This is where we broke up." She forced the words over the lump rising in her throat. "Where I gave you back the ring." The pretty, heart-shaped diamond flashed in her memory then winked back into darkness. How it'd hurt to give it up. "That was the worst day of my life."

She felt Cole tense behind her. "Mine, too."

"I don't want to leave you again."

"Then don't."

"It's not that easy. People depend on me. Plus, I still have twelve months on my contract. What if I asked you to give up the ranch and move to LA to be with me?"

"My family's here. There's nothing for me in California."

She gasped. "I'd be there."

"But…" His voice trailed off.

"That's not enough," she finished for him, sadly.

"It's just different. You'd be coming back to your home. To your family. I'd be leaving those things. I can't quit the ranch when it's on the verge of bankruptcy, not when we finally have a chance to turn it around and save it."

"I'd be leaving a career I've worked hard to build," she countered. "I don't care about being a star anymore, but I still love journalism. It's selfish to ask me to make all the changes."

He drew in a harsh breath as if she'd slapped him. "I only want to make you happy."

"But on your terms. What would you be giving up?"

Silence swelled between them, filled with unspoken words, unnamed emotions and incomplete thoughts.

"What do you want me to do, Katie-Lynn?" Cole's voice broke. "You want me to be a concrete cowboy? Maybe I could be an extra in a Western movie? A stuntman?"

She dropped her head in her hands. "I don't know," she groaned. "I just want to make this work between us."

Cole gently pried her fingers from her face, tipped her chin up and kissed her cheek. "Then we will. I don't want what happened to Pa and Joy happening to us. They refused to compromise, and it ruined their happiness. To lose the love of your life is bad the first time… A second time means losing everything. Even hope."

"We won't let that happen," she whispered.

He stood, grabbed on to a branch above them with one hand and helped her to her feet. She tucked herself against him as his free arm wrapped around her. "We'll find a way to compromise," he vowed, fierce.

"Love always does. Or should." The vision of Boyd and Joy, cuddled on the couch during the interview, returned to her, sharp and sweet. "And we need to figure out how to get Joy and your dad back together. A grand gesture…"

Cole stared out at the yellow-rose sky. "We could get the siblings and the Cades together and call a truce…a permanent one this time?"

A short laugh escaped her as she climbed down the tree. "Middle East peace would be easier to negotiate."

Once on the ground, they trekked through shadows to Cash.

"Ouch!" Cole hollered beside her, grabbing his foot.

"Did you hit something?"

"That old spring cover." Cole rubbed his toe. "Remember it? I should have been on the lookout considering how many times one of us tripped over it in the past."

"Cole." She dug her nails into his arm, a hunch seizing her. "Covers are put on springs when they dry up, right?"

"Right. Why?"

"This could have been a natural spring back in Maggie and Everett's day, right?"

In the weak light, she discerned scarred rocks and younger tree growth, evidence water had once run here.

Cole's eyes glittered. "That's a possibility…and since it's capped, it wouldn't have been marked on our survey map. Are you thinking this could be Maggie and Everett's spot?"

"Columbine's growing here."

"There's mulberry bushes."

"And Scotch pines over there."

Her heartbeat drummed in her ears as they edged toward the bluff and stopped beneath the towering trees.

"Feel this!" Cole pressed her hand against grooves cut into a scaly trunk.

She traced the faint marks, four letters and a heart. Her mouth dropped open.

"You feel it?" Cole asked, urgent, his voice electric.

"E.L. and M.C.… Everett Loveland and Maggie Cade! This is their tree." For some crazy reason, tears sprang to her eyes and she laughed, not from amusement, but from pure, unadulterated joy. This. These moments of incredible discovery were why she loved her job. And sharing it with Cole made it all the sweeter. "It's their Say Anything spot. All this time…they were right here with us. It's got to be a sign." She threw her arms around Cole's neck. "It also says *forever*."

"Where? I didn't feel that…"

She pressed his hand to her heart. "Yes, you do. Right here."

He captured her lips then in a brief, electric kiss, his mouth curved in a smile when he pulled back. "Now I feel it." Then he nearly yanked her off her feet. "Come on!"

"Where?" she gasped, hustling.

"Back to the ranch for shovels." When they reached Cash, Cole lifted her effortlessly into the saddle, swung himself up behind her and directed Cash back down the path.

"Can't it wait until I get my crew? A backhoe?" she asked.

"Not if we're going to find Cora's Tear in time."

"In time for what?"

"To make a grand gesture." Cole lightly kicked Cash, urging him on. "We're going to save the wedding…"

CHAPTER FIFTEEN

"WHAT ARE *YOU* doing here?" Justin Cade snarled through his screen door three hours later.

Perspiration trickled down Cole's cheek beneath the intense noon sun. He counted backward from ten and relaxed his grip on the hat he mangled in his hands. He was on enemy territory... "My pa's come to speak to Joy."

Justin snorted. "Ain't happening."

Cole laid his hand on the doorjamb and leaned close to the wire mesh separating them. "You've got two choices, Cade. Open the door or get out of the way when I open it for you."

"Or what?"

"You'll be flattened," Cole calmly vowed. Justin was scrappy, but Cole had him by three inches and twenty pounds.

"Go on." Justin propped his shoulder on the door, crossed his arms over his chest and cocked an eyebrow. "I need a good laugh."

"Who's here?" Joy's worried frown eased into a faint smile when she spied Cole. "Oh. Cole. Morning. Would you like some coffee?"

"Thank you." Cole shot Justin a triumphant grin and strolled inside. A pouch holding Cora's Tear burned in his pocket. Finding it with Katie-Lynn an hour ago, buried beside Maggie and Everett's Scotch pine, hadn't fully sunk in yet. "Brought someone else with me, if it's not too much trouble." Boyd and Katie-Lynn mounted the stairs behind him.

"Not at all…" Joy's voice trailed off when she turned from the coffeemaker, spied Boyd and dropped an entire bin of ground beans on the tiled floor. "Oh!" she gasped and crouched to clean up the mess.

"Let me help," Boyd said softly, joining her.

Joy flicked red-rimmed eyes his way then down again, nodding. With quick, efficient strokes, Boyd scooped up the mess as Joy mopped the last remaining bits.

"Thank you," she whispered when Boyd held out a hand for the mop.

"Joy, I—"

Her head shake stopped Pa's entreaty. "There's nothing left to say."

"Outta here, Lovelands," Justin growled. "Ma doesn't want to talk to you."

"Boyd's not the only one who's got something to say," Cole stated, firm. "Katie-Lynn and I have news."

"You're getting married?" Sofia, James's wife,

asked as she strolled into the kitchen holding Javi's hand. His hair stuck up every which way and his eyelids drooped at half-mast.

"No," Katie-Lynn answered, fast. Too fast... They'd vowed to find a way to work things out. To compromise. Was she having second thoughts?

"Pregnant, then?" teased James as he entered the kitchen, his pink-clad daughter in his arms. His smile disappeared when he spied Cole and Boyd. "What are you doing here?"

"Yeah!" Jewel stomped into the room. "Ma's been crying all night because of you."

"I'm sorry, darlin'." Boyd squatted beside Joy's chair. "I never meant to hurt you."

Joy nodded but refused to lift her eyes from her lap.

"Let's all take a seat." Cole pulled out chairs for Katie-Lynn and Sofia. Jewel spun hers around and straddled it, glaring up at him.

"I prefer to stand." James jiggled his fussing child. "Unless you're dropping the lawsuit, we don't want to talk."

Joy looked up sharply. "Are you, Boyd?"

He shook his head wearily. "Cole and Katlynn said they uncovered something important, but they'd only share it with both of us."

"We're not leaving Ma alone." Jared crossed to the fridge and grabbed a carton of eggs.

A knock sounded on the screen door.

"Who is it?" James called.

It creaked open and a stampede of boots clattered on the floor. The sight of Cole's siblings in the kitchen's archway filled him with exasperation and pride. He'd told them to stay at the ranch. Clearly, they'd had other ideas. Lovelands always stood with each other. Through thick and thin.

"Don't recall inviting you inside," James drawled.

"Door was open." Heath, ever the peacemaker, gazed briefly in Jewel's direction then tipped his hat before doffing it. "Morning, Joy."

She returned his smile, looking a tad stronger. "Morning."

"You're trespassing." James nodded at a uniform-clad Travis. "*You* should know that."

"I'll report it to the proper authorities," Travis intoned, sardonic, his lips twitching.

Cole's siblings guffawed as the Cades advanced, their faces dark.

"Enough!" Joy cried. "I can't take any more senseless fighting."

Jewel hurried to her mother and wrapped an arm around her. "It's not senseless, Ma. We've got reasons to hate the Lovelands going on over a hundred years."

"Yeah. About that." Katie-Lynn held up Maggie's journal in one hand, the stack of letters to

Everett in the other. "My show's about to dispute that claim."

"Come again?" Jared stopped cracking eggs into a blender.

"We know what really happened to Maggie Cade." Cole leaned against the granite kitchen island and calmly met everyone's astonished stares.

"Everett killed her for the jewel. Case closed." Justin grabbed a pear from a nearby bowl and took a savage bite.

"No. It's a story about star-crossed lovers denied their chance at happiness by tragic fate, missed opportunities and outside interference." Katie-Lynn swiftly filled them in on their findings. When she finished, the group crowded around the large table, peering at letters and reading journal entries.

"Who talks like this?" scoffed Justin before quoting, "'Souls, soldered by the moon, spun together by the stars.' Sounds fake."

"A woman in love." Jewel sighed, the tough, no-nonsense cowgirl surprising everyone. Her eyes connected with Heath's for a moment, and Cole spied her brothers exchanging meaningful glances. Seemed his hunch from the line-dancing night was right; she was soft on Heath. Given the way Heath returned her stare called into question Heath's on-again-off-again girlfriend's claim of an impending proposal.

"You think these are real?" Justin asked Katie-Lynn.

"We'll authenticate them for the show," she assured him. "But I'm certain they're genuine."

A blender whined, filling up the silence as the group digested the feud's new facts. Something in the air shifted, a new weather front moving in, milder. Warmer. Heralding better times ahead?

"Poor thing." Joy swiped at her streaming eyes. "Pregnant, alone and about to marry a man she didn't truly love."

Boyd produced a handkerchief and gently dried Joy's cheeks.

Cole recalled how she'd been in a similar predicament once. She had loved Jason Cade, but Pa was her first love, and you never forgot your first love. His eyes strayed to Katie-Lynn, who now read passages from Maggie's diary to a rapt Javi. Sunlight blazed on her white-gold hair, setting her aglow. She was beautiful, intelligent, funny and caring. He was a lucky man to have won a heart as big as hers.

"Everett loved Maggie." Daryl rubbed his chin, peering down at the open journal. "And he worked hard to earn enough money to win her family's blessing. Doing things properly. Sounds like a Loveland."

Nods circled the room, including a few of the Cades. The sight caught Cole with an unexpected warmth. They might reconcile and become one family after all. Who would have thought it? His gaze drifted to Katie-Lynn again. When she'd returned home, he'd considered her a threat. Instead, she'd become his family's salvation... His, too.

His hermit existence had been comfortable. And miserable and lonely, he amended. Katie-Lynn dragged him back into life, proving the outside world, beyond his ranch and family, wasn't a minefield of threats after all.

"What if Everett killed Maggie out of jealousy? Maybe he didn't want her marrying another guy." Justin accepted a glass of beaten eggs and juice from Jared, and downed half in one gulp.

"Of course he didn't." Sierra held up the last letter. "That's why he came home when Maggie wrote him about the new wedding date. Strange how he worked for Maggie's betrothed."

"It wasn't a coincidence." Cole shook his head at Jared's offered orange-egg smoothie. "Clyde William Farthington hired Everett to get him out of the way. He'd had Maggie followed and discovered their secret meetings."

The group listened, rapt, as he repeated Clyde's deathbed confession. When he finished, the only sound was James's baby, now gnawing on a teething ring with tiny, satisfied grunts. Their oversize tabby cat, Clint, leaped to the floor, seemed to forget why, then stretched out on the tile.

"Clyde the fourth admitted this to you?"

Katie-Lynn nodded at Pa. "Got it all on tape, and he signed on to be part of the episode."

Joy reached over her shoulder and grabbed Boyd's hand. "Clyde Farthington killed Maggie Cade," she said slowly, her voice full of wonder. "Not Everett Loveland."

"Doesn't change the fact you Cades strung up Everett without investigating the facts," Travis stated flatly, in full-on lawman mode. "Your family exacted vigilante justice."

"We're hotheaded," James replied, his grave eyes on a scowling Justin. "And we did wrong. Can't change the past, but we can ask for forgiveness. Please accept our apology."

"Did hell just freeze over?" Javi asked his mother in a loud whisper. "Pa said it would before we ever said sorry to the Lovelands."

James's frown gave way to a smile, then a guffaw. Sofia giggled, Boyd chuckled, and the rest of the room erupted into gales of laughter.

A couple minutes later Joy blotted her streaming eyes, stood and tucked herself into Boyd's open arms. The room quieted, but the smiles remained.

"We accept the apology," Boyd pronounced. Cole and his siblings nodded.

"So we don't have to hate each other anymore." Jewel ducked her head, then peeked up at a blushing Heath.

"Wouldn't go that far," Justin joked, "Cole's still a pain in the—"

"Who'd like some cupcakes?" Joy hurried to say, speaking over him. "We've got plenty left over after last night." Her voice lowered. "Boyd. I'm sorry about acting so rashly. Reading about Maggie and Everett…it reminds me true love's too precious to squander."

"Are you saying you'll marry me?" The lines of Boyd's face smoothed, his color returning. For the first time since last night, Cole dragged in a full breath.

"Guess we might as well since we can't get the deposit on the cake back," Joy teased. "And my wedding dress was on clearance. Can't return it."

"And I already rented the tux," Boyd said, tweaking her right back. "Nonrefundable. Don't want to waste good money." He spanned her waist and grinned down at her. "Or love."

Joy's eyes glowed as she smoothed a hand down the side of Pa's face. "I love you, Boyd Loveland. The wedding's back on."

The group cheered.

"Hey! We'd better hurry." Jared pointed to the wall clock. "We're supposed to be at the church in a couple of hours."

"We'll make it," Joy said, her eyes on Boyd.

"Yes." He kissed the tip of her nose and grinned. "I believe we will."

"What about the lawsuit?" Justin asked, somber.

"We'll discuss it another day," Joy pronounced. "As a family."

Nods circled the room.

"One more thing." Cole held up a hand to stop the mass exodus. "It's about Cora's Tear."

All eyes turned to him expectantly.

"Did you find the buried treasure?" Javi bounced on the balls of his feet.

Cole patted the little guy's head, withdrew a faded velvet bag from his pocket, then shook the jewel into his palm. Brilliant light sparkled on the large sapphire brooch. Gasps erupted, and the group pressed near for a closer look.

"Is that…?"

"What's he got?"

"Can't be…"

"Katie-Lynn and I found this where Maggie buried it for her and Everett's future." Cole passed the jewel to Joy. "Now you and Pa can use it to start yours."

He leaned down and bussed Joy's damp cheek. "Glad to welcome you to our family."

She caught him in a tight hug. "I couldn't be

prouder to become a Loveland or your step-mother."

"That can be your something blue, Ma," Jewel said. "And you're borrowing it from Maggie."

"And having the wedding she never did," Katie-Lynn added. "The brooch will finally make it down the aisle."

It took Boyd several tries before his shaking fingers successfully pinned the brooch to Joy's shirt. He stepped back and beamed at her. The large blue stone grabbed every bit of light in the room, sparkling like blue fire.

"Pretty!" Javi rose on his toes to touch it.

"Thank you, Cole, Katlynn," Joy said, fingering the brooch. "You've given us our happily-ever-after."

Cole caught Katie-Lynn's smile and returned it, ready for their happy ending, too…

They'd vowed to make things work and like his grandma always said, "Where there's a will there's a way."

They had plenty of will; now they needed to find their way.

"You're awfully quiet." Katlynn gazed up into Cole's handsome face as he waltzed her on the crowded dance floor a few hours later. In a fitted black tux, he cut a fine figure, broad-shouldered and slim-hipped, his deep blue eyes and square jaw putting any Hollywood leading man to shame.

A slow country tune wove through the converted barn Sofia used for her event-planning business. Flower garlands, hanging from the rafters, filled Katlynn's nose with their heady scent. Outside the large windows, she glimpsed the sinking sun finally relinquishing the day to a soft, lavender dusk.

"Cole?" she prompted, touching his chin lightly.

Laughter mingled with clinking glasses and the muted shouts of children playing outdoors. A peaceful happiness stole over her, sweet and sharp. She wished she could press this moment into a memory book and keep it forever.

If she gave up her job and returned to Carbondale full-time, she wouldn't need a memory book. This would be her life—simple, uncomplicated and full of love. "Earth to Cole…"

His eyes swerved to hers. "Got carried away."

"With?"

His strong arms tightened around her. "Thinking about us. How lucky I am."

"I think you've got that backward."

He shook his head and one side of his full lips tipped up. "You make me so happy, sweetheart."

"Joy and Boyd look happy."

They turned to watch a laughing Joy, garbed in

a simple, high-necked ivory dress, place a piece of wedding cake into Boyd's mouth. Cora's Tear sparkled at her throat. The surrounding group, bloodthirsty for a cake-war, egged on Boyd. With a shake of his head, he ignored them and carefully dropped a bite into Joy's mouth. The long kiss he planted on her, however, satisfied the cheering crowd.

"Do you think Maggie and Everett are watching?" Katlynn glanced outside at the first twinkle of stars.

"Yep. Bet they're pleased to see us all come together." Cole waltzed her past a shuffling couple, twirled her under his arm, then reeled her back with one smooth, effortless pull.

Her breath caught. Her heart raced. A rugged, protective, loyal cowboy was a catch. Add in a tender heart, old-school charm and grace and you had a keeper. Her fingers gripped Cole's broad shoulders. She wasn't letting him go... He'd vowed they'd find a way to a compromise. With twelve months left on her contract, they had to figure out a path forward.

Cole smoothed his fingers over the top of her head and guided her cheek to rest against his drumming heart. His warmth enveloped her. Was there anything sweeter than dancing in the arms of the man you loved? A blissful sigh escaped her. Let tomorrow take care of itself her pa always said… Speaking of whom…

"Mind if we stop by to stay hello?" She pointed at two large tables pushed together. Her brothers, sisters, nieces and nephews dined on the steak and baked potato meal while her father carefully cut her mother's meat.

"Sure."

"Hey, y'all," Katlynn called when they neared her family.

The children launched themselves at her, throwing their arms around her legs. "Aunt Katie-Lynn!"

How much had changed since she'd begun stopping by her ma's house on her free time, working around their schedules instead of hers. She no longer needed to be the star. She was happy to orbit around others' lives, nothing to prove except to herself, a lesson she'd learned from Cole. She felt a complete trust with him to be exactly who she was. She didn't have to be any other version of Katlynn/Katie-Lynn Brennon for him to love her.

"Guess you'll be leaving us soon," her father said. When he held a bite of steak to her mother's mouth, she good-naturedly swatted it away with her arthritic hand.

"Stop fussing." She motioned to the empty seats near her. "Won't you sit a spell?"

"Thanks."

Cole pulled out her chair then grabbed one for himself.

"The cable guy you hired came by a couple days ago. Set up the whole thing. He's even got my DVR-thingy taping your show now. I won't miss another one." Her mother patted her hand. "We're so proud of you, Katie-Lynn."

A strange look crossed Cole's face, swift as a speeding cloud over the sun. Was it regret? Second thoughts about compromising?

"Thanks, Ma." She leaned over and kissed each of her parents' cheeks.

"Go on," her stoic father protested. He swiped at his face but looked pleased by the gesture nonetheless.

"Just found out your father needs back surgery," her mother announced. "And you know how the roof's leaking... Keith was hoping to have his cannabis business going by now, but he's hit a bit of a legal snag..."

Cole choked on his water and plunked the glass down so hard the liquid sloshed over the rim.

"Are you all right, Pa?" Katlynn touched his calloused hand. He'd worked hard all his life until an injury forced him on disability. She wasn't sure which took a bigger blow, his health or his pride.

Her father nodded stiffly. "Don't you worry about me, darlin'."

Katlynn held in a sigh. Pa never wanted a fuss. Still, given his pronounced back hunch and the line of strain around his eyes, he was clearly in pain. Her family shouldn't have to choose between health care and a roof...

"I'll send money for both," she vowed.

"Oh. Now. We don't want to impose, Katie-Lynn," her mother tutted. "You help out plenty."

"I don't mind. I'm happy to do it."

Her mother sighed. "Well. It'd be a big help. Michelle's promotion at the market fell through yesterday when her boss refused to give her time off for Timmy's preschool graduation and she quit. John's working overtime just to make his alimony and child care payments, Martin's car needs a new transmission...so..."

"We'll pay you back someday," her father vowed, his fingers tight around his fork.

"I know, Pa," Katlynn agreed, knowing she'd never take a dime from her parents. They'd given her so much more than she could ever repay. Growing up, she'd thought she'd lost out on their attention. What they'd really given her, though, were valuable life lessons like independence, a strong work ethic and responsibility.

What would happen to her family if she left *Scandalous History* and couldn't help them financially? They depended on her as did the show's cast and crew.

Yet Cole needed her, too. Would a compromise mean splitting their time between Colorado and California? She could live here as her main residence and travel to LA when taping a season...

"Katlynn, you look ravishing."

She turned and spied her producer, Tom, beside her chair. His dark hair was slicked back, and he wore a tailored gray suit, his expensive Italian loafers gleaming under the soft light cast by hundreds of flickering candles. "Tom. This is my family." By the time she finished introducing the large group, he appeared faintly shell-shocked.

"We could develop a reality show with a family this big," Tom murmured, eyeing a teething Frankie as he gnawed on a flip-flop.

Cole recoiled like he'd been stung.

"And I believe I met another of your siblings. Keith?" Tom continued, oblivious. "We had a—ah—transaction outside. Quite the businessman. Perhaps we'll call the show *In the Weeds*. What do you think? The first legalized pot-selling family. Gives new meaning to the old mom-and-pop operation..."

"Pot?" Katlynn's pa sputtered. "No hippies in our family."

"It's okay, Pa," Katlynn soothed, guiding her

red-faced father, a Vietnam veteran, back down in his chair. "Tom's just joking."

"Don't see the humor in it," Cole muttered, giving voice to the horror still contorting her father's face. He tossed down his napkin and rose to his towering height.

Tom backed up a step and swallowed hard. "Cole Loveland. Didn't see you there. I hope you'll accept my apology for what happened yesterday. We meant no offense. It was just business."

"That's all that matters to you Hollywood types," Cole charged, his expression hard. "Money. Not people."

Tom began to nod, caught Katlynn's slight head shake, grabbed a glass of water and downed it in one gulp.

"Hey!" Katlynn's father protested. "My teeth were in there!"

Tom spit out the water.

Her entire family cracked up. Katlynn's brother Martin slapped Tom on the back as he coughed. "Pa was just foolin'. He's still got his teeth. Look."

Katlynn's father parted his lips to reveal an impressive mouthful for his age. "Got ya."

She chuckled. Once she'd been awestruck by the sophistication, the intelligence, the savvy, of the LA crowd, yet here was proof country people were just as clever in their own way. And warm and welcoming, too. She appreciated her roots and was proud, not ashamed of them.

Tom dabbed at his wet chin with a napkin. Red stained his spray-tanned face. "You got me, all right. Katlynn. I need to steal you away for some quick shots with the bride and groom."

She nodded, resigned.

"And Cole—" Tom extended a hand "—no offense meant. We have plenty of footage without using the rehearsal dinner clip, thanks to Katlynn interviewing your grandfather."

Cole's expression froze. His hand dropped. *No!* She'd meant to tell Cole about the interview once she'd heard which angle the production team had chosen; a decision she'd expected to be included in…

Cole's gaze slowly glided to Katlynn. "Did you interview my grandfather?" he asked, his voice low, taut.

"Senator Reardon!" Tom crowed, answering for her. "Quite a chatty man, but I suppose all politicians are." Tom eyed her. "Katlynn? We need to finish filming, or the crew goes into overtime and you know how it is dealing with the union…"

"Tom. I need a minute," she said without taking her eyes off Cole. Grabbing his elbow, she led him out a side door.

When they reached an empty picnic table, he ripped his arm from her grasp. "How could you?"

"Your grandfather heard about the taping and insisted on being interviewed or he'd go to the papers. Again. I knew you didn't want controversy before the wedding, so…"

"You just volunteered," he cut in, his voice low and burning as if it'd been raked over coals. "You promised me three things, Katie-Lynn. Three. Not to drag my mother into your show. To shield my father and to include me in the investigation. You said you'd let me in, keep me in the loop, but you shut me out."

"I refused to do it at first," she insisted, frantically trying to catch Cole's eye. "But Tom said they'd have Ashton Reince interview the senator instead, and he's a shark. I had no choice."

"You had the choice to tell me you were interviewing my grandfather." He averted his eyes and scrubbed a hand over his face as he prowled up and down the grassy area. "The choice between going for an Emmy or supporting me. You choose the show. Your ambitions. Again. They've always mattered more than me."

"That's not true," she denied.

Was he reliving his mother's rejection? Feeling like the unloved boy of his past? Remorse banded around her chest and squeezed. "I'd convinced them to consider another angle—Joy and

Boyd's second chance. It didn't make sense to upset you until I knew which one they picked. I gave it my all during Boyd and Joy's interview to make their decision easy."

"And who's Ashton Reince?" Cole stopped pacing and stared at her, frustrated and confused.

"He broke the story about who really stole Katy Perry's backup dancers."

"Katy who?"

"The whole Katy Perry-Taylor Swift scandal… It's…it's…" She was going to say epic but here, in the shadow of the mighty Rockies, with the love of her life staring at her like she'd betrayed him, the petty squabbles of rich Hollywood stars seemed inconsequential.

"It doesn't matter." She slumped down to the picnic table. "If Ashton had interviewed your grandfather, the sleazy segment would have been too much temptation for the producers not to include."

"Did you ask him about my mother?" The rawness of Cole's expression grabbed her by the throat and shook her.

She nodded, glum.

"About her death?"

"Yes. He tried to give me the same pack of lies he fed to the press years ago but Cole—" she grabbed his cold hand "—I didn't believe him back then and I don't believe him now. I swear,

I didn't make it easy on him. In fact, I think… I think I did a good job of revealing him for what he really is."

"And who's that?"

"A grieving father unable to accept his daughter's disastrous choices."

"You sympathized with him!" Cole yanked his hand away and stomped to a pole holding an overhead light. "You actually feel bad for him?"

She hurried to join him. "A little." She blew out a breath. "Okay, more than a little. It doesn't mean I forgive him for what he did to you and your family. But I'm trained to see two sides to every story. I understood his misguided perception of events. His pain."

"His pain…*his* pain?" Cole stormed. "This had nothing to do with protecting my father, my family. You were just doing your job, a job you love more than me."

Anger rose to mingle with her regret. "It *is* my job. One I happen to be good at."

He turned sharply to face her. Overhead, moths banged against the light then fell, their wings singed by what had attracted them most.

She could relate.

"Have they decided to show his segment or not?"

"Based on what Tom just said, I'm thinking

yes, though I thought they'd include me in the final decision."

Cole clamped his hands around his ears as if he didn't want to hear anymore. "This will kill my father."

"Even if the segment airs, it'll reveal more about the senator than reflect badly on your father."

Cole's scoffing sound scorched her. It was the sound of everyone who'd overlooked her, dismissed her, failed to believe in her. And in a flash, she was a meteor, burning up when it entered the atmosphere, disintegrating, falling, tumbling to earth, too small and insignificant to be noticed.

"You don't trust me as a professional?" Why couldn't he be happy for her to have this opportunity and trust her to take care of his family?

"Your show is called *Scandalous History*, Katie-Lynn."

"Have you even watched it?"

He shook his head.

"Then you're judging it based on what? Your preconceived notions? Your bias? People in LA aren't all that different than folks here. Most want the same things. A steady job. Family. Love." She choked on the last word, feeling it slip through her fingers.

"Money," Cole added.

"And you don't care about that?" she countered. "You're suing the Cades for five million dollars in damages they don't even recall making."

"It's different."

"Is it? How?" She blinked back the sting in her eyes.

Cole shoved his hands in his tuxedo jacket's pockets. "I'm trying to save my family's ranch, my legacy."

She flinched. "In other words, your job has worth and mine doesn't? You said we'd find a way to compromise."

"Compromise," Cole mumbled under his breath before turning around, his eyes meeting Katlynn's. There were a thousand thoughts mirrored in their depths—anger, disbelief, pain, disappointment… But regret, regret was the one that hit her the most. "A compromise isn't possible," he sighed out. "Not then, not now. Not when we clearly want different things out of life…out of love."

"Cole," she breathed, reaching for his arm.

He shook her off, a calm resolve settling over him, one that had her fearing the words she knew were coming. "No matter your reasons, you broke your promise and chose the show, your career over me. You'd never be happy living here in Carbondale, putting us first."

"I am ambitious, and I love my job, but if you believe I'd put them ahead of you, then you don't really see who I am, after all." Her old insecurities rose to clog her throat. Katie-Lynn the invisible—only she'd come too far to let anyone make her feel that way again. She wasn't worthy because she was a star, but for simply being herself, flaws and all. If Cole couldn't accept her, all of her, then he couldn't truly love her.

"Your actions speak louder than your words."

"Then you don't hear me, either."

Cole shoved his hands in his pockets and stared up at the moon. "Maybe I've only been hearing what I wanted to hear."

"What's that mean?"

"I fooled myself into thinking you cared more than you do," he said, sounding betrayed. "You got what you wanted from me. With my grandfather's story, you'll score more ratings and fame than ever. You advanced your career at the expense of my family...of me. But what about your vow that I'm what you really wanted?"

"I do want you—above everything else."

"Then prove it."

"How? By moving home and quitting *Scandalous History*?" she demanded once a loud group of wedding guests got into their cars and drove away.

"Yes," he fired back. "You can get another job.

I can't get another Loveland Hills. It's my heritage. My life."

"Then who am I?" she cried, the threatening tears thickening her voice. "You said I'm a part of who you are."

Cole hung his head and blew out a breath. "You and Loveland Hills. That's who I am."

"What if I asked you to choose? To put us first and come to LA?"

"Come on, Katie-Lynn." Cole stepped closer. "You can't ask me to do that."

"Why? You asked me. Which would you choose?"

"I won't answer that."

"Because the answer is the ranch, isn't it? Again. You still put it first and won't compromise even the slightest bit for me. You've given up everything, including love, for that piece of land, which I think is selfish."

"Selfish?" He jerked back as if slapped. "You just named every sacrifice I've made for my family."

"No," she countered. "You said it yourself. Loveland Hills is a part of you. The things you gave up were the things you knew you could live without—one of them being me."

In the sudden silence, when Cole failed to disagree, she heard the faint tinkling of her heart shattering in a million pieces.

356 A COWBOY'S PRIDE

"I'm not part of your heritage," she whispered, swiping furiously at the tears flowing from her eyes.

"I want you to be."

"But only on your terms. Love can't be one-sided. My career is a part of me, a part you don't accept."

"Katlynn," Tom called from the doorway, his hand over his eyes as he peered into the darkness. "We need to film."

Cole gripped her hand. "Stay," he urged.

"No," she said without looking at him. If she did, she'd lose her resolve, lose herself in a much deeper way than she'd ever imagined the first time she fled Carbondale. "I've got a job to do."

CHAPTER SIXTEEN

COLE SLOUCHED AGAINST the half wall separating the Cades' kitchen from their massive living room and rolled his stiff neck. Near the flat-screen TV crowded his new, blended family. They'd all come together for the first time since last month's wedding to watch their *Scandalous History* episode.

Everyone seemed to be speaking at once and their animated chatter grated on Cole's last nerve. Since Katie-Lynn left, he'd spent most of his time alone, recuperating from the arm he fractured when he tumbled from the silo's ladder. According to the doctor, it'd healed enough to let him resume his ranch work.

Too bad his heart hadn't healed, too.

Every thought of Katie-Lynn was like pressing on a bruise. His mind replayed their last conversation on a nonstop loop. It still confounded him how she'd turned the tables, calling him selfish and unwilling to compromise, when *she'd* betrayed *him*.

Used him.

"You okay?" Jewel Cade passed him a soda as she leaned into the wall beside him.

"Why?" With a flick of his fingers, he popped the tab, releasing the slightest scent of ozone.

"You're scowling." She eyed him over the lid of her can. "Standing by yourself. Then there's that strange noise you just made."

"Noise?" The cool, sweet drink soothed his burning throat.

"Sounded like someone stepped on a cat...in heat."

His mouth curled, despite his foul mood. "If I'm such lousy company, why don't you join them?" He nodded to the lively group now hooting loudly as Jared and Maverick tossed peanuts into the air and caught them in their mouths, competing.

"Misery prefers company," she said obliquely and lifted her soda again.

He glanced from her drooping, freckled face to his brothers. All were here minus Heath, who'd left for Nashville to try to get a contract with a record label. Was she pining for him?

"Appreciate your pitching in at Loveland Hills while I was laid up."

Jewel nodded. "It wasn't so bad."

Given the faraway look in her eyes, he wondered what'd really gone on while she and Heath had ridden the range together. They'd driven

Loveland cattle in search of water while they awaited their court date to reinstate the easement.

"Have you heard from Heath?" he asked, off-handed. Casual.

Jewel jumped. "Wh-why would I hear from him?"

"You two faced a lot of challenges together. The flashflood. Cattle getting sick. The wolf attacks. Poachers…"

"We were busy."

Cole eyed her flaming cheeks. Busy doing what?

"What about you?" Jewel asked, turning the tables. "Have you heard from Katlynn?"

When he opened his mouth, she interrupted him. "And don't even ask why I'm asking. I saw you two at the wedding. You looked as in love as you were in high school."

The directness of her stare left him nowhere to go except with the truth.

"We were."

"*Were*? What happened?"

Cole gulped more soda, thinking hard. What had happened? Everything fell apart so fast he still hadn't figured it out. "Seems she cares more about her job than me."

"So?" Jewel challenged, her dark eyes flashing. "You're too selfish to share her affections with something else? Got to have her all to your-self?"

"No," he protested, defensive. "I just—"

"Need to come first?" she finished for him, shooting him a scornful look. "You realize this is the twenty-first century, right?"

"Yes," he ground out, not liking the direction of this conversation. "I'm not a male chauvinist."

"So why can't her job be a priority, too?"

He stared at her, flabbergasted. This must be what cattle felt like when they were driven from the herd, prodded and blocked until they finally went in the right direction.

"Women need their independence," Jewel insisted. "It makes them a real partner. Don't you want an equal?"

"Yes," he conceded. If Katie-Lynn had given up her career to be with him, then she wouldn't have anything for herself. Jewel made sense. He had been selfish. But that didn't excuse her betrayal.

"So why don't you go to her? Tell her you've been a blockhead Neanderthal and now that you realize fire and the wheel have been invented for thousands of years already, you're ready to evolve."

Cole snorted. "A blockhead Neanderthal?"

Jewel reached behind them to grab a bag of

M&Ms from the half wall. "Just calling it like I see it."

He extended his hand when she offered the candy. "There's more to it than my being stuck in the Ice Age."

Jewel shook an overflowing handful into his cupped palms. "Like?"

"She broke a promise to me. Three, actually."

A stream of colorful chocolates fell to the floor before Jewel caught herself and closed the bag. "Now that's serious. What were they?"

"Not to talk about my mother in the show. To protect my father from getting hurt. And to include me in every part of the investigation."

Jewel nodded, chewing. "But didn't you hurt your pa by keeping the lawsuit a secret?"

A cough erupted from him when he swallowed the wrong way. "I had a good reason," he wheezed.

"And Katlynn didn't?"

Cole sifted through the candies in his hand, stopping on a blue one matching the color of Katie-Lynn's eyes. "She thought she did."

"So did you."

"You're starting to get on my nerves."

Jewel grinned at him, chewing. "Good. The truth hurts."

"You're saying I'm being hypocritical?"

"You said it, buddy, not me."

He chuckled.

Her grin stretched even wider. "Sometimes men are idiots."

"So I'm an idiotic, hypocritical man?"

She patted his arm. "Don't worry. You're not the only one. How'd Katie-Lynn hurt your pa?"

"She went behind my back and taped a segment with my grandfather for tonight's show."

Jewel whistled. "You didn't want her bringing up old gossip."

Cole shook his head. "She knew how much it hurt my family…me."

"She was with you the whole time. Remember how she'd talk to the reporters and run interference?"

Cole recalled how strong Katie-Lynn had been while he and his family had fallen apart.

"Always thought that took a lot of guts," Jewel said, her tone appreciative.

"It did."

"What was her reason for giving your grandfather airtime?"

"Her producers were going to tape the segment regardless, and if she didn't do it, some guy named Ashton something-or-other would interview him in her place."

"Ashton Reince?" Jewel gaped at him. "The guy who started the Katy Perry-Taylor Swift feud?"

"How does everyone know this but me?" he asked, mystified.

"Because you're living in the Dark Ages, remember?"

"Ice Age," he corrected with an involuntary smile. Jewel wasn't half-bad, for a Cade.

Jewel chewed, lost in thought, then said, "Ashton Reince is one of the snarkiest tabloid reporters in Hollywood. He'd have to be if *I've* heard of him. If Katie-Lynn stepped in, dude, she saved your family. By the time Ashton finished with your grandfather, he would have looked like Liam Neeson from *Taken*."

He eyed her quizzically.

"Lord." Jewel rolled her eyes. "I forget you live under a rock. It's this film where Liam's daughter gets kidnapped and he's a heroic avenging father… Anyway, if Ashton interviewed your grandfather, Investigation Discovery channel would be taping a show on your mother's death faster than you can say *ratings week*."

"You're saying Katie-Lynn did me a favor?"

Jewel pointed at the TV as *Scandalous History*'s opening credits rolled. "I'm betting she saved your life."

The sight of Katie-Lynn's pretty face filling the screen ripped every ounce of air from him. When she smiled, it transported him to their *Say Anything* tree, to line-dancing, to baking strawberry-rhubarb pies in his family's brick oven to an overflowing mess. Every moment, with each of her smiles, rushed through him like the first spring breeze after a harsh winter. It carried away the bleakness inside and replaced it with a warm, yearning hope.

God, he missed her.

"It's Katlynn!" Javi shouted then shushed, instantly, at James's subtle head shake.

"Carbondale, Colorado, a sleepy town nestled in the foothills of the Rocky Mountains, is a peaceful, family-friendly place to live in America's heartland," Katie-Lynn intoned. Her beautiful, melodious voice floated from the television's speakers to wind through his heart, swelling it. "Unless you're a member of the Loveland and Cade families, that is."

His pulse raced fast enough to leave him dizzy and slightly sick. Soaking up the spotlight as if it were her natural habitat, Katie-Lynn relayed his family's feud with empathy and authenticity. It was like hearing it for the first time. With expert pacing, the tale unraveled, both the Cades and the Lovelands portrayed as sympathetic families whose star-crossed lovers were duped by Clyde Farthington.

With each commercial break, the family broke into excited chatter then hushed when she reappeared. Near the end of the episode, Katie-Lynn segued into her interview with his grandfather and everyone seemed to hold their breath. Cole had warned his family of the segment, had prepared himself for it mentally, too. Seeing his relative's hateful face, however, struck him hard in the gut.

Yet as he watched, Katie-Lynn's empathetic listening and pointed questions portrayed his grandfather as a grieving father struggling to accept the reality of his daughter's suicide—just as Katie-Lynn had assured him. A quick glance at his pa showed his parent gripping Joy's hand, a slight smile on his wet face.

When Cole's grandfather expressed his regret for alienating his grandchildren with false accusations, Sierra gasped. Cole froze. Had has grandfather just admitted he'd been wrong and abandoned the rumors about his mother at last? Like Katie-Lynn promised, the segment wouldn't ruin his family's truce or his father's happiness. In fact, she'd done the exact opposite…she'd helped them heal.

"Maggie Cade and Everett Loveland are America's Romeo and Juliet," Katie-Lynn concluded at the end of the segment. "Their tragedy demonstrates how squandered opportunities, misconceptions and pride create rifts instead of peace, and disappointment rather than love."

Her eyes lasered from the screen and into

his heart. It was like she spoke directly to him, about *them*. Katie-Lynn was right, and he'd been dead wrong. Anger at himself fired inside. He'd messed up their second chance at love because of his misconceptions, selfishness and pride. Insisting she give up her dreams to live the quiet life he preferred was self-centered and shortsighted. He couldn't shut out the world any more than he could keep Katie-Lynn from his heart.

Jewel punched him in the shoulder. "Verdict?"

"I'm a Neanderthal blockhead." He rubbed the spot, marveling.

Just then a teaser segment began, informing the viewers of a live Q&A session with Katlynn Brennon on set tomorrow.

"You have to go to that and speak to her," Jewel said.

"In front of a live audience?" He recoiled.

"Just think of them as friends you haven't met yet."

Cole groaned.

"It took a grand gesture to get Ma and Boyd back together. Katlynn deserves nothing less."

Cole nodded. Jewel was making a lot of sense. Maybe too much. "I'm not sure if you're trying to ruin my life or save it."

"What do you think?"

"My money is on the last one."

"Go get her, caveman—just don't club her over the head and drag her home, okay?"

"No promises." He winked at Jewel, grabbed his keys and headed for the door.

"Where are you going?" his pa called. Joy cast worried eyes his way.

"Katie-Lynn's studio." He donned his hat. "To make a fool of myself at her live taping tomorrow."

"A fool in *love*," Jewel added.

"We'll be watching," catcalled Daryl.

"That's what I'm afraid of." And with that, he headed out the door, no longer worried about his pride. Keeping his guard up, and others out, might avoid hurt, but it also prevented happiness, too. It was lonely inside the fortress surrounding himself; no one could get in.

Now his heart and life were open, and he wasn't resistant to sharing them anymore...not when it came to the woman he loved.

KATLYNN PERCHED ON a stool and stared into the darkened studio audience. Blaring lights nearly blinded her. A faulty earpiece buzzed with intermittent static. Oh, the joys of live television. With her ankles crossed, hands folded on her lap, she hoped she projected serenity and confidence during today's Q&A session...neither of which she felt.

Not even close.

"Hi, Katlynn." A woman with a brown bob and large-framed glasses waved to her from one of the aisles' microphone stands. "Are any of the Cade or Loveland brothers single?"

The largely female audience tittered.

Cole's handsome face flashed in Katlynn's mind's eye, and her smile disappeared.

"Say something," Gabe urged through Katlynn's earpiece.

"Sorry, ladies, but the Cade brothers are happily married."

The group collectively groaned.

"However, all of the Loveland brothers are single except Daryl."

A couple of catcalls and a few whistles mingled with the cheers.

At today's staff meeting, the marketing department announced America had fallen hard for the Cades and Lovelands. The higher-ups even proposed a one-year reunion to check in on Joy, Boyd and the blended families.

Cole would hate another camera crew.

Hope rose at the prospect of seeing him again, though, checking in under the guise of work. Would he slam the door in her face?

Katlynn held on to her slipping smile while she waited for the bubbly crowd to quiet. Usually she caught her audience's mood. Today her heavy heart wobbled sluggishly in her chest.

The Cade-Loveland episode earned *Scandalous History* its highest ratings, critical praise and a three-year series renewal. Her agent currently negotiated a producer credit and a twenty percent salary increase for Katlynn's next contract.

Yet happiness eluded her.

She loved her job, but she also missed Cole and Carbondale. Everybody knew everybody there, the pressure to be "somebody" nonexistent. She was herself and liked for it...even loved...

Did Cole miss her? Love her, still?

"Hi, Katlynn," another woman asked from a mic farther back in the studio. "First of all, I'm your biggest fan."

Katlynn's hand rose to her heart, touched and grateful. "Thank you." The adoration of strangers, however, was no match for the love of a good man like Cole.

"Maggie and Everett's love story was beautiful," the woman gushed. "And tragic. Why didn't Maggie just tell her parents the truth? Or why wouldn't Everett elope with Maggie and win over her parents later?"

Answers shuffled through Katlynn's mind, none of them easy. "Societal pressures played a factor, I suppose." She paused, sipped her mint tea, then continued, "But I believe it's really an unwillingness to compromise. If they'd told her parents everything, maybe it could have worked out. I guess we'll never know." She fidgeted with her silver bracelet, thinking of herself and Cole.

Would she spend her life wondering "what if"?

Cole had insecurities and flaws, as did she. At the wedding he'd felt betrayed and she diminished. And just as they had in the past, he'd shut down, and she'd run away. Big mistake. She wished she'd stayed and insisted on a compromise.

After this Q&A, she'd fly to Carbondale. If Cole refused to see her, she'd camp on his doorstep until he relented. She was an investigative reporter who knew a thing or two about persistence.

A middle-aged woman wearing sandals and a linen dress tapped on the closer microphone. "Is there truth to the rumor you once dated Cole Loveland?"

Katlynn gulped air and struggled to respond.

"I can answer that question," spoke a familiar bass voice from the rear mic.

Her heart fluttered madly in her chest. Cole? What was he doing here?

Speaking at a live taping of all places?

"You…you're one of the Lovelands," the woman in the sundress gasped.

"Cole Loveland, ma'am."

Feminine squeals echoed in the studio.

"Katlynn and I were childhood sweethearts." Cole pulled the mic free and ambled down the aisle. "Each other's first love."

"Awwwwwww," the audience cried.

"Hello, Cole." Katlynn tried to smile but fell short.

"Hello, Katie-Lynn."

Had he seen yesterday's show and forgiven her? Hope spread through her, sweet as lavender honey.

"Thank you for joining us," she said formally, swallowing back a sigh. In gray slacks and a navy dress shirt, he'd never looked handsomer or dearer.

"Are you two still in love?" pressed the woman at the mic.

"I can only speak for myself." The sight of Cole facing an avaricious crowd, declaring himself to millions of viewers, filled her with confusion and delight.

He mounted the stage. Security personnel fell back at her head shake. "She's the one. She's always been the only one for me. And I love her with all my heart."

The audience exploded into ooohhhs and aaahhhs.

Katlynn slid off her stool and smoothed damp

palms over her dress. "What are you doing here?" she asked beneath her breath.

"Making a grand gesture… You know…the kind where some lucky guy wins the girl." He ducked his head. "I want to be that guy."

"But people are watching. Listening."

"That's the point of a grand gesture."

His lopsided grin took her breath away. "Let's go to commercial break," she announced.

Gabe's head shake cut her off.

"In a few minutes," she amended. Shoot. Suddenly, she was the one wishing for privacy, not Cole. He seemed determined to expose his heart in the most public way possible.

"I was an idiot and a hypocrite for letting you go. I should have trusted you. Supported you." Cole's voice was low and rumbly, his tension evident in his wordiness. "Will you give me another chance? I want to be in your life, if you'll let me."

"Cole," she gasped, surprised and delighted. "What are you saying?"

"Marry me, Katie-Lynn." His loving gaze touched her face like a caress. "I know I'm not perfect. And the life I have to offer isn't much. But I promise no one will ever love you, love *all* of you, like I do."

She gulped. "I have another year on my contract. And I'm planning to renew it."

He set down the mic, framed her face with his hands and gazed at her tenderly. "We'll split our time, here in LA when you're filming, and home on Loveland Hills when you're not. We're each other's missing pieces, and I want—need—to be whole again."

Her eyes stung. "I'm not whole without you, either. I thought I was meant to fix you, but you were sent to heal me, too. I love you," she whispered. "Let's never be apart again."

At first, he looked as if he hadn't heard her. He didn't move a single muscle, just continued to stare at her, then released a shaky breath, and a fierce wonder sparked in the glittering blue of his eyes.

"Marry me," he breathed as his lips lowered onto hers, stilling every word in her mouth, every thought in her whirling brain.

A strong arm wrapped around her waist as he deepened the kiss. She was floating. Time stood still. She must be in heaven.

"Marry him! Marry him! Marry him!" chanted the audience in response to a cue-card-holding intern.

When their lips parted, and their eyes connected, his darkened, intensifying the emotion in them.

"You don't want to marry someone like me,"

she said sadly. "Red carpet events, paparazzi, parties with strangers."

"I thought I wanted to hide from the world, to be somewhere no one would bother me. But you wouldn't let me languish there. Since the day you returned home, you've dragged me into the wide world." He drew his mouth over hers slowly, gently. "Thank you for that. It's much less comfortable out here, I'll admit. But I wouldn't miss it for anything since it includes you."

"Me neither." She struggled to see him through her blurring vision.

"I want to marry you, a woman who has a heart as beautiful as her face and body, a woman with ambition and purpose, who loves me and my family fiercely," he said, his voice hoarse. "I want you, Katie-Lynn. Katlynn. All of you."

When he dropped to one knee, she couldn't believe it was really happening. She looked in his eyes and sailed among the stars. Long ago she'd wanted a big wedding where she'd be the center of attention. Now she only cared about catching one man's eye, and heart, and miracle of miracles, she'd won both.

"Marry me." He produced a small, black velvet box from his pocket. A familiar, heart-shaped diamond ring gleamed inside, the one she'd worn twelve years ago.

She could barely think with the sensation of bees swarming in her stomach as his eyes searched hers, but she wasn't befuddled or at a loss for her voice any longer. "Is that…?"

He nodded. "I couldn't part with it, not when my heart kept on loving you," The words were issued in an aching whisper. "Will you do me the honor and be my bride?"

"Say yes!" cried the audience as another intern walked in front of them holding a different cue card.

Happiness radiated from a deep inner core, shining through her. It seemed so long ago that she'd fought to prove herself rather than be herself. Everything was clear now. Her destiny had been written on her heart forever, and she could finally see it, finally give voice to what she'd wanted all along.

"Yes." Tears slid down her face, unchecked. "I'll marry you."

He lifted her hand to his mouth and gently kissed it. Then he slipped the ring on her finger.

"She said yes!" Cole sprang to his feet, caught her around the waist and twirled her around. His infectious exuberance sent the crowd into hysterics.

"Break!" Gabe yelled once the camera lights turned off

Katlynn grabbed Cole's hand and dragged him offstage to her dressing room. "What just happened?" she gasped once the door shut behind them.

"Us." His arms closed around her so fiercely she couldn't breathe. Not that it mattered when he'd told her he loved her. Wanted to marry her.

He buried his face in her hair, and she felt him shudder against her. For several heartbeats he did nothing more than hold her. Never had Katlynn felt such peace, such contentment.

"What changed your mind?"

"Someone calling me a blockhead Neanderthal and I agreed when I saw your interview with my grandfather. I should have never doubted you."

"Who called you a blockhead Neanderthal?"

"Jewel."

Katlynn snorted. "Sounds about right."

"I love you, Katie-Lynn." He slid his fingers in her hair, tugged slightly to angle her face up to his and lowered his mouth. "Love you like crazy." His kiss was hard and fierce but so tender she wanted to cry and laugh and dance at the same time. He murmured words of love between kisses, and she held each one to her heart like a precious jewel.

This was good and right and wonderful.

She hadn't disappeared when she'd returned home; she'd discovered herself, through Cole.

Tumultuous seconds later he lifted his head, and his hold on her relaxed slightly. He expelled deep, uneven breaths. His eyes sparkled with emotion, deep as blue sapphires, and she was clinging to him, trembling faintly as his calloused palm smoothed slowly over her cheek.

"I have to go back on camera in a sec," she whispered, already resenting her show for taking her from Cole. Good thing this was the last taping of the season, and she'd have six glorious months to focus solely on the man she loved.

"But you'll come back," he said, a smile evident in his voice.

"Yes." Katlynn laid her head on his chest and heard the rapid, staccato beat of his heart. "I'll always come back to you."

"Counting on it." His breath stirred the hairs at the crown of her head. "I can't wait to marry you."

"Then let's do it quick," she said softly, knowing in her heart that it was time to take that leap. They'd waited too long already. "Next weekend."

He drew back, and his look was tender and searching. "Don't weddings take months to plan?"

"Not if it's on a mountaintop," she told him, misty-eyed. Her heart overflowed with unrestrained happiness.

He blinked and stared. For a moment he looked

as if he didn't dare believe he'd heard her right. "You don't want a big wedding?"

"Just you and me and the world at our feet," she vowed, giving him back the words he'd used twelve years ago. Now she'd return them to him—a concession to show how much she valued him, had grown to want the same things as he did on many fronts.

Feeling freer and lighter than she had in a long time, Katlynn smiled up into Cole's serious face and watched his answering smile start in the corner of his mouth and spread into his eyes.

He cupped her face with his hands. His thumb traced her lips. "And heaven will be at our fingertips, my angel. My star." His reverent words were said in a husky voice just before his lips sealed the vow.

He kissed her again in a tender, slow joining that reached deep inside, drawing warmth straight through her heart and claiming a piece of her.

It was such a powerful feeling, as if they'd each had half a soul inside them that finally found its match.

Their missing pieces.

Her goose bumps got goose bumps.

"Say anything," he whispered a moment later against her temple.

She slid her hand beneath his chin, turned his

face to peer into his intense blue eyes and whispered the most important words she'd ever say in her life. Not anything. *Everything.* "I love you."

* * * * *

*If you loved this novel, don't miss
the other books in Karen Rock's
Rocky Mountain Cowboys series:*

Falling for a Cowboy
Christmas at Cade Ranch
A Cowboy to Keep
Under an Adirondack Sky
His Kind of Cowgirl
Bad Boy Rancher

*Available now from
Harlequin Heartwarming!*

Get 4 FREE REWARDS!

We'll send you 2 FREE Books plus 2 FREE Mystery Gifts.

Love Inspired® books feature contemporary inspirational romances with Christian characters facing the challenges of life and love.

FREE Value Over **$20**

HOME *on the* RANCH

Get 4 FREE REWARDS!

We'll send you 2 FREE Books plus 2 FREE Mystery Gifts.

Love Inspired® Suspense books feature Christian characters facing challenges to their faith... and lives.

FREE Value Over **$20**

LIS18